AFTER
DISASTERS

Center Point
Large Print

**This Large Print Book carries the
Seal of Approval of N.A.V.H.**

AFTER DISASTERS

VIET DINH

CENTER POINT LARGE PRINT
THORNDIKE, MAINE

This Center Point Large Print edition
is published in the year 2018 by arrangement with
Amazon Publishing, www.apub.com.

A version of "Two Ruined Cities" was first published in
Witness, Vol. XXIV No. 1 (2011) as "The Ruined City."

The text of this Large Print edition is unabridged.
In other aspects, this book may vary
from the original edition.
Printed in the United States of America
on permanent paper.
Set in 16-point Times New Roman type.

ISBN: 978-1-68324-639-8

Library of Congress Cataloging-in-Publication Data

Names: Dinh, Viet, 1974- author. Title: After disasters / Viet Dinh.
Description: Center Point Large Print edition. | Thorndike, Maine :
    Center Point Large Print, 2018.
Identifiers: LCCN 2017046264 | ISBN 9781683246398
    (hardcover : alk. paper)
Subjects: LCSH: Earthquakes India—Fiction. | Survival—Fiction. |
    Rescue work—India—Fiction. |.Large type books. | BISAC:
    FICTION / LGBT / Gay. | FICTION / Literary.
Classification: LCC PS3604.I477 A67 2018 | DDC 813/.6—dc23
LC record available at https://lccn.loc.gov/2017046264

To my parents, my brother, and my sister,
the family I was given,
and to Matthew and the children,
the family I earned.

TABLE OF CONTENTS

AFTER DISASTERS

PROLOGUE

The Future

The moment the earthquake hits, Ted has a premonition: a burning sensation on his feet. Not the pins and needles from sitting cross-legged for too long, but like the restlessness of the soles after standing on the subway for an hour. Like the blood wants to burst from his skin. No blinding vision, no sudden trance—it's not until weeks later that he realizes what the feeling was. But in the future, he won't tell the story this way. In his version, he knows the premonition's exact meaning when he feels it. The strange friction on his feet is a harbinger of subterranean plates, tectonic movements, earth grinding against earth, playing out on his skin, as if he were indistinguishable from the world, and the world from him. And if anyone challenges him about his predictive powers, he will simply say, *But it happened. It really did.*

For now, though, it's the end of January, and the city outside is covered in a crystalline mist that fails to coalesce into snow. Soon, definitely, it will snow. But not tonight.

Though, why not? Take last year: the Y2K bug threatened to plunge the country—maybe the

11

global grid—into darkness. Ted was still doing his USAID training in Washington, DC, and when he stopped into the CVS on Dupont Circle on December 31, 1999, the shelves were almost bare. Seeing its stripped-down state, he began to panic. Another man in the store, proud of his preparedness, asked him, "Do you have medical supplies? A backup generator?" And Ted realized he wasn't ready—for anything! He hit every supermarket, pharmacy, and hardware store in a two-mile radius, and back in his apartment, he took stock of his supplies: canned food, bottled water, batteries, Band-Aids. He called John and asked if he and Dr. Mark were prepared, and John said, "Yep, we've got everything we need. Champagne, vodka, and mixers." But the new millennium crept in without the lights so much as flickering, and Ted felt disappointed. You expect the end of the world, and: nothing. You expect nothing, and: the end of the world.

But thinking about John means that Ted won't be able to sleep. Any rest is fitful, even with blue pills that promise addiction-free slumber. He stretches on his couch, head propped with pillows, and when he dozes off, he breathes through his mouth, until the gumminess on his tongue wakes him. He never dreams during these minor instances of sleep; instead, the sounds filter through his consciousness into new forms: traffic whooshing past becomes a fast-flowing river; the horns of pissy drivers become gulls. Dogs yipping and straining against their leashes are children running by with heavy footsteps. He hears cattle in the street, with bells around their necks, lazy whips with a dried reed.

John is dead, Ted reminds himself. He died on a wet day early in November. Ted had always known that John would die first, and not just because of what was in his blood, but he never expected that John would die so soon, so ridiculously soon, simply from his inability to look both ways before riding out into the fucking street.

A few minutes later, Lorraine calls.

"Are you ready?" she asks. "We've gotten reports of an earthquake."

"How big?"

"Big enough. You've been to India before, right?"

Yes, he has. That visit two years ago, in fact, brought him to USAID. He spent a year training in DC, then another six months in New York with Lorraine and Piotr. He knows how much food and water a person needs a day (1,500 kilocalories; one gallon) and how to bribe armed rebels with bottles of cologne to cross a border. He knows about rioters and bureaucrats and military generals. He knows the best way to help is to know things, and right now, he knows things because he's read Piotr's careful reports, official documents filed with the secretary of state, handwritten notes, pages warped and dirty with sweat. He's as ready as he'll ever be.

"I want you on observer status," Lorraine says. "I'm arranging the flight now. We're going to scramble within the next few hours."

She will call back soon. Ted retrieves his go bag from beneath his bed. It's prepacked: a battery-powered tape recorder, some blank notebooks, a stack of pens bound with a rubber band that clack against each other like gnashing teeth. The rest of the bag is full of clothes he doesn't mind ruining: frayed jeans, faded underwear, socks that have lost elasticity. He finds room for a razor, floss, sample-size antiperspirants.

From the living room, the CNN anchorman announces: "We've just received word of a major earthquake in the Gujarat Province of India." Initial readings of 6.5 on the Richter scale. Reports of serious damage. Numerous injuries. Ted listens for more information, but none is forthcoming. In fact, it will be a year before he hears of Gujarat again, but not the Gujarat he remembers. Not the Gujarat he tried to save. A five-second video clip shows the smoke-streaked skyline of Ahmedabad, as if a storm has descended on it. The city burns: shops and houses and mosques and temples. Bodies too. Ted can't see the rioters in the blurred video feed, but they're there, in plazas between the buildings, gathered around the charred metal of cars. In the neighborhoods just beyond the city, the rioters hold the addresses of Muslims from the voter rolls, and those houses will soon feed the charcoal haze above the city.

But at the present moment, he waits for Lorraine. Maybe he can shut his eyes until the phone rings, at which point he'll make his voice alive and alert, as if he'd been waiting for this moment, whatever this moment may be.

Here you go, he thinks. *The start of your new life.*

On the red-eye from New York to Heathrow, Piotr, pressed between him and Lorraine, spreads maps on the serving tray. He licks his fingertips to flip between them. With a metal compass, the type Ted hasn't used since geometry class, he draws concentric circles. He chews the tip of his horn-rim glasses until the earpieces are white from bite marks.

The luminous corona of New York fades into the darkness of the ocean. Ted tries to determine when the critical mass of electricity fails to penetrate across the water, but it's like trying to pinpoint the exact moment day turns into night. He rests his head against the window, and the subzero temperatures outside push in on him. Lorraine, in the aisle seat, has her ear glued to the air phone, which disappears in the nimbus of her hair.

Theirs are the only lights on in the cabin. Even the flight attendants catch shut-eye. Lorraine becomes more and more agitated. She can't secure transport of the food supplies from Mumbai, and organizations are already hording medical supplies. "We have at least ten tons already set aside," she says. "I don't care, just find them. No, I will not call again. I will stay on the line until you have them." She sits back with a thud. The seat to which the phone is attached jerks, and a man peers over the headrest.

"And tents," she says. "I need tents and all the grain you can spare. From the Delhi warehouse."

Piotr jostles Ted's elbow off the armrest. He wears a pink striped button-up shirt. The overhead beam makes it seem as if his chest is awash in blood. The fabric between his buttons buckles, and Ted can trace Piotr's body hair inching up from his stomach and across his chest. Ted should be doing something too, but doesn't know what.

Piotr places his hand on Ted's left knee, holding it in place, and it's only then that Ted understands that he's been jittering. It's a firm gesture—how a father would calm a frantic child—and Ted stares at Piotr's hand until he moves it.

"We should already have everything," Piotr says. "We were just in India last year."

Lorraine muzzles the mouthpiece with her fist. "Wasn't it two years ago?"

Piotr shakes his head. "Fifteen months. Orissa. Typhoon."

"Oh," says Lorraine, "that's right."

Piotr returns to his notations. His hand—accumulating faint liver spots and excess skin around the knuckles—pushes out numbers, cross-referencing, calculating. His hand already knows who can be saved, and who cannot. Later this year, in Arequipa, Peru, Ted will look at the damage estimates and think, *This is nothing compared to India,* and, *Only seventy-five killed? In India it was twenty-five thousand.* He will try to resist comparisons of scope and scale and misery. Really, he will. Suffering is not a zero-sum game. He won't want to feel tired, not yet, but maybe he poured the entirety of his being prematurely into India. Aid organizations have a term: *donor fatigue,* the point at which people desensitize and can't engage any more bad news. And as he accompanies a mule-drawn cart laden with shelter kits and irrigation tools up a mountain, he will wonder, *Is there such a thing as disaster fatigue? What if a person has a limited store of strength, and once it's depleted, it's gone for good?* He's not a person for whom good deeds recharge the batteries. So why did he choose this line of work? What did he hope to accomplish? He will see a group of shirtless children on the side of the road. They will look like tree stumps, frozen in place. He will wave, and they will disappear into a copse of trees like rabbits, a flurry of legs and feet, and even if Ted were to pursue them, he knows that he will never catch them.

Lorraine asks Piotr, "What's the time difference between New York and India?"

"Nine and a half hours," he replies.

With the tip of her fingernail, she holds down a button on her watch. The hours flick by. Ted does the same, spinning the minute hand until he realizes, *My god, the future's already here.*

RESCUE

TWO RUINED CITIES

Four hours after the earthquake, Dev knows that Dr. Sengupta is dead. Presumed dead, at least, which is the same as dead. Dev learned of the Bhuj earthquake as soon as it happened, and within an hour, Médecins Sans Frontières put in a call for medical personnel from New Delhi General. Dev responded without thinking, and only after he boards the Bhuj-bound army plane does he remember that he should have had Geeta cancel his appointments for the week. But he can't raise a signal in the air. Geeta will know what to do.

Both hospitals in Bhuj have collapsed. It makes sense that Jubilee Hospital, erected in celebration of Queen Victoria's golden jubilee, did not survive. It had been built as a showcase: a band of carved stars circled the second floor and along the roof, a crenellated border of stone pennants. Jubilee was the older hospital, in need of an upgrade, an expansion. But Bhuj Civil—modern, second-best in Gujarat behind Ahmedabad—was an acclaimed service hospital, and Dr. Sengupta had been scheduled to arrive at eight. Dev remembers how, even on the hottest Delhi days, Dr. Sengupta wore a suit and tie and the same pair of polished black wing tips. Dev can see him now, walking into the hospital lobby—*One must keep oneself busy,* Dr. Sengupta had said—as crisp and pressed as when he was Dev's advisor in medical school.

The earthquake struck at 8:47. Dr. Sengupta was never late.

Dev last saw Dr. Sengupta five years ago, at Padma's urging. Dr. Sengupta had retired to Gujarat, and Dev had offered Padma her pick of any place in India, any luxury she could imagine, but she remained steadfast.

You made a promise, she said.

She had her own reasons for visiting Gujarat, of course. She had once entertained the dream of becoming a museum curator, long before she realized her dream of being a dutiful wife and, later, mother. In those days, she had converted her art-history degree into a job working with an antiquities dealer specializing in architectural salvage. From a soon-to-be demolished house on the outskirts of Delhi, she rescued a matching pair of stone pedestals, both in remarkably good condition for being in a home that, once abandoned, grew full with vagrants. Squatters had stripped and sold everything: furniture, bathroom fixtures, copper pipes, and wiring from within the walls. Yet the pedestals remained, blackened with soot from campfires stoked with garbage. Scraps of plastic hung off the heads of devas like shawls.

Padma cleaned them with a soft toothbrush until her employer told her to stop because if they were too clean, buyers might think them a repro. He sold them to a Delhi restaurateur who used the pedestals as a repository for toothpicks, matchbooks, and fennel seed.

In particular, she wanted to see the Islamic mausoleums in Lakhpat, a stone's throw from the Pakistani border. At Lakhpat's height, she told him, the city had been a port housing nearly ten thousand people; merchants from Karachi sailed down the Indus in wooden ships to trade spices, silk, and fish. From Lakhpat, they continued into the Gulf of Kutch, the Arabian Sea, the Indian Ocean, and the world beyond. The Portuguese built two-storied houses with red-tiled roofs, whitewashed walls, and balconies overlooking the salt marshes of the Great Rann. But perhaps the gods took offense when Jamadar Fateh Muhammad built a wall around the town thirty feet high and eight feet thick. In 1819, the earth shook Lakhpat, sending the sea rolling up Kori Creek as far west as the Goongra River, and when the earth could not completely dismantle the walls, the Indus River himself moved thirty miles westward, abandoning Lakhpat altogether. People evaporated from Lakhpat, a port without water, and now, only a handful of families remained, mud huts among deserted houses, years of sun and sand scourging the whitewash to reveal gray concrete underneath. This was a city cursed by land and water alike.

It was also, Dev thought, a poor place for a honeymoon.

But Padma didn't mind the dust, the heat, the barren landscape. It was as if she were trying to prove that she hadn't married him because he was a doctor, that this arrangement was legitimate. Or perhaps she was emphasizing her responsibilities as a wife, because she was as uneasy as he about marriage. At their first meeting in the nayan's office, she didn't look at him; she focused instead on the portraits of happy couples on the wall, the groom's dhoti knotted to the bride's sari, an inextricable bond, and Dev watched the small flittering movements of her head.

Dev had told Padma only once about the promise he had made. Shortly before he left for his residency at Columbia, Dr. Sengupta had taken him into his office. He was in his sixties and preparing to retire. For Padma, Dev imitated Dr. Sengupta's voice, the precision of his vowels, the pauses that held uncertain meaning. *When you have your own family,* Dev repeated, *you will come and visit mine in Bhuj.*

This was easy to say. Dev kept his voice light and playful, reciting this friendly promise between teacher and student. He did not repeat, however, what had led Dr. Sengupta to that promise.

I see you, Dev, he had said. *Rootless and frightened. You think what you cannot find in India, you can find in America. But this is never the case. You cannot find what you need. You must create what you need for yourself.* Dr. Sengupta clasped Dev's hands. The gesture made Dev break into a sweat. The world seemed more immense and frightening than it had ever been previously. Dev had seen classmates swallowed whole by America, its carelessness, its selfishness, and he was as susceptible as they were, perhaps more so.

You must make a family for yourself, Dr. Sengupta said, *or you will always be incomplete. You must promise me that when you have your own family, you will visit mine in Bhuj.*

Dev nodded, but this wasn't enough.

Promise, Dr. Sengupta insisted.

And, as her first wifely duty, Padma made him keep his promise.

There, in Lakhpat, as they walked, round stones ground against each other. When Dev stooped to pry one from between the treads of his shoe, he discovered that it was a shell, nearly translucent. He held up a handful, ranging in size from his pinkie fingernail to a lozenge.

—Look at this, he said. He poured the shells into her hands, and she shook them, as if separating rice from its panicles.

—There's a legend, Padma said, —that in

ancient times, these shells were used as money. It's false, of course, since the currency of Kutch was the kori. Lakhpat itself was supposedly named after the fact that it brought in a daily income of one *lakh* kori.

Dev scooped both hands full.

—You've married a millionaire, he said.

—Only a millionaire? What a disappointment.

Padma circled the Ghaus Mohammad *quba*, a single dome upon an octagonal base. The mausoleum housed the body of a Sufi mystic, whose spiritual practices were said to have been half-Hindu and half-Muslim. The water from the adjacent tank was said to cure skin diseases. In it, dark-green algae clung to its sides; small white larvae gathered in the corner, roiling like foam. Weeds had overtaken the area, growing around an unmarked tumulus until the area looked cobwebbed. A hole had been knocked out of a nearby wall. Dev squinted; the architecture hurt his eyes. Nothing had a plain, solid surface. He didn't understand all this effort. The sun worshiped by casting shadows; the pigeons worshiped by building their nests.

Padma examined the corner pilasters, solid columns of stone with the tree of life carved into them. She ran her hands over the lattice like a blind woman committing the image to memory. If she could have, she would have taken it home and rebuilt the entire mausoleum in Dev's apartment.

Dev had wanted to marry, but marriage, family—these seemed like a mirage in the distance. What he saw in the foreground was his career, the long queue of patients waiting for his clinic to open, as they had once waited for his father's. He remembered running among them as a child, marveling at their ills: open sores the color of currant jelly, broken limbs hanging at impossible angles. And then, after an hour with his father, they reemerged, arms and legs returned to their original orientations. Dev's father taught him how to bind a wound in gauze, squeezing Dev's wrist and saying, *It should feel this tight:* the correct pressure to save a life.

And now, an adult, he ignored the rumors regarding him as the jealousy of gnats—*the head of an HIV clinic, unmarried at thirty-five; what do you think?* He lobbed away his colleagues' offers of matrimonial representation. It was bothersome, these blessings people wished upon him, the pujas they wanted to perform. It had been his mother's idea to place a matrimonial ad in the newspaper. She fielded possibilities during his residency, letters and photographs in thick files marked *unsuitable, possibility, suitable, unavailable.* That last folder grew increasingly fat, fed by women who could not wait for Dev to return from the States or, after his return, could not wait while he made up his mind. His mother lamented: *Will you be an orphan before you marry? Or until you have become too old to be suitable?* To which he replied: *Mother, I am a doctor. I will always be suitable.*

On Padma's hands, the mehendi had not yet faded, though the images had begun to bleed. Dev's name, hidden in the tail feathers of a peacock, had blurred. It was now an inscription as ancient and indistinct as anything here on the *quba*.

—Such a pity, Padma said. A camera hung around her neck, resting just below her breasts. She traced her fingers across cracks filled in with white mortar. Architectural scars. Designs interrupted, careful carvings discolored with moss and grime and only half cleaned, as if the task were too burdensome for one person to complete alone.

—These beautiful buildings, she continued. —Look at how those cornices have shifted so that the floral design no longer matches. And this latticework. It's like someone threw plaster at the holes to repair it.

This was natural selection at work. If Lakhpat hadn't been meant to survive, then it should have been allowed to die. But its residents persisted: an occasional motorcycle wound through the streets. Children called to each other. Two radio communication towers stood within the fort walls, like spikes driven into the city to keep it from blowing away. Dev understood the city's significance—Padma, more so—but historical knowledge was like all things past: enlightening but hardly practical. The medical profession no longer relied on leeches, or bed rest, or admission to a sanitarium. No, these things were best left behind.

Padma left dainty tracks around the *quba*. Dev had chosen her from his mother's files. In the photo she had sent, she posed with three school friends in Varanasi. If she had not circled herself, Dev would have assumed that she was one of the others. Other prospects sent carefully photographed studio portraits, lights positioned to catch cheekbone structure or the luminous sheen of glittered eyelids. This, apparently, was the best picture Padma could produce of herself, her eyes the color of the Ganges, as if she had reluctantly emerged from the water. He slipped her folder from *possibility* to *suitable*. If his mother recognized her when he presented Padma's file, she said nothing.

—Let's go to the fort walls, Dev said. —We can see the entire town from there and then move on.

Padma smiled and followed.

As she navigated the narrow path atop the fort, Dev walked a few paces behind. Travelers had left their mark: scratched-in graffiti, hieroglyphics of initials and dates. He wondered if, a hundred years from now, this writing would have more meaning than the fort itself. Once the fort had crumbled into its component parts, these letters would be framed in a museum—"PSK," whoever he may be, memorialized forever.

Padma stopped to snap pictures—a cannon on the ground like an amputated leg, a crumbling lookout window—and as she did, she regained her enthusiasm. She cupped her hand out before her.

—Look, she said. —I can hold the entire city in my palm.

Dev knelt to look—one wall to the other, balanced between her fingertips and wrist.

—Be careful not to drop it, he said. —You don't want to break it.

She laughed, a sound that startled Dev. Padma stretched her arms as if she could embrace the entire desert, the heat and salt and beige light, as if she wanted to embed this place of unlimited possibility and desolation in her skin. And for a moment, he didn't see her as Padma, the shy one—he saw her as Karisma Kapoor, seated on a throne of broken rocks, a dupatta wrapped around her head, and he was Akshay Kumar, a man haunted by a dark secret.

Padma pointed to the horizon. —Boats! she said. She clambered off the fort walls and walked into the Great Rann. Areas were still moist from yearly flooding: the tidal surges that presaged the monsoons, then the monsoons themselves. The muddy patches reminded Dev of skin under a microscope, the irregular cracks of the cells' borders. Padma could not completely avoid the mud and left skids where her balance wavered. Her tracks joined others: tridents left behind by birds, wishbones left by antelopes. Where the earth had dimpled, reservoirs filled with white flecks of salt remained.

Nothing grew here, except the *gando baval* and its vicious thorns. Jumbled nests of it, gray and dried, snagged his pant cuffs. It was an illness, this tree. It erupted from the ground, green tentacles leaching what little sustenance lay in the soil. The residents of Lakhpat fought its slow creep, cutting trees at the root and leaving the branches in the sun to desiccate, but its spread could not be halted, only maintained. It sent seedpods into the floodwaters, spreading itself across the breadth of the landscape.

Dev wondered if any of his patients had come here, to Lakhpat. He knew of many, too many, who had come to Delhi for work, contracted HIV, and then returned to their towns of origin, often remote, rural locations, where no one knew of their infection, rather than continuing in his care.

Not that he blamed them. He remembered, R____, twenty-eight years old. R____ had died in the hospital after five days of high fever and respiratory problems. In his final hours, he was delirious, speaking nonsense, spittle frothed on his lips. The nurse, who for weeks had cared for him, now refused to approach, not even to lay a wet cloth across his forehead. Dev could feel R____'s body heat from the doorway, unnatural, radioactive. *His situation is declining,* Dev told R____'s wife, *and you must make arrangements.* She said, *Yes, yes,* as if she'd understood, but when he died, no one came to claim the body. Shame and fear overwhelmed even grief. Dev summoned the other HIV-positive patients with whom R____ had grown close. It was decided: as a group, they would give him last rites. The next day, the others—*devadasis,* homosexuals, *hijras,* unlucky wives—arrived. Why Dev felt a kinship with them, he could not say. Dev listened to their breaths and knew who had acquired thrush and who had only recently recovered from pneumonia. In the mortuary, the staff stood back. *We know why his body is covered in plastic,* they said. *This man has died of AIDS.* The driver to the temple demanded three times the normal fare. *I have a family too,* the driver said. *What will happen if I catch it?*

S____, whom Dev suspected was the man's male lover, said, *We should wrap the body in a bedsheet, so that it looks*—and S____ paused. The very word, unspoken momentarily, seemed absurd. *Normal,* S____ said.

32

What if the priest sees the plastic sheet? someone asked. *What if he asks about it?*

The whole day, Dev had been silent: his relationship with these people was professional; he wasn't religious, and yet, here he was, with R____ and his friends. Dev said, at last, *Once we reach the cremation ground, I will ask the priest to hurry.*

Padma reached the first boat, set off the ground on rocks. The anchor, a thin hook of rust, was mired in the ground, stretching the rope tied to the prow taut. Someone had taken pride in this vessel: roses and twining vines were carved in the wood. It had once been painted blue, but all that remained were flakes of color on the knobs that never touched water. Padma seemed disappointed that this boat was intact—she pointed at the plastic bottles for ballast, the discarded work gloves in the center, the old tire that someone used as a seat.

—Those farther out look more interesting, she said.

And if by *interesting,* she meant *decrepit,* then she was correct. She found something beautiful in their decomposition: the curved wood, a rib cage; the planks, rotted and bleeding rust where they had been nailed together. Mud had seeped through the hull. These boats had long been abandoned. Perhaps the owners had sacrificed them, scuttling them to beg the Indus to return. *We will give you our livelihood,* they said, *if you return ours.* Even Padma had her superstitions. She kept a bottle of Ganges water in the kitchen—filtered, purified, deionized—and added a squeeze from an eyedropper to every pot of rice.

Three figures moved along on the horizon, black dots like fleas. *Goat herders,* Dev thought. *Nomads.* They walked as if time had already forgotten them. Padma was busy taking snaps; every now and then, she halfheartedly tugged at a piece of wood to see if it would come loose. Perhaps she understood these artifacts belonged stuck in the ground, or perhaps she could think of no way to salvage them. Or perhaps she was simply bored.

As the figures drew closer, Dev saw they were not herders after all. Their clothes were not loose drapes and turbans, but fitted and regimented. They carried not sticks, but guns.

—Padma, he said. —People are coming.

She hmmed, still in reverie. But when she saw the men, she said, quickly, —We're not doing anything.

One soldier waved; another beckoned them to come closer; the last held out his hand as if to hold them in place by sheer will. Two Sikhs: an older one with his nylon turban shimmering in the sun, the other with a beard as bristly as a scrub brush. The younger *jawan* who had been waving had a sparse mustache. None were Gujarati, as far as Dev could tell. They had been stationed here, perhaps against their will. Lonely men, scattered about the country, far from what they knew. Anything could happen to them.

—I'm sure it's nothing, Padma said.

The letters *BSF* were stitched in brown on their epaulets—Border Security Force.

—What are you doing here? the elder Sikh asked. —ID cards.

Dev reached for his wallet, and the other Sikh called in on his communications radio: —We've found some people. He waited for a reply.

The elder looked at their papers and held them up as if he'd be able to see a watermark reading "Counterfeit." —What's your address? he asked.

—We just married, Dev said. —We live in Delhi.

—I study ancient architecture, Padma interjected. She gave him a business card. —I wanted to study the buildings here.

He shoved the card into his pocket without looking.

—You're not supposed to be here. How do I know you're not trying to sneak across the border? How do I know you're not spies?

—We're not, we're not, Dev said, and Padma said, —We weren't doing anything wrong. Her voice intensified. Her hand balled into a fist, a petty gesture, like a woman diverting the flow of a river with a teacup.

—Do you know how close to Pakistan you are?

—I read we'd just signed a cease-fire, Padma said.

The Sikh laughed. The young man squatted on his haunches, and the butt of his rifle dug into the ground like a flag. A piece of camouflage cloth was wrapped around the muzzle, and the magazine cartridge was transparent. The bullets inside were sharp-tipped, severe. The other soldier still couldn't raise anyone on the radio.

—We are never at peace, the older Sikh said.

—What would you know? Living in Delhi. He opened a canteen, took a swig, and spit onto the ground. —Why do you have a camera? he asked.

—I'm taking pictures. Of the buildings. And the boats.

—I have to confiscate it, he said.

—That's preposterous, she replied.

—We can't allow pictures of our border stations circulating. Who knows what people are planning.

—It's just of the old buildings, she said.

—You, he said, menace in his voice, —are in no position to argue.

—But— said Padma, and the young man cut her off.

—Hey! he called to Dev. —Control your woman.

This caught Dev unawares. Here was a clause in their marriage contract that he had not thought to exercise. They were far from the modern world. This was a hopeless place. Dev had sought to appeal to the soldiers' sensibility, but now he knew he had to appeal to their brutality.

—For goodness' sake, Dev told his wife. —Hold your tongue.

Padma looked like a bird that had flown into a pane of clear glass.

—I apologize, Dev said. He took the camera from Padma's neck. —Sometimes we need to be reminded of our place, he told them. He opened the back of the camera and pulled loose the film. The brown exposed coils curled around his wrists like manacles.

They waited a half hour in the sun until the commanding officer came. The officer lectured them as if they were unruly children—*this is a time of great tension, this is for your protection*—and Dev said, *Yes, sir, yes,* until he lost track of what he had agreed to. He could no longer say he was even annoyed. He felt less than nothing, really. This show of authority was as empty as a hand puppet; the soldiers had already proved what they wanted to prove. They were the lords of this expanse, keeping an endless vigil on this dead city. Lakhpat's walls had been built as the first line of defense against Sindhu invaders. Now, it was the Pakistanis.

—You are not allowed beyond the city walls, the officer said, and Dev said, —Yes.

In the car, driving toward the guesthouse in Narayan Sarovar, Padma turned her head away from Dev, as if the landscape, an expanse the color of underbaked bread, was worth looking at. He asked how she was feeling, and she tilted her head in a maddeningly noncommittal way. —Things were going badly, he explained. He hadn't meant to insult her. No reply.

—Very well, then! he yelled. He didn't care if her tongue shriveled inside her mouth.

The guesthouse Padma had chosen was adjacent to a Dwarkadish temple. She went straight to the room while Dev registered. The only other person there was a young foreign tourist, the type that lived out of a backpack. Foreigners were a rarity here in Kutch. Dev guessed he was German.

The tourist acknowledged him with a nod and a smile.

He could understand Padma's anger, up to a point. It was unfair for him to be cross with her for speaking, and then to be cross with her again for being quiet. But if she had wanted fairness, she should not have been born a woman.

Dev felt no better than those *jawans*. He had never before been disrespectful to a woman. Even in their short marriage, he was pleasantly surprised when she challenged him, correcting his admittedly incomplete knowledge of history.

He placed no demands on her: he had not forced his way into her arms or come home demanding meals. Asking her to be silent—just for a moment—should have been of no consequence. He had apologized, and still a barrier he could not comprehend remained.

In the room, Padma unfolded the sari she would wear tomorrow to visit Dr. Sengupta. She brushed it to straighten the creases, to remove the dust that had infiltrated their luggage. Her hands glided against the fabric. It was a vermillion silk; the edges were hemmed with gold thread. Dev had chosen it for her, a traditional gift, something his mother or grandmother would have worn. It seemed out of place among Padma's other clothes: the pantsuits, the blouses in colors unknown to nature, the saris she had named after different artists. Hand me my Pollock, she would say. My Picasso. My Chagall. Such a clever wife he had. His colleagues had been duly impressed. The ring he wore was proof against speculation, against rumors. It was proof of his duty, of the affection that had not yet had a chance to grow.

Dev lay on a pad that he had stretched across the floor so that his wife could have the bed.

—I know you're disappointed with me, she said.

—I'm not disappointed, Dev replied. —Not with you.

But Padma stared at the ceiling, as if learning

39

how to endure this, the first of the lies in their marriage.

Dev woke during the night, uneasy. Padma's quiet breath filled the room, and from the high, arched window on the wall, a solid stripe of moonlight entered. What the soldier said disturbed him. The words ricocheted in his head.

Control your woman.

He left the room and paced the guesthouse. It wasn't the thuggish command that bothered him—*control*. It was the other part. *Your woman.* He could no longer ignore it: Padma was *his* woman. Dev's mother and father had embraced her as their own, as she had embraced them as new parents. And Dev, whose responsibilities had always been diffused among humanity, now possessed a specific set of responsibilities to which to attend. He felt bound to her in ways he could not—maybe could never—understand.

He knelt before the German's room, this unfettered young man, free to wander the ends of the earth. He aligned his eye with the keyhole, resting his cheek against the wood. His aperture of vision revealed the German's bed lit up by the moon. He had thrown off his sheet; it bunched on his shins. He slept nude, but the light ended just below his belly button. His stomach moved steadily. His right wrist bent awkwardly in front of his pubis, and Dev knew that when he woke, that hand would be numb, unresponsive. It would flap uselessly until blood returned to the nerves, and it would prickle as if on fire. Dev held his breath to still the terrible racket. His heartbeat pounded so loud it could have woken everyone in the city.

As he stood, his bones creaked. His joints popped. Adrenaline burned the back of his throat. He felt his way back to Padma, tracing the painted wall with his fingers. He could tell where the brush hadn't fully covered a crevasse, where a drip had run in a vertical line. Shoddy workmanship, one incomplete project after another.

Back in the room, Padma hadn't stirred. She gave off a floral smell, sweet in the salt-tinged air. He sat on the edge of the bed, the mattress so thin he could feel the metal springs underneath. Padma had the sheet up to her shoulders, and he caressed the outline of her body. He had once deemed Padma *suitable*. He had never considered if she considered him *suitable* in return. Perhaps they were suitable only for each other. He stroked her, as if smoothing out a piece of velvet, until she stirred. When she tried to rise, his lips found hers in the darkness, and he knew that he could not abandon either Padma or his duty to her.

They left shortly after sunrise, but the German had left even earlier than they. —These tourists and their backpacks, the guesthouse manager said. Dev nodded, and his heart thudded, emptying entirely of blood. On the ride to Bhuj, Padma had a smile that Dev could not place. It was not the previous day's girlish glee. It was more settled, a smile with wrinkles at its borders. Padma napped when she could with her head on Dev's shoulder. He sagged under her weight and balanced himself against the unsteady road.

The street on which Dr. Sengupta and his wife, Sushrita, lived had no two houses alike. They stood, one-, two-, and three-storied, balconies bulging like hernias. The architectural chaos was constrained only by the size of the plot. The other houses were so colorfully garish that Dr. Sengupta's white paint seemed quaint. Dr. Sengupta would have been astounded at the buildings continually rising into the Delhi sky, thin and spindly as young bamboo. That's where Dev's future lay: years from now, he and Padma and Arusha would live in a block of flats in Noida, and from his window, he would see other gray constructs replicated across the length of the land. In the distance, cranes would herald the next step of progress. This was his life at its apex, comfort that others would envy, a beautiful stability. Perhaps he would shift away from his HIV clinic and into teaching, like Dr. Sengupta. Perhaps Padma would morph into a dutiful doctor's wife, pleasant and content.

In Dr. Sengupta's living room, Sushrita set out bowls of chaat. Dev nibbled nervously.

Padma insisted that she could not eat a thing, and Sushrita insisted that she should, and since Sushrita had the force of age behind her words, Padma relented. —Delicious, she said. Dr. Sengupta's portraits of his grown sons and their children hung on the walls. Generations smiled down upon the newlyweds.

Dr. Sengupta emerged. —Dev! You kept your word.

—Padma would never forgive me if I had forgotten, he replied.

—Is that true?

—When women are involved, Sushrita said, —it's always true.

—Not even a week and she's running your affairs, Dr. Sengupta said. —Sushrita had me by the collar as soon as the ceremony had concluded.

—A good thing too, Sushrita said. —Padma will be a good influence on you, Dev. Now, if you don't mind, I need Padma in the kitchen.

Padma excused herself.

—Lovely, Dr. Sengupta said. —You should be very proud.

—I am, Dev said. —You were right. I feel—

Dev stopped on the last word, unsure how to continue.

—Yes, Dr. Sengupta said. —Marriage changes boys into men. You look the same as the first time I laid eyes on you in class. Ambitious, yes. But also curious and stubborn. Unprepared for

the rigors of life. Dr. Sengupta raised his hand.
—Don't misunderstand me, he said. —I saw my
own, younger self in you, Dev.

—And now?

—And now, Dr. Sengupta said, leaning forward
and lowering his voice. —You will discover, as I
once had to, that—

At that moment, Padma and Sushrita brought
out cups of tea, steaming hot. In each cup, the
ground spices accumulated in a vortex. As she
served him, Dev touched Padma's hand, a small
gesture, a finger on the base of her wrist. Dr.
Sengupta paused. He blinked as his thoughts—
disrupted and now shifting—seemed to take on
a new form. Sushrita sat next to her husband,
heedless that she had interrupted anything.

—Dr. Sengupta? You were saying?

—That nothing is more important in this world
than family, Dr. Sengupta continued. —They are
both history and future, your inheritance and your
legacy. When the trappings of this world have
fallen away, they remain. I see you changing,
Dev, in ways that you yourself cannot. And I
know that you and Padma will know the joy that
Sushrita and I have felt these many, many years.

This was a speech Dr. Sengupta must have
recited many times. It slid off his tongue like
a piece of candy. It meant little, of course, but
Dev would always wonder what Dr. Sengupta
had meant to say before Sushrita and Padma had

emerged from the kitchen. That—that would have been a real truth, a guide that heretofore had been hidden. And now—it was lost. Dev's life contracted and expanded before him in one long breath. He smelled tomatoes stewing on the stove. Sushrita had Padma's earlobe between her fingers, admiring the delicate gold hoops that Dev had given her. Dr. Sengupta pooh-poohed the women's fuss over jewelry, but Dev knew that he would soon purchase a pair for Sushrita herself. Dev felt himself growing older, his cells dying and replicating more slowly, losing chunks of DNA. He would have his own students, and he would tell them that their own destinies would lie with their own families, and they would believe him. He foretold his own decay: the unsteadying of his hands, the loss of sexual vigor, his senses shaving off and fraying, until he and Padma could no longer attend to themselves and moved in with their children and grandchildren. Perhaps Dr. Sengupta was on the cusp of promising another life, an alternative, a secret that he had discovered too late to take advantage of it. But the one he had offered was the one Dev knew he had already accepted.

It's near three in the afternoon when Dev arrives in Bhuj. A young soldier ushers him and four others into a Tata Sumo, which normally has room for ten. The rest of the space has been given over to equipment. Dev keeps a hand on the neck-high pile of boxes next to him. Others sit folded, like letters in an envelope, to make room for supplies.

Debris has choked off roads, points of exit. A caravan of Sumos stretches from the army base into the heart of the city, which bears no resemblance to the city Dev visited five years ago. All around them: rubble the color of clotted cream, and among the rubble, darker spots, which Dev imagines are bodies, clothed, crumpled. In the car, a collective gasp: some pray, and the remainder weep. Nurses weep; doctors weep. Dev, however, does not weep. Both he and Bhuj have changed irrevocably; there can be no crying over it now.

As they enter, others escape. The car in front of them has been consumed by the mass of evacuees on foot. The soldier blows the horn, but no one moves. There is nowhere to go. People press their palms against the car, heads bowed. Their knuckles rap on the windows, leaving rosettes of blood.

—What should we do? asks a nurse. She reaches for the window crank, and Dev yells, —Stop! They'll swarm us. She is on the verge of tears but crosses her arms. In the box next to her, glass tinkles, the sound like ice crystals forming.

Men stand behind the tailpipe and hold up both hands, mouths downturned in anguish:

Why do you not stop? The car moves forward, the engine whinnying as the driver presses the pedal.

—How much farther? Dev asks, and the soldier gestures as if waving away a mosquito. Somewhere in the distance.

The nurse asks, —Would it be easier if we got out and walked?

The driver shrugs.

Triage has been set up where Bhuj Civil used to stand. The peaks of the tents look like points of skin where the stitching needle has not yet broken the surface.

Speed is the key. Much of the groundwork has been prepared: the ambulatory and lucid are separate from the immobile and the dazed. The unresponsive lie on the ground on blankets, and Dev moves up and down the rows. Colored rolls of tape dangle from his right arm like bracelets. He holds a silver penlight and peels back each person's eyelids. He cannot look at other wounds, not now; he stares only at their eyes. He focuses on the retina, on the iris, waiting for a contraction as the beam grazes the eye. And just as quickly, he attaches a strip of tape to each person's chest, right beneath the collarbone.

He does not want to use the black tape, but more and more, the situation warrants it. As the roll runs out, he attaches small pieces of the black tape along his fingers until his entire left hand is covered, a dark semaphore.

New Delhi General has been the site of emergency simulations: terrorist bombs, poison gas leak, nuclear attack. The administration insisted that all personnel participate.

Dev refused. *The HIV clinic is long-term essential services,* he argued. *Not emergency.*

This is a government-mandated exercise, the director told him. *Besides, it is always better to have a preparedness plan.*

So, Dev said, *you would have my HIV patients evacuate? Mingle among the other patients and reveal their identities?*

No, said the director. *Just you.*

The operating theater is functional nine hours after the earthquake, and even then, far too late. Limbs that might have been saved are now gangrenous: rancid, black flesh. Concussions have bled into subdural hematomas, leaving patients disoriented, unable to sit for examinations. A doctor sits with three patients in front of him in a radial pattern so that he can stitch all three in one go. He shouts, —Needle! I need a needle!

With the surgical team in place, Dev can now perform more thorough triage with borderline cases. The man before him has an indentation in his temple the size of a walnut. The skin is unbroken.

—What is your name? Dev asks.

The man stands, as if late for an appointment, and Dev holds his shoulders. He's a marionette. He looks fifty, pockmarked with evidence of a hard life. The blank intensity of his stare reminds Dev of a taxi driver.

Soldiers move the dead to make room for more living. *They should,* Dev thinks, *keep better track—write down names, post a list.* People come to the medical area, searching for loved ones. They fill the air with plaintive inquiries— *Are you there, Ramesh? Please answer*—and push at the tents with a desperation so violent that the soldier guarding the tents cocks his gun, on the verge of firing.

—Your name? Dev asks again. Still no response.

Dev administers a prick test with a safety pin. He starts at the man's middle fingertip and makes his way down the hand and up the arm. —Sharp or dull? No answer. He repeats the test with a chip of ice. —Hot or cold? The man seems impervious to sound, light, pain—to any sensation. At best, he rates a seven on the Glasgow Coma Scale. Four grades away from death. The man once again tries to leave, but Dev detains him.

—Where do you need to go? What's so important? This man needs a CT scan, a PET scan,

MRI, EEG. Any number of unavailable devices. The man turns his head to Kalpataru Road. His chin tilts up, a tremulous nod. His pupils contract, and for a moment, Dev thinks he's indicating a direction, someplace that he needs to be. The man's moment of clarity disappears as soon as it appears—his pupils re-dilate, and he turns back toward Dev. He opens his mouth, and between his lips, thick cords of mucus distend.

—I can't let you go, Dev says, but the man ignores Dev's insistence. He belongs *out there,* the man seems to say. His family awaits, be they dead or alive. Dev takes a self-adhesive label and writes, as neatly as he can, "RAJIV." If the man's being has leaked out of the indentation in his skull, the least that Dev can give him before he wanders back into nothingness is a name.

Dev sees Sushrita wandering the hospital grounds. Of all people! Her poise—straight-backed, regal—makes it seem as if she is in charge, and the soldiers do not hassle her. She is too composed for chaos. She reaches into a bag slung on her arm and gives a nearby nurse a parcel. Dev is relieved to see her, but all the same, she shouldn't be here.

They embrace. —I'm thankful you are safe, he says.

—Yes, she replies. —The earthquake gave

me quite a scare. But our house was solid. She mumbles a quick puja.

—Sushrita . . . , he says, but he's unable to continue. He doesn't know how to say what he has to say. He has informed thousands of their serostatus and knows how to guide the conversation to what he has to say: *I understand what you must be going through. There are treatment options. It's not a death sentence.*

But here, he cannot find the words to comfort Sushrita.

—Oh, where are my manners? She hands him a samosa, wrapped in newspaper. Dark spots of oil seep through yesterday's news.

—What is this?

—The power has gone out. Didn't you know? It probably won't come back for days, and the food in the refrigerator will spoil.

—The army brought emergency rations, he said.

—Yes, yes, but those are for everyone. Look at you, working so hard. You should have something better.

—What about you?

—I have plenty, she said.

—Are you feeling all right? Did you fall? Hit your head? Dev gives her a cursory visual examination. She may be in deep shock.

—Such fuss! she says, waving him away. —I'm an old woman, nothing more.

The sun sets, bathing the world in dirty orange light. The dust and particulates diffuse what remains of the day. Soldiers have set up generators, jerking the start cords with their entire bodies and cursing the machinery, until, one by one, the engines sputter into life. Dev becomes aware of a sound—the *tink tink* of metal upon stone. Over at the ruins of Bhuj Civil, soldiers and civilians alike chip at the stones with screwdrivers, hoping to free survivors. The electric lights project jagged shadows. The dead are piled shoulder-high. Still—*tink tink tink*.

—About Dr. Sengupta—, Dev says.

—Mithram. Call him Mithram. Still so formal after all these years!

—I'm sorry, Dev says.

—He's around here somewhere, she says.

—Always helping. I knew when I married him that the lives of others would always come before mine. It's my duty as a wife. My burden.

She looks around, as if realizing for the first time where she is.

—I shouldn't keep you from your work, she says.

—Sushrita, I'm so sorry . . .

She holds up a hand.

—When you see Mithram, please give him a message.

And with that, she continues west along Mandvi Road, back toward Pithorapir. Surely Sushrita must be living on the street. No one trusts the indoors. The city has been turned inside out. Whole neighborhoods huddle on the sidewalk. Nothing vertical seems safe: walls, pillars, roofs, what has not collapsed still bears the weight of that possibility. Sushrita hands out samosas until she has no more, then walks in a straight line, weaving to avoid the families spilling onto the road.

Dev walks to the base of Bhuj Civil, away from the lights, away from the people hammering at rubble, away from their painful, futile optimism. He places a hand on a broken chunk of concrete. In the concrete, there are smaller stones of different colors—individual cells in the cross section of a torso. It feels warm beneath his palm, throbbing gently, matching Dev's own pulse. He puts his face next to the stone and whispers, —Mithram, Sushrita says she's having trouble falling asleep; call her before you get home.

Broken hands, broken legs, blunt-force trauma, burst intestines: patients from nearby villages— Anjar, Bhachau, Dhamadka—come to Bhuj. Doctors amputate mangled limbs with scissors. The hospital in Ahmedabad, despite suffering damage itself, has offered to take the most serious cases, provided they survive transport. Dev must make decisions, and make them quickly: *You, who have lived a long life, will stay; you, who have not yet begun to live, will go.*

Then come the aftershocks: sleepers wake, the rubble shifts ominously, and the lights sway. One falls and bursts into stars. People scream and scramble.

Dev crouches low and puts out his arms to steady himself. His heart jumps. The aftershock finishes as quickly as it comes. Dev hyperventilates; his fingers and toes buzz from excess oxygen. He feels dizzy, as if he might topple. Around him are desperate screams, a deafening cacophony. Panic is as palpable as rain. But Dev—he feels more alive than he has for a long time.

The generators chug out black fumes and heat and electricity. But they also stall out and fail. The sudden darkness sends people into terrors. One soldier has been given generator duty; he patrols with a canister of petrol and a funnel, trying to keep all of them functioning simultaneously. In this patch of night turned back into daytime, the light dries Dev's eyes—each time he blinks, his eyelids stick to the balls.

These small emergency generators aren't powerful enough to run a full refrigeration unit, so plasma is stocked in a tent walled with slabs of ice. The bladder bags grow skins of frost, and the nurses melt windows with their thumbs to uncover the type.

The night brings its own cold. Dev has no other clothes than what he wears, and his sleeves are smeared with blood and lymph and who knows what else. Impossible to keep sterile conditions. Latex gloves are scarce. He has one box, which he guards between his feet. He would share with his colleagues, but he remembers the times they snubbed him, when they passed him in the halls of New Delhi General and turned their bodies to avoid even accidental contact. Two years ago, after his testimony before the World Trade Organization, *India Today* featured him as "the new face of the struggle against AIDS," and they avoided him even more. Jealousy. Cowardice.

He has been up for nearly twenty-four hours. While Dev was a resident, he worked thirty-six-hour shifts but always sneaked a few minutes of rest: a quiet office, an unoccupied gurney, his head in his hands in a toilet stall. But he is no longer a young man, and one patient shuffles after the next.

He sets a broken arm as best as he can, and the woman screams as bones scrape against one another. Her screams meld into the others. The surgeons have no anesthesia.

—Don't cry, says Dev. —Save your energy for breathing.

He has no plaster with which to stabilize her

arm. He looks around for a plank of wood, a roof tile—even cardboard. At his feet, empty packets of gauze, ankle-deep.

Dev summons a group of soldiers. He sends them into a nearby store to bring back pants, shirts, saris, shawls. Bandages are their first priority.

—Cotton only, please, he instructs them. —The wounds must breathe.

They shred the cloth with bayonets. The unusable clothes—rayons, polyesters—are given to those who have nothing to wear. One young man had been in the bath when the earthquake struck and walks naked, dust crusting on his skin like a shell. He puts on a shirt that extends past his fingertips and pants that expose his ankles, and for these, he thanks the soldiers.

Dev fashions a sling out of a pair of panty hose for the woman with a broken arm.

The *jawan* watching the generators stands idle.

Dev calls: —You! Break into that chemist's shop and grab supplies. The soldier, little more than a boy, should be used to taking orders. —Go, Dev says, —I will take the blame.

He breaks the window with the butt of his rifle and emerges with a few boxes: syringes, needles, bottles of glucose.

—Get medicines! Dev yells.

—What kind? the boy asks.

—All of them. Everything you can get your

hands on! Dev had almost forgotten what his own voice sounded like; his shouts are a vestigial organ rediscovering its function. —Quick, now, he says. —*Quick!*

A man, barefoot, approaches. He resembles a ghost who has been wandering for eternity. The lights have brought him here. People have grown inured to the night, vanquishing it with a flip of a switch. Now, it has reconquered them. They cower before its immense power. Even Dev has forgotten how incapacitating darkness is: its unyielding hunger. To banish night, even for a moment, is to reassert humanity's dominance over nature.

The man carries a girl in his arms. She dangles as limp as laundry.

—Please, he says, —my daughter.

—Her name, Dev says. He tires of asking this question. A formality now.

—Lakshmi.

Dev motions to a nearby cot, and the man places her there. The muscles in his arm tremble. He must have been carrying her for hours.

—Doctor, he says, —please treat her first.

—There are others, Dev says. Screams have faded to moans, the sound a wall that threatens to crush him at any moment. Triage is almost complete; tomorrow, Dev will find a scalpel and enter the surgical theater. There are, perhaps, lives that can be resuscitated. This girl—nine, at most, dressed in a woolen jumper with her school's seal stitched to the right of her heart—perhaps she was to play some part in the India Day ceremonies. Dev thinks of Arusha briefly—but this girl is not Arusha. This girl cannot be saved.

—Please, the man says again. His voice is flat; his hopes have died with his daughter. —Please examine her, he says. —If she is dead, then I need to look for my wife.

—Go, Dev says. —Go search for your wife.

The man steps back into the all-consuming dark, and only later does Dev realize what he should have said. A simple, elegant statement—a response that should have bubbled up from a place that Dev can no longer recognize. He should have said: *Go, and I will attend to your daughter.*

Because of the false afternoon cast by the overhead lights, Dev misses daybreak, but now he can see people who were hidden. He recognizes colleagues from conferences and gatherings. He sees the generator guard—not a boy, but a man in his thirties with a wedding ring. And he sees what devastation looks like in the light, how shock gives way to despair.

People resume their efforts to save the trapped, clawing at the stone with whatever they have:

hammers, chisels, hands. The rows of injured, laid across the ground, covered with gray army blankets, look like freshly dug graves, even as they stir and respond to the sunlight. The living dead. And then he sees Sushrita. She has changed her clothes.

—Sushrita, he says, —you shouldn't be wandering. It isn't safe. Another aftershock and—

—And what? she replies. —If it is my time to die, so be it. But while I live, I will do what I can.

He can't muster the will to fight. Not with Sushrita, not now. It's like arguing with his mother—he will never win.

—You should get some rest, she says, and Dev laughs. How bizarre the world has become, that she treats him like a child even while death surrounds them. Dev feels like he's bleeding, that he's been bleeding for some time.

—Have you eaten? she asks.

He can't remember what he did with Sushrita's samosa. Gave it to someone. Or someone took it. But Dev isn't hungry. He places his hand on his stomach. There is blood pooling inside of him.

—I knew you wouldn't eat, she says. —Mithram is the same.

She hands him a cold piece of roti wrapped in a napkin. —Here, she says.

He accepts, too tired to argue.

Then—unexpectedly, like the sun rising in the

west—Sushrita asks, —Have you called Padma?

Dev hasn't even thought about Padma since leaving Delhi. Even if the telephone lines were operational, which he is sure they are not, it would be a drain on resources, a waste.

—No, he replies.

—*Tch.* Sushrita unzips her purse and, from within its depths, retrieves a moist towelette. The Indian Airlines logo has almost completely rubbed away from the wrapping. It must be years old. She rips it open and unfolds the small square.

—You and Mithram are two of a kind, she says. She takes Dev's chin in her hand. They look into one another's eyes. He wonders if what he sees there swimming in her gray irises is sadness. He wonders if she sees something similar in his eyes. Perhaps he's as blank as the towelette she holds in her hand.

She wipes his forehead in long strokes. The cool moisture; the rough, scouring paper; her strong fingers pressing into his skin. She brings it over his nose, and he inhales the evaporating alcohol, the false, chemical lemon. He remembers when Arusha was one, when he had given her medicine to bring down a fever, but after twenty minutes, it still hadn't taken effect. She fussed mightily, and he thought she would squirm out of his arms and fall to the floor. Padma took her from him and cradled her in her right arm. With her left, she dripped cool water from her fingertips onto

Arusha's forehead and blew gently on her face.

—Both of you, Sushrita continues, —attending to strangers and leaving your loved ones to worry. Both of you, very careless and very noble.

This is our duty, Dev thinks. *Our burden.*

But it excuses nothing. If he and Dr. Sengupta are indeed the same, then Padma and Sushrita are the same as well. After all, both women would rather believe that their husbands are saving the world, when, in truth, both men have slipped silently into a landscape of ruin.

THE VIRGIN RESCUE

Twenty-Eight Hours after the Earthquake

Before the flight to Bhuj, Andy jitters with nervous energy. His fingers thrum against his knuckles. Not just him, though: the four on-call rota UK Fire Services Search and Rescue Teams gathered at RAF Brize Norton can't keep still. They circle the perimeter, greeting old chums, handshakes all around. *Armenia, right? No, Turkey.*

Andy envies the men's easy camaraderie, the shared experiences that harness them to one another. For every fire that Andy's battled, he's done twenty times as much outreach: going to year one and two classrooms, teaching fire safety—matches, electrical outlets, the like. They listen to him, bright-eyed. They ask about the engines, the sirens. They touch his helmet. Important, necessary work. But not always exciting. It's silly to expect a burning building every shift, but he's getting paid to wait around for a pan of bacon fat to catch flame.

The other members of the UKFSSART remember their first time like it was a birth or death—so momentous they can't shut up about it. Every detail is etched in their memory: the time, the place, the date, the quality of the light, the color of the air. It drives Andy mental.

Boarding the RAF TriStar for his first mission is like boarding a can of spray paint: he's the little metal ball clattering around inside. The men make themselves comfortable. They roll their suits into lumbar logs and cross their arms across their chests. Andy sits between Les and Colin, not entirely at ease. Les has been his mentor since he first joined the fire brigade, sharing mundane duties on their shifts: stacking the dishes in the fire hall mess, running to the nearest chip cart. Les cheats when they play cards, but Andy hasn't quite figured out how. Les doesn't try to change the channel when Andy's watching telly but plops down and watches along. Les was the first to ask Andy to dinner outside work, and Andy listened as Les talked about his wife and children, about his burgeoning beer gut, about what a twat Reg was. Everything Andy had to say seemed small and useless. He lived in a tiny flat and sent money home to his mum.

"Jesus," Les said, "don't be so hard on yourself. You just started shaving, what, yesterday? If my son grew up half as set as you, I'd be happy."

Even if your son was queer? Andy had grown used to all manner of insult; he was even adept at using them, putting the same force into the words as he would into his shoulder to break down a door. When Andy told Les that he was, in fact, gay, Les was more than surprised but less than shocked.

"Fuck, man," Les said. "I didn't know. How long have you been looking at my ass in the shower?"

"You're not my type," Andy said.

"What? You don't think I have a nice ass?" Les turned to check himself out. It was true: Andy *had* seen Les's ass in the shower. He had seen Les's cock, along with the cocks of all the men in the company. What intrigued him most about Les's body was the blotchy scar running the length of his left arm, a burn from two years ago. Les had been holding a support beam when a cherry-hot cinder fell into his coat sleeve. He let the cinder singe his arm rather than drop the beam.

Les tapped Andy's chest with an open palm. "You're a good lad and a good firefighter. To me, that's what matters. But I wouldn't go telling just anyone. You understand me, right?" Not just anyone. Right. It sounded odd coming from Les, who wasn't above calling someone a dirty queer. But Andy knew that if the rest of the crew found out, he'd be sent to Coventry. Les, bless his heart, ran interference. If someone razzed Andy about not having a girlfriend, Les interjected, "Give the kid a break. He only hit puberty last week." And even though Les continued to call people dirty queers, he always mouthed a silent *Sorry!* afterward.

On the plane, Les snores louder than the hum of the propellers. Andy wants to check him for apnea. Jostled from all directions: the airplane's vibrations through his feet, Les's snoring into his brain.

Colin, the DCO, sorts through papers. He passes some to Mike, who shuffles and returns them. Colin catches Andy trying to read them. "Nothing you need concern yourself with," he whispers. "You just be ready to go when we land."

Be ready. Crikey, for what? Andy's first major call with the brigade was the Paddington train crash at Ladbroke Grove. Two trains, head-on. The firehouse got the call at 8:15, two hours into Andy's twenty-four-hour shift. *Major emergency,* HQ said, *major emergency. Respond immediately.* The house was halfway across town, but as the Atego pulled out of the house, Andy saw the streaks of smoke dredged across the sky. He steeled himself for unbearable flames, the trapped and the burning, all the horrors he'd read about in simulation exercises. Unnavigable chaos. Severed limbs. Dead children.

But they were the fifth brigade on the scene, and there was nothing more to be done. The diesel had burned itself out. Twisted, charred wreckage fumed in the crisp October air. Andy led survivors to the nearby Sainsbury's car park, where the doctors of St. Mary's Hospital had set up. Ambulances from Hammersmith Hospital and the Royal Free Hospital stood at the ready. The car park was all emergency lights and sirens, and the bruised and abraded queued as if waiting to check out groceries. Andy pointed those who could walk toward a nearby school playground, toward a larger transport from Wexham Park Hospital. *Move this way; move that way.* The people couldn't hear him, dazed and shocked as they were, ears ringing from the explosion, but they could follow his finger.

The evacuation took three hours, and afterward, he and Colin walked the tracks, marking smoldering scraps of metal for investigators. Wheel casings and bogeys strewn about, blackened with seared grease. In the scrub far to the left of the tracks, a sheet of steel with the First Great Western logo, blown far from the rest of the wreckage. Survivors described a fireball coming down the center aisle of the car, a great whomp as the fire sucked away the oxygen. No one could avoid it. The heat melted armrests into their skin. How small Andy felt, spritzing pulped metal with a handheld extinguisher, the foam sizzling as it hit the ground, a strange frost. He smelled burning polyester and remembered how, at sixteen, he set an old pair of gym shorts on fire. He picked out the acrid tang of burned leather from the seats.

"That's not leather," Colin said. "That's flesh."

And so it was. Andy counted to ten, tensed and relaxed his stomach muscles until he stopped heaving.

"I'm all right," Andy said. "Really, I am."

Forty Hours after the Earthquake

They debark in Ahmadabad, down a rolling set of stairs to the tarmac. The asphalt is crisscrossed with tarry repairs. Inside the airport, people lie on the floor, the lines stretching out the door and into the street. These are the lucky ones who can afford a ticket. They don't budge, and Andy walks around them. He slips his thumbs underneath the straps at his shoulders and pulls tight. If he takes a tumble, his three-stone bag could do serious damage.

A few blocks away, the face of an apartment building has sheared off to show its insides. Rubble is heaped on the ground, a barricade. Men stand in the street—not walking, not milling, just standing. But then, prompted by nothing, one throws his head back and howls. So raw, so animalistic; Andy shivers. He's attended memorial services for fallen brothers before. Last year, one was killed in a motorway accident. The funeral was a dress uniform affair, shoes polished, bell caps low and tight on their heads. The tears jumped from one man to another, like pinkeye, but nothing excessive, nothing embarrassing. Andy didn't cry. Sadness hit a dam within him, no spillway. It was OK for them to cry, but not for him.

"We're arranging transportation," Colin says.

"We haven't arrived yet?" Andy asks.

"The army wants us farther in. They've already got Swiss and Turkish teams working here."

"Fucking hell," says Reg. "Turks?"

No one's awake enough to take proper offense, but whoever's here isn't working fast enough. Andy's palms itch. It's right in front of him, so close that he can smell the plaster in the air, the sting of particulates.

"And the Swiss," Reg continues. "What are they doing? Bringing everyone cocoa?"

"For fuck's sake," Colin says. "Shut up."

Reg looks like he's just stepped in shit, and Colin glances up the street, as if waiting for a bus. Reg makes a *wanker* gesture behind Colin's back. Andy's hands are still fists.

"Have you worked with the Swiss team before?" Andy asks Colin.

"Yeah, in Montserrat." Colin swings his hands, like it's his first day of work. "They were first on the scene there. And the Brits fucking own Montserrat."

We used to own India too, Andy thinks, but

feels bad for thinking it. Maybe that's the difference between him and Reg: Reg doesn't apologize for what comes out of his mouth. Andy isn't scared of Reg. Reg reminds him of men he's brought home, the ones who want to prove they're stronger than he is. They grapple him in massive bear hugs, and he squirms in their embrace; they put him in shoulder locks and dare him to escape, which he knows is his cue to submit. Grizzled and burly men who gnaw on his nipples as if they're taffy, and he wakes sore, sensitive to the touch, flushed with heat and blood, and can't put on an undershirt because even cotton hurts.

Sometimes he doesn't get the whole gay thing. Well, he *gets* it, but doesn't get *it*.

Two buses pull up. Their panels read "Himalayan Tours," and they have tinted windows set high above the ground. The door opens with a pneumatic sigh. "Welcome aboard," Mike says. "Next stop, Bhuj." The team of seventy splits between the buses, not just the UKFSSART, an acronym that reminds Andy of a deflating tire, but the International Rescue Corps and Rapid UK as well. Andy, at twenty-five, is the youngest. He's also the shortest. The rest of his crew has nicknamed him Fireplug for his height and his thickness. Most of the men duck to avoid the top of the doorway as they board. Not Andy, of course, who has room to spare. During his initial firefighter recruitment session, one poor sap three or four centimeters shorter than Andy was dismissed, and Andy thought, *Should have worn platforms, mate.*

He and Colin sit up front. Colin glares at Reg. Mike and Les settle across the aisle. Outside, people are shadowy versions of themselves. Orange dots move about in the distance. The Swiss team, maybe the Turkish team. At last.

"Back in Montserrat," Colin says, "the Swiss had done a pretty thorough sweep of the immediate area. Everything around the volcano had burned to a crisp. Ten-kilometer radius. You could smell it. I nearly swore off meat."

The burning pine, Colin explains, couldn't cover the bittersweet stench of burned skin. Ash, ankle-deep, had seared villagers fifteen kilometers away. The Swiss team had spray painted large *X*s on the doors of the houses where there were no survivors. Village after village, x-ed out. Even outside the blast wave, ash smothered everything. What seemed like life had been choked in place: livestock suffocated while standing, human bodies solidified as if they'd been dipped in plaster. Colin entered a chapel where people had sought sanctuary. They had collapsed in the pews: an elderly man in a brown suit, head lolling back as if bored by the sermon; a mother holding the hands of her daughters in white dresses, sashed at the waist.

Colin stopped checking pulses after the first few. His breathing apparatus was a cheat. He put an *X* across the double doors, the fingertip of his glove black with paint, and, on a hunch, went back inside. He crossed the nave and went up the chapel stairs to the sacristy. There he found the pastor, unconscious, but alive, his chest moving shallowly. He was in his vestments, crisply ironed. Colin administered oxygen, sharing his breathing mask, until the man woke. The pastor said he'd come up for additional prayer books and must have fallen asleep. *Alléluia*, he said. *Un miracle*! God had saved his children in their hour of need. The pastor's words steamed inside the mask, a damp hope. *Un miracle*, he said again as they descended. Colin kept a tight hold on the pastor's arm as they walked toward the door. He called out, *Guillaume! Sophia!* He knelt by the mother and her two daughters and took the younger's hand. *Anne Marie,* he said softly, realizing at last. *Claire.* He stroked the girl's hair with the back of his hand, kissed his fingertips, and brought them to her lips. His strength waned, his arm hanging limp across Colin's shoulder as they entered the sunshine. The village was gray and silent. The pastor hid his face, praying into his fingers.

"But how did he survive the oxygen displacement?" asks Andy.

"I don't know," says Colin. "See, that's the thing. Maybe it was a miracle after all."

Forty-Five Hours after the Earthquake

A jolt shakes Andy awake. The other crew members look asleep—eyes shut, hands crossed in their laps, heads resting on rucksacks. The packs stowed in the cavernous luggage compartments below shift. Metal scraping metal. During firefighter training, trainees put one pound into a beer kitty for every piece of equipment damaged or missing, from a popped-off button to a burned-out bulb in a headlamp. At the end of the course, there was enough for drinks on the house three times over. How strange that damage could warrant a celebration.

Andy looks out the window, picking out shapes on the landscape. The flatbed lorries with the heavy-lifting equipment trail far behind them, their lights distant specks. The headlights seem like the only lights in a blacked-out world. He expects electricity—proof of life—and reminds himself that this isn't London, or even the countryside. This is middle-of-nowhere India. He remembers Bombay and Calcutta from geography class, placing the cities on a blank map for exams, but he's never even heard of this place they're going to—never mind that he'd failed geography. Bhuj. It sounds like a bad word, something you'd get in a fight over. *Your mother's a Bhuj!*

Once in a while there are factories, huge,

tubular structures glowing from within like paper lanterns. The three-quarters-full moon reflects off puddles of the salt marsh, and the ground glows phosphorescent. Andy's eyes tire of squinting into the darkness, omnipresent, thick and consuming, impenetrable, filled with pain.

"You think you're ready for anything," Les had told him once. It was during his induction ceremony into the UKFSSART. All thirteen brigades—even South Wales—had gathered at the Charter Accountant's Hall. They choked the place in noise. Bronze sconces lit the room golden, and near the ceiling, above the balustrade, portraits of old men peered down, judging the revelry. The men sat bicep to bicep, filling the empty space with muscle. The chairs had been removed in favor of benches the length of telephone poles, and as they ate, they knocked elbows, each bite a wrestle for supremacy. A burp from one end of the hall could be heard at the other. They were red-cheeked from lager, good cheer, and the heat of the room.

Andy had always been proud of his wiry, taut physique, and sure, the London Fire Brigade had a fitness requirement, and the Search and Rescue Team an even stricter one, but his new comrades-in-arms were made of sterner stuff than he. They were tempered and honed, forged in heat and disaster; he, at twenty-two, was still a shapeless, molten mass.

"Your first time'll hit you like a brick wall," Les said. "When your time comes, it'll be beautiful. It'll make this feel worthwhile."

Mike, the chief officer from Leicestershire, had the new recruits stand, starkers, on the table. Andy thought about how unattractive the men were around him, how warm the air was in the room, how this humiliation was nothing. He unbuttoned his shirt and unbuckled his pants. The table was dotted with beer and coagulated fat. Andy had shaved his chest recently, but not recently enough: small sprigs of blond hair sprouted, making him look dewier than ever. Other inductees were older and had barrel chests of hair. Andy stared at the ceiling, where cigarette smoke accumulated, tinting the plaster gray. Other inductees hunched to obscure their tackle, but a few had accepted the futility and let everything hang, arms spread like they'd burst that way from the womb. Andy was surprised to see how pale they all looked under the hazy yellow lights, proof that they were unready for the world.

"If you fall backward right now," Mike asked, "would you trust your brothers to catch you? On the count of three." Andy had done this exercise before—usually with clothes. But that was the point. If you couldn't trust your crew naked and ashamed—whom could you trust?

"Three!" Mike said, and Andy fell. For a

moment, his body rejected this new vertigo; it wanted to stay upright, but even before he'd tilted thirty degrees, hands cradled his calves. Andy kept his body rigid and locked his knees. *If you're going to save me, you'll have to save me as I am.*

"I've got you," Colin said. Anonymous hands supported his weight. Trusting these men wasn't something he could simply choose to do or not to do. Either they would save him, or they wouldn't. So be it. If they were going to let him down, he hoped they would do so gently, but just in case, his body tensed for the hard fall.

Fifty Hours after the Earthquake

Andy's legs grow numb. Everyone's restless. Men walk up and down the aisle, swinging their arms. Any energy they had at Tikar had worn off by Maliya and by Gandhidham completely dissipated. It reminds Andy of a school trip. Once the initial raucousness fades into fatigue, all that remains is the want for home.

Les rifles through his bag. He could probably do it blindfolded. "My first time, I was completely out of sorts," he says. "I mean, we're set up for earthquakes and fires and all that, but in Mozambique, it was floods, and I didn't bring a pair of macs. My boots got so swollen that my feet didn't fit."

He takes out his hammer, cuts through the old grip tape with a pocketknife, and peels it back like a banana skin. He finds the edge on a new roll and rewraps the handle, rotating the hammer, flattening the tape with his thumb.

"When we arrived, we rode motorboats up the river, and I'd see huts along the shore that didn't look too bad. Then all of a sudden, we crested, and the river opened up onto a lake that used to be a town. Nothing but dead animals floating in the water. Chickens and pigs and cows, rotting.

"I went to a collapsed schoolhouse. I was thigh-deep in mud. It was warm like pudding. I felt like I'd pissed my pants. All I saw was little bodies. They looked like they was made from mud. But you'd touch one, and the mud rubbed off, and you saw skin. The bodies were warm from it. The stuff poured out of their mouths.

"And then I heard someone gasping. Real faint, like I was imagining it. In the corner, a chalkboard had toppled against a wall. When I moved it aside, there was a little boy in an air pocket. He'd managed to keep his head above the water. I dug around him with my hands until I reached his knees, and when I pulled him out, the mud gurgled, like it didn't want to give him up. And for a moment, it all made sense. All the medical training, all the workouts. Everything."

"Did it make you feel better?" Andy asks.

Les restashes his hammer. "Almost."

Mike briefs them on the chain of command: although they are working under the auspices of the Indian Army, they are to take directions only from him or Colin. They will deploy as soon as they set up camp, so they need to be ready at a moment's notice. Bring any problems to his attention immediately. Take the time to make sure that their packs are fully stocked and set to go.

"Let's calibrate our watches," Mike says. He stands at the front of the bus, shifting his weight as if he's lived his entire life at sea. "On the count of ten, it'll be ten thirty." Andy holds out his watch, his finger on the button. "We should be there at any moment."

Fifty-Nine Hours after the Earthquake

As Andy steps off the bus, his body cracks. They are in a large green, next to what's left of town hall. It must have once stood three stories high, but now it's an outcropping of timber beams and broken doors. Wires dangle, as if reaching out for attention.

He takes in a deep breath and coughs it back out. Too much dust. Others clear their throats and spit. The air roils overhead from the earthquake. The breeze creates swirls. Andy wants to slip a mask over his face, but sees no one else has, so he doesn't.

One team is dispatched to where live contact has been reported, but Andy gets volunteered to set up camp. Fine: there's work to be done. He drives metal spikes into the ground. Hitting the hammer against the metal, the sharp *ting* it produces, eases the crimps in his body. Gets the blood flowing. Andy strips to his T-shirt. Steam sizzles off his skin. During drills, the team constructed camp in under twenty minutes, but those were practice conditions, where the aluminum support poles sunk easily into green turf and held fast. Fresh air, the sun at their backs, Colin standing off to the side with a stopwatch. "Let's pick it up, men!" Andy could secure a spike with just two strikes; now it takes five before the dry clay and dead grass give way.

Mike meets with the interior minister and the state police chief. The chief strides around as if the situation were well in hand. The brass bars on his epaulets are shiny, his mustache is ruler trimmed. Two Indians soldiers carry cartons of bottled water, followed by another with two red petrol cans. Other soldiers mill about, awaiting orders, their uniforms the color of the earth, their skin like strong tea. The police chief points at Andy and waggles his fingers, as though shooing away a gnat.

As Andy wonders what the policeman said, his hammer glances off the head of the spike and smashes his left thumb. He brings his fist to his mouth. *Fuck!* He sucks his thumb. It tastes of iron and two days' worth of dirt. The nail is unbroken, and only half of it is purple, but when it throbs, each throb is a sparkler of pain.

He'd injured this thumb four years ago during training. During his search-and-rescue obstacle course, he tried to climb the three-meter vertical wall and, halfway up, lost his grip. He landed with his thumb beneath his body, and it wrenched away from the rest of his hand, and as he rolled on the ground, Reg, the drill leader, called him a cunt, a weakling, not fit to rescue a cat from a tree. That night, he could have cried about it—the pills the med officer gave him were a step above Panadol—but he wanked off to Reg's face moving closer and closer, repeating *cunt, cunt, cunt,* until Reg was whispering in Andy's ear. As Andy came, he tilted his head on the pillow to let the word leak out. The next day, hopped up on painkillers, hand taped and immobile, the world unbearably bright, he returned to training and stared down Reg, and Les called him a stubborn fucker.

But even with his newly smashed thumb, Andy lashes the overhead tarp and proofs it against aftershocks. The heavy-lifting equipment hasn't arrived, which makes Colin uneasy. They're supposed to have a scissor press that can lift and hold ten tons indefinitely. Andy has watched videos of it in action. The motor whirs and whines, blowing out hot exhaust, and the press moves imperceptibly. Patience is the key. It takes twenty minutes to lift that much weight—a combination of hydraulics and leverage so arcane that it might as well be magic—but even three centimeters, the length from the tip of his thumb to the first knuckle, is enough to free someone.

"We'll have to start without it," Colin says, cracking his knuckles. Colin's a postbox, solid and thick, with a jaw that juts out like it's ready to accept letters.

Andy secures the sides of the tent, unfolds and aligns the cots. He empties his pack of his protective fire gear and slips tools into the loops on his utility belt. He cradles his helmet in the crook of his arm, the straps undone and hanging about, and takes his place in line, where they stand at attention. He tucks his injured thumb into his fist.

"Right," says Mike. "Let's get to it."

Dusk. The Balaji apartment complex.

This is the third building Andy has searched. These buildings once had names and windows and exterior features; now they had fuck all. At the first building, on his first tunnel down, he shone his torch onto a man's scalp—"Are you all right? Can you move?"—only to realize that it was a head on a torso. The other half of the body had been pincered away. He'd wasted his breath, unable to tell the living from the dead. For the next two hours, he kept quiet, lips tight against the airborne plaster until Colin called off the search. At the second building, dust sifted down from above, and the interior rumbled and hissed as it rebalanced. Pebbles tumbled from an unknown height, and Mike simply shook his head. *No.*

The sun slides beneath the horizon, and light struggles into the air, a bloody glow that drains from the atmosphere. Civilians, dressed in civilian rags, pick at the wreckage to reach the twenty-five or so missing persons reported trapped inside the Balaji. Their friends and family. They haul bricks and cinder blocks with their bare hands and relocate the rubble down a line. Some men look as if they haven't eaten in days, skinny enough to break in two. They heave rocks into one another's arms, shirttails out, and where they wipe their hands on their pants, they leave smears of blood. Nosebleeds cake into their mustaches, dark as pitch, and when the soldiers tell them to make way, they shift the line. They're determined to do something.

Andy and the crew approach the central staircase of the lobby, the only part of the Balaji that hasn't compacted, and Colin sends Andy in with a warning, "You feel anything go wrong, hear anything out of the ordinary, and you get the fuck out." Andy clamps his hands into fists to keep from shaking because everything he's learned feels useless. During training, he had to crawl through a twenty-meter concrete tunnel no wider than a body. The tunnel was worn smooth by endless recruits before him, and a trickle of water ran down the center for authenticity. Even outfitted with a breathing apparatus, Andy made good time, being smaller than the others, but toward the far end, the pipe tightened so that the tunnel pressed against his back and stomach with each breath. His own odors concentrated, and he wondered if his light-headedness was a lack of oxygen, the onset of claustrophobia. If he couldn't do this, then this was the end of his career. He curved his shoulder toward his chin and let his left arm lie limp as his right pulled him forward. He reached the end of the tunnel, where it opened enough for him to rise onto his hands and knees, and he turned himself around, sitting on his ankles and rolling backward, readying himself for the long crawl back.

The opening before him is a mouth, as far and deep as he can see, full of teeth. Andy secures the mask around his face, clicks on the torch attached to his helmet. Ready. Phil and Reg hold the line circling his stomach, and from elsewhere, he hears team members call, "Please respond if you can hear me."

Andy musters the strongest voice he can. His voice needs to penetrate the filter mask into the space ahead. Bent girders deflect the sound. Around him, shorn steel cables: sharp, impaling objects poking his body. Floors here were raised without support beams, and the walls, thick as a slice of bread, stood without plinth. It's no surprise that this building collapsed; it's more of a surprise that it didn't collapse long before. The upper floors lean against each other awkwardly. They threaten to tear away at any moment, and as if Phil and Reg sense his reticence, they pull at his cord to confirm that he's fine, and he replies, a single tug. He drops to his knees and faces a dark void—"Anyone here?" The staircase is a broken back, and the debris, like splintered bones, grabs his clothes, and Andy doesn't realize how badly he's scraped until he notices rust-colored pinpricks on the orange surface of his suit. If it weren't for his torch, he wouldn't be able to count the fingers in front of his face, and a chill settles on his cheeks and eyelids. The air is stagnant, and Phil calls, "Anything?" and Andy says, "No, I'm going farther."

He can't be more than five meters in, but the void he's working in is less than a meter high. He uses both hands to undulate forward on his belly like a snake. He won't let himself imagine what this place must have been like, how it must have once been filled with the noise of children and families, how it smelled like the curry carts in Whitechapel. With each movement, Andy sends plumes of white dust into the air. Desks, frying pans, cribs—all effaced, indefinite. Up ahead, a bundle of black-rubber-coated wires sway as if in a breeze, and these wires are connected to a gray blouse, and Andy says, "Hello?" in a paper-thin voice, then louder—it's hair, a woman's black hair, and her head tilts back, and he sees her eyes, and Andy calls out, "Reg! Reg! We've got a live one!" and turns back to ask, "Are you all right?" but her eyes glaze over, and her face contorts, as if she had given up hope long ago, and he says, "We're going to get you out." She snaps to life—her eyes widen, and she speaks rapid-fire Hindi, which he can't understand, and he says, "We're here for you," which she can't understand, and Reg asks, "Can you reach her?" If his arms were three meters longer, he'd be able to, but there's so much between them: cinder blocks and rubble, boulders and Sheetrock, and he tells her, "I'll be right back. I promise," and once he's out, Mike does a rapid assessment: "Physical condition? Head and shoulders visible. Good. Rest of body? Unknown. Obstructions? Many. Working space? Tight."

Mike requests a translator, a thin Indian man who puts on a harness and shimmies into the void like a cat. Andy can't get the woman's face out of his head—suffering from dehydration, shock, bottomless fear. He's made a promise to her, hasn't he? And even if she didn't understand, he's bound to it. The translator tells them, "It's her foot. Her foot is caught," and Andy's heart jumps—*amputation, we're going to have to amputate to get her out*—something Andy never imagined doing, but the option hangs like a dark cloud, and the Indian fellow says that he can't get close to her, and Mike asks, "Who's the short man in your unit?"

Andy says, "Me. I'm the short man."

It's up to him; he has to do this, and the U clamp goes back onto his waist, and he crawls in as the others clear the entrance, giving him every bit of space they can manage. Andy clears what he can, rock by rock, and anything he can't push aside, he breaks with his hammer. He lies on his stomach and taps away impediments; the sound echoes around him, and the woman calls out now and then, as if reminding him of her presence. His gloves make a tight grip on his hammer difficult, and it sometimes slips out of his hand. He shifts a chunk of debris and wonders if he's going to cause a rockslide, if he's going to need a rescue himself, and his breaths grow louder, and he can smell her fear, its acridity, and his own perspiration, his body steaming in the suit. So close. The woman stretches out her arm, her fingers wiggling toward him. Almost. He reaches out until the skin at his armpit feels ready to rip and—he makes contact. He takes her hand and squeezes it; he's there, he's kept his promise, she's going to be OK, and he's going to bring her out of this hole, and their lives will be there waiting for them on the other side.

But the woman lets go and makes a waving motion with her fist. She's angry with God and cursing her fate. Or she's angry at him for his uselessness, the fact that he hasn't saved her yet, or—maybe she's angry at nothing at all, because Andy realizes she's making a hammering motion—she isn't weak; she isn't helpless; she wants to free herself. Andy hands her his hammer, and she bends at the waist to reach her foot. Stone grinds against stone, and Andy winces as she strains and tugs, but—but she moves closer, a cascade of pebbles like rain, her skin washed of dust by sweat; she puts her arms up above her head, a surrender, and Andy grabs her wrists and inches backward; her arms pop in their sockets, and she shakes her torso, trying to get free; she looks up at him, the skin tight on her skull, and she nods, and Andy pulls, every muscle tense and straining, and it's a cork coming out of a bottle: her chest, her waist, her legs, her feet; as soon as she's loose, she crawls after him with fire in her eyes, and soon, Reg and Phil have his feet, and the world opens up, filled with overhead lights, and it's so blinding that Andy turns off the torch on his helmet because nothing can compete with that light; medical personnel load the woman onto a stretcher; the light blots out the moon and could overpower the sun if it wanted to; the medics speak to the woman, and she closes her eyes because perhaps she has lost everything, her family, her children; she has nothing but this brightness, and Andy squints in its intensity, feels crushed by it, and an Indian fellow hugs Andy full throttle, an assault for which Andy is unprepared; he stands, awkward, as the man cries into Andy's suit and says incomprehensible things; Mike steps forward to shake his hand, then Colin, and, off to the side, Les nods, and Andy feels oddly alone, because he can't stop thinking about the hammer the woman has left behind in the darkness. His best hammer, his only hammer.

At the end of the night, exhaustion covers Andy like cling film. His head buzzes. His nerves are alight, twinkling. This must be the way superheroes feel when they transform from ordinary humans into vessels of power. He can hear the trapped miles away, frightened heartbeats, shallow breaths in dry throats. *I will come for you.*

Les, standing as far from the cots as possible, motions to Andy. "I've got something for you," he says, conspiratorial. He roots in his pack and, from its bowels, produces a can of Guinness. It's completely forbidden—contraband—and the can is dented and scraped and nicked and bruised, but never before has Andy wanted more to give Les a big, sloppy kiss. Les gestures toward the others. "They asleep?"

Ian, Marc, and Oliver are lumped in their cots like sacks of laundry. Ian gurgles, making clicking noises as he switches from nose breathing to mouth breathing.

"We should celebrate," Les says. They shouldn't; they need to be alert as soon as they wake tomorrow, but one beer isn't going to kill them. Les pries back the flip top in microscopic increments until the seal breaks and foam spurts from the breach. He passes the can to Andy, who slurps the overflow as quietly as possible. It geysers over his sore thumb, down the side of the can, onto the ground. He has a mouthful of head. His cheeks bulge until they hurt. His lips pucker tight. The bubbles pop against the top of his mouth, and the residue sticks like candy floss. He imagines burping, the smell invading everyone's dreams.

After what seems like minutes, the can stops foaming, and Les kicks dirt over what's on the ground. Andy takes a sip and feels like a dying man who's been granted one last wish. He's never thought about the flavor of beer before. It's always been a social convenience. A method to meet men. *Can I buy you a pint?* Simple, generic, effective. But tonight, he swishes it in his mouth, bathing his tongue. He tastes roasted barley, hints of caramel, flavors that don't materialize in cigarette-choked pubs or clubs suffocated by coconut-scented smoke machines.

"Brilliant," Andy whispers.

He'll be up to his ears if Colin or Mike catches him, but it's worth the dressing-down. He loves Les, but not in a romantic or sexual way, and anyway, he doesn't want to fuck up things between them with those sorts of feelings. What he wants most of all is for Les to put his arm around him and kiss him on the forehead.

"You've earned it," Les says. His smile disappears. "I have to warn you. It doesn't get easier from here. After pulling that one kid from the mud, I didn't find another living person. It fucks with your head, it does. You're a good kid." Les smiles again, no longer celebratory. "I shouldn't call you kid anymore, should I? You've had your first."

"You can call me kid if you want."

Les pats Andy's head, the closest they'll ever get. He's OK with that.

"I know. But I shouldn't." He stretches both hands above his head. "I'm going to hit the sack. You should too."

Andy nods.

"And for fuck's sake, dispose of the evidence."

Andy's too wired. He steps out of the tent into the open air. He looks to where city hall should be. Something once existed there. High above him, a cascade of stars, a sight he's never seen in London before, never seen in his life. They remind him of embers spraying against a soot-black chimney when a burning log breaks in half.

Huh. He doesn't understand the fuss people make about stars.

This is the first time he's been out of the UK. The closest he'd come was the holiday he took when he was thirteen, the last vacation he'd taken with his family. Back then, his father was still normal, and his mother still had an air of youth. They were in Dover. He remembers salt in the air, salt on his tongue. On the ferry that rounded the cliffs, his mother turned away from the spray, throwing her head back when she laughed, sending good cheer into the clouds. Andy and his father stood at the rails, taking the full brunt of the sea, and Andy imagined himself a sailor, a pirate, a traveler from afar, and his father put his hand on Andy's shoulder, as if to keep him from going overboard.

Things turned into shit quickly after that.

The can is half-full, but he can't finish it. Not because he's incapable of drinking it, but because around him, soldiers shuffle back and forth, maintaining some sort of order, while civilians claw at the rubble or themselves. Tomorrow, he has to be back among them. His fingertips buzz, not from the alcohol, but from the need to do *something*. He's had his moment, but inertia is a fatal trap, and if he rests for a moment, he will dissolve into nothing.

Up ahead is a campfire where people have gathered. The firelight falls across a pair of shoes, a man sitting cross-legged, an open notebook in his lap. Andy's surprised to see another Anglo.

"Sorry," Andy says. "Didn't mean to disturb you."

"No, no, you're fine." He sounds American.

Andy moves closer. "I didn't expect to meet anyone out here."

"I understand," the man says. "It's strange being surrounded by . . . *this*." The man gestures with his chin, and the lines on his face darken.

Andy cocks his head. He's here for a job. That's not strange in the least. If anything is strange, it's the fact that nothing is strange.

"Mind if I sit?" Andy asks.

The man pats the ground. "Be my guest." He's writing, a pen entwined in his fingers. "So who are you with?"

"UK Fire Services Search and Rescue," Andy says. Saying it makes him puff his chest. He flexes his right bicep, a pleasant show of vanity.

"That's great," the man says.

"I had my first save today." The story spills out, like he's reliving a love affair. Just thinking about it, eagerness pulses through him, and his muscles twitch in anticipation. Tomorrow seems far away.

"What are you doing here?" Andy asks.

"I'm with DART—Disaster Assistance Response Team. From America."

"And what are you doing?"

"Me? Helping as much as I can, I guess."

"Cheers to us, then," Andy says, and he raises the can. "Have some."

The man laughs. "Leave it to the Brits to find a way to smuggle beer into a disaster."

"Have a sip anyway," Andy says. The liquid sloshes. The man swallows a token amount, as if not wanting to offend his host.

"You're going to spoil me," he says. The man sighs and takes another sip. "But I'll take any little bit of happiness I can find."

"You should, you should," Andy says, and finally, he *does* feel strange. He and this stranger, sharing a drink amid death and destruction. It's as the man described it. *Any little bit of happiness.* A woman is alive because of him, and all that she is—all that she will become—is because of him. The truth of it overwhelms him; it's on his tongue, behind his teeth.

"You do good work," the man says, in a tone of

voice more apologetic than complimentary, and Andy says, "We both do." Andy stands, holding out his hand, as if asking the man to dance. The man flips his notebook shut, takes Andy's hand, and rises. Andy wraps him in a bear hug. It's ridiculous and impulsive, but it's all he can think of. The world is full of life, all around him. Even under compacted rubble, even injured and in pain, even in grief so deep that it suffocates: the life is there. He will discover it, and he will rescue it. The top of Andy's head comes to the man's chin, and the man's body tenses, then relaxes, then relents.

And—he isn't quite sure of when he first realizes its presence, but it's as unmistakable as the nose on his face—Andy feels the man's erection. This is a pleasant surprise. Andy feels himself growing hard and locks eyes with the man, who looks mortified.

"I'm so sorry," he whispers. He tries to pull away.

But Andy won't let him. In lieu of apology, Andy grasps the back of the man's head, brings it to his, and kisses him. A strange embrace in a strange place. Their lips are chapped and rough, and Andy tastes dust and stout, but he knows that this is the breath of life: the air from his lungs fills the man's, and oxygen revitalizes the blood. Synapses light up, like a row of matches laid end to end.

But this is not enough. The real secret to resuscitation, Andy knows, is returning life to the spirit as much as the body, and out there, out in the dark, are people waiting to be saved.

STETSLOVICH'S CONJECTURE

Piotr smells coffee in the predawn darkness, when the world should be silent, but isn't. He has always prided himself on being first to rouse, but for the last two mornings, before he wakes, someone has prepared a communal stockpot of coffee. It hangs over an open fire as an incentive to join the day.

His Walkman has run all night. The plastic is hot and smells of ozone. The cassette, Chopin's preludes and etudes, has played an endless loop and is stretched so thin that the sound emerges tinny, as if he's listening through a long, hollow tube. He peels the Walkman off his chest. The inside of his ear canal is soaked, as if he's been underwater.

No one sleeps soundly. It's impossible. Ted snores lightly beneath a gray blanket with the consistency of fiberglass; Lorraine's empty cot looks remarkably neat. But the team is lucky even to have cots: two tents down, Monika from the UNDP simply lies across plastic bins pushed end to end.

Piotr's task is to know things, and either he can give answers or he can't. It's like being a pianist: one either plays the notes on the page or doesn't.

Playing the notes poorly or giving an incorrect answer—these are unacceptable.

But first: coffee.

The pot appears next to a hand-lettered sign in English warning not to scoop the grounds at the bottom. Others have appended translations: French, Swedish, German. As additional workers arrive, new translations appear, and the sign looks as though it's grown a beard. People sip cupfuls of the black liquid and sit on their haunches. It's a ritual, watching the fire flicker, stoking it, thinking about what lies outside camp. As the pot empties, someone adds more water, emptying bottle after bottle until the liquid browns again, and people resume drinking. By afternoon, someone sets the pot aside, and in the middle of the night, the process starts anew. Piotr does not know who the mysterious brewer is. Not yet, at least.

He hits the "Stop" button on his Walkman, and the day begins.

The Walkman was a gift from his former DART lead, Connor Gibbard. The infamous Connor Gibbard, who, at Christmas parties in his Georgetown home, greeted his guests wearing his lucky flak jacket. He bragged that it was tailor-made. He festooned it with ornamental bows, the red and green representing, he said, blood and gangrene. Good luck charms. In the foyer hung a gas mask stuffed with mistletoe. Beneath it, Piotr gave Connor's wife, Beth, a peck on the cheek. "He has quite the morbid sense of humor," Beth said. "Merry Christmas." She suddenly looked concerned. "Oh, dear. You're Jewish, aren't you?" Technically, yes, but not practicing. "Well, I hope I didn't offend you. If you'd like a beer—" She gestured toward a body bag laid across the kitchen table, bottle tops poking out of the zippered gash.

Connor was known in USAID circles as the "aid bully." He rejected the image of the aid worker as a silent figure. No, Connor argued, the aid community should have a prominent role in shaping international policy. Aid workers were not merely deliverymen, he said; they were public advocates for the dispossessed. Connor insisted on placements in conflict areas, and in the ten years Piotr worked with Connor, they'd dispatched to Somalia, Rwanda, Colombia, Haiti, Chechnya, Tajikistan, and Bosnia. It was after Bosnia that Piotr left Connor's DART.

When Piotr was first hired, Connor told him how everyone in the field needed a distraction. Knitting, books, whatever. Something to blot out the shells whistling overhead, the encroaching gloom, the screaming. Piotr told Connor that if he concentrated on his work, he could quell the voices around him.

"You're wrong," Connor said. "They only get louder."

They were eating lunch at Eastern Market, in southeastern DC. Sweet smokes filled the air. Booths sold African masks and sticks of incense bundled in mason jars, and the vendors shouted and cajoled, outdoing each other.

"You can't simply give things away," Connor said. "Governments have to be coaxed—or coerced—into taking aid. Imagine that! They see aid, especially from the US, as an intrusion, as colonialism. First come the aid workers, then the governmental advisors, then the military." Connor was in his fifties, magisterial and iconoclastic. "So we need to change the system into which we deliver help. Otherwise, it's a black hole. A waste of money. We need to be part of the negotiations."

But Piotr had no aptitude for negotiating. As a child, his mother haggled with department store saleswomen, pointing out every uneven stitch, every crooked button, until the saleswomen offered 10, 15 percent off. Piotr, on the other hand, accepted fixed prices, nonnegotiable stickers. Haggling played no part in his cost/reward analysis.

"If you can get tangible concessions," Connor said, "then your efforts are worth it. Nothing comes for free."

They wandered the interior of Eastern Market.

T-shirts with unfamiliar slang. Stained glass sun catchers and wind chimes. Carved-wood elephants. Piotr needed none of it: in his one-bedroom apartment, he had all that was necessary. He tapped a wind spinner, reticulated glass bars glued into a spiral. The edges undulated, a golden ocean wave. If only all beautiful things could be so simple.

A salesman spread Walkmans of dubious origin on a blanket across the floor. One was the size of a deck of cards, thin and silvery as a fish. "Do you like music?" Connor asked Piotr. The salesman flashed a crooked smile. Connor picked one off the ground.

"Beauty, huh?" the salesman asked. Connor shook his head and stepped backward, then forward again. He pointed to the thin one.

"How much?"

"For you, my man, ten bucks."

"Ten! Maybe if it were new. But look here—" Connor pointed at a scratch in the silver paint, revealing plastic beneath. "It's damaged. How do I even know if it still works?"

From his pants pocket, the salesman produced two AA batteries. He found a cassette squirreled inside his jacket. He detached the headphones from around his neck and plugged them in. Connor and Piotr pressed their heads together. The music that came forth wasn't to Piotr's taste.

"Headphones ain't included," the man said.

"Not included? I'll give you a dollar if you're not including the headphones."

"No way," he said.

"These things are antiques. How many have you sold in the last week? The last month?"

"Five, then."

"Do they even still make cassettes? I should just buy a CD player." Connor started to move away. "Let's go, Piotr."

"Hold up, *hold up*. You're killing me, man. OK. One buck."

Connor had been palming the dollar since the start of the encounter, the paper soft from overuse. On the Orange Line back to Federal Triangle, Connor pressed the Walkman into Piotr's hands: *See how easy it is?* he seemed to say. *You could be me in no time.*

The military airport in Bhuj has been overwhelmed by incoming flights. Planes idle on the tarmac nose to tail. The previous day, USAID sent a C-5 Galaxy's worth of goods, and the air traffic controllers said the plane couldn't land. The runway, they feared, would crumble beneath its massive weight. What the earthquake had not destroyed, the Americans would. Typical.

But the pilot found a way. The wheels left a river of melted rubber as they touched down. The plane seemed as big as the base itself. Its belly opened to a city of boxes secured to the floor with fist-thick ropes.

The military now reserves Bhuj for food aid, rescue equipment, and medical personnel. Today, housing materials—canvas tents, plastic-sheeting roofs, galvanized-metal walls—are to arrive at the Gandhidham Military Base. Piotr will see to their distribution.

"This might be an all-day affair," Lorraine says. "The roads are a mess, so I don't know how long it'll take to get there." Her hair has expanded like a sponge in water, her head a fibrous mass of dark-brown curls. She hands him a dossier: maps and charts and graphs. Seismic activity, population density, estimated damage, loss of life. The sheets curl around his arms, a ceaseless rustle of paper, and he clamps them in his armpit to keep them stationary. His skin smells of a fax machine's insides.

"Have you been getting any sleep?" she asks, and he shrugs. She breathes out long and slow, as if frustrated. She is nearly ten years younger than he is and has also worked in disaster relief for nearly her entire life. Piotr admires the commitment to her work: no family other than her elderly parents, no distractions to take her away from her precise, unrelenting focus. And yet, she treats him and Ted with a maternal softness, as if she holds what she feels for them like a golden stone within her heart.

"It's going to take us a few more minutes to finalize transport," she says. "Try to get some rest."

He returns to the tent, where he removes his glasses, puts down his pencil, and rubs his temples. White hairs have established a stronghold there. He pinches the bridge of his nose. A rare moment of calm, this moment after sunrise, when morning stains the sky blue. In a nearby field, trucks rumble, engines low. Behemoths dreaming of a stampede.

An Indian gentleman, dressed in clean clothing, steps in. "Hello," the man says, unaccountably cheery. He introduces himself as the special government liaison for Gujarat. The locals refer to him as "babu," both an insult and an honorific. He is a fixer who greases the wheels of Indian bureaucracy—if one needs a building permit or a new irrigation canal, he can help. Sometimes even out of the goodness of his heart.

Babu Roshan clasps Piotr's right hand. "I understand that you're arranging housing," he says.

"We will be distributing materials, yes."

"Good, good," he says, with a distracted air that suggests that anything Piotr says will be good. "The housing here." He shakes his head. "Unsatisfactory."

"It will take time to rebuild."

"The work you do is truly commendable.

Truly, truly." He folds his hands together and places them on his belly. "I come with a simple request. A minor one. If you can acquire semipermanent housing, would you be able to set one aside?"

Piotr puts his glasses back on to get a better look. Babu Roshan has a well-fed, flush complexion. He reeks of cologne.

"If it were me alone," he says, "I would happily sleep on the ground in the open air. I am accustomed to having little. But my wife and elderly mother—Oh! You should see how they shiver. I must do anything I can do to ease their suffering. Are you married, sir?"

Piotr nods.

"Then you understand the lengths you would go to protect your family."

"The situation is the same for everyone," Piotr says.

Babu Roshan nods vigorously. "We are glad you are here," he says, "but when you leave, you leave behind nothing but canvas tents and good intentions. Surely you want to do more."

"I can promise nothing," Piotr says. Hopes are double-edged swords.

"I understand," Babu Roshan says. "But if you need anything, I have considerable knowledge of the area. I can aid you." He bows. "Should you need my aid, that is." He leaves, trailing cologne into the sunshine.

Distractions, Connor had once told him, keep one sane. Piotr slips his earpieces back in, and Vassilov begins his repertoire once more.

The cassette of etudes and preludes was a gift from Rana. She bought it during a shopping excursion in Astoria. It featured the great Ukrainian pianist Arkady Vassilov, recorded in 1969 at Durgatev Concert Hall in Kiev. As a child, Piotr wanted to be a concert pianist, and even though he showed no signs of being a prodigy, he practiced rigorously, religiously. But at thirteen, he realized his small hands and short fingers would never achieve Vassilov's grace. He couldn't play chords of more than an octave, and his fingers tangled trying to chase arpeggios. So he abandoned his lessons. His parents were disappointed, but Piotr knew, as much as anything else, his own limits.

Rana placed the cassette on the kitchen counter as she put away groceries. They had invited Lorraine and Ted for dinner. Rana was hesitant about having a homosexual in her home—she'd never met one before—but Piotr reassured her that Ted would be most gracious.

"Music," she said. "For dinner." She tossed a lump of ground beef from one hand to the other until it was the shape of a thumb. Tomato sauce bubbled on the stove. A head of cabbage waited for Piotr to cut it into salad. He picked up the shrink-wrapped cassette. He had not thought of Vassilov in years. He did not recall telling Rana about his childhood fantasies. But she remembered things he could not, and perhaps as they had lain together, his hand encircling hers, he had whispered to her, *Once, when I was young . . .*

During dinner, Ted's deferential charm won her over, and by the end of the night, she reprimanded Ted for his rough face. "I will show you where to get a proper shave," she said. "So smooth, your face will forget what hair is like." As she cleared the table, Lorraine played with their son, Mikhail.

"Like Gorbachev?" she asked.

No, *not* like Gorbachev. Rana laughed. Mikhail was named for the economist Mikhail Stetslovich, he of the elegant theorems about needs and desires. Stetslovich had formulated a version of Maslow's hierarchy, years before the publication of "A Theory of Human Motivation."

"We must chart a population's needs and desires on separate graphs," Stetslovich wrote in his last manuscript. "For although certain constants remain as points of reference between the two, the curve of the desires always rises faster." Stetslovich ignored the base of Maslow's pyramid, the physiological needs, which Stetslovich considered overly self-evident: breath, food, water, sleep, excretion.

Also, homeostasis and sex. If Stetslovich had included those base needs, he'd be celebrated today. But the pogrom caught him, and all that remained of him was an homage: a young boy living in Queens.

Lorraine held Mikhail in her lap, and Mikhail flailed his arms and clipped one of her ears. Rana chastised him, and Lorraine said that she was all right.

"Take a look," she said, holding out her left earlobe for Rana to inspect. A chip of flesh was missing. "Compared to that, his little hands are nothing." She squeezed Mikhail's fist as if testing how ripe it was.

Piotr knew that Mikhail would be good at baseball. His arms were strong and sure of their position. But his unsteady walk, even at five, meant that he would fail at American football. Mikhail had inherited his father's gangly legs and big feet, which Piotr had, in turn, inherited from his own father, whose feet had been just big enough to stay one step ahead of the Germans. Piotr had not yet formed opinions about Katia. She was still an infant. But she had her mother's beauty and olive skin, delicate features that seemed so fragile.

"Have you ever thought about family?" Rana asked Lorraine.

"Yes," she replied. "Sometimes." Lorraine kept her eyes on Mikhail's, as if trying to hypnotize him. Rana was about to ask another question, but Piotr stopped her with a hand on her shoulder. Lorraine, he guessed, had made her peace with her decision long ago.

As Ted put on his shoes to leave, he whispered, "Beautiful family." Katia had been put to bed. "You're a lucky man." Piotr knew that Ted felt a little envious. He waved at Rana, who waved back. After Piotr shut the door, Rana said, "I will find him a nice Muslim girl." And unexpectedly, Piotr saw memories swirl across her forehead, a dark vortex, but the moment passed, and she continued: "And if he does not like the girl, then I will find him a nice Muslim boy."

The bus to Gandhidham lurches, stops, and swerves, seemingly at random. Above every other seat is a small mounted fan. Piotr requests his neighbors not to turn them on, as the breeze disrupts his papers. Piotr gives calculations to Stefan, the head of this United Nations Disaster Assessment and Coordination mission, who draws up a tentative distribution path based on the number of trucks and personnel available. They have contacted local drivers in Gandhidham, and Stefan wonders if he has hired enough. Piotr prefers silence when he works, but when that is impossible—with rumbling tires and ceaseless coordinating and strategizing—he snakes the cords of the headphones up the inside of his shirt and hits "Play."

By the time they reach Gandhidham, the tape has repeated three times. Piotr has not only memorized every note and pause, but also Vassilov's exhalations after a vigorous arpeggio, his feet working the pedals and tapping the hardwood floors of the concert hall. Midway through the octave study of op. 25, no. 10, the driver pulls the brake. The bus hisses. The metal arch welcoming visitors, crowned with a carved wooden sign announcing "Gandhidham," bends, as if disappointed in the city whose name it bears. Gandhidham was built in 1960, but that did not save the city from damage. At the bus station, the buses lie crushed beneath their own shelters.

The military base remains intact. Atop a shoulder-high rock wall, painted pink, concertina wire curls between bayonets. Outside the gate, the implements of war—a long-range shell launcher, an old Soviet tank the color of moss—now serve as statuary, as if peace weren't the absence of war, but merely war repurposed and disguised. The base's squat, boxy buildings, built with beige efficiency, are cracked but functional.

Most of the soldiers have been deployed to the countryside as peacekeepers, emissaries of the military's goodwill. The few who remain work with ruthless discipline; the distribution trucks are loaded and ready.

This pleases Stefan, but the trucks are uneven. Some have equipment piled high until their axles bow and groan; others are almost bare. The routes have been planned assuming equivalency among the vehicles.

Without prompting, Piotr unfurls maps from his sack. He licks his fingers, skimming through maps printed on yellowing fax paper, maps on whisper-thin onionskin, maps that bleed color from one region to the next. Area of effect. Population centers. Per capita income. Roads and rivers, points of transit, possible landing sites. He punches numbers into a calculator and scribbles notations, performing a necessary, heartbreaking calculus: *If we distribute here, we can reach* x *number of victims; here, only* y.

Only a handful of drivers speak English, and Stefan relies on those who do to explain the routes to those who do not. The most heavily laden trucks will go with four workers each; the lesser ones can make do with two. Two men are enough to lift a sheet of galvanized iron and bend it to their will.

Turquoise-blue tarps are folded into parachute-tight bundles; when opened, they display a yellow UN symbol printed in the center. Plastic, but waterproof. Two representatives from CARE mention constructing semipermanent housing, but this is a longer-term goal. Despite his quid pro quo venality, Babu Roshan is correct: aid workers fly in, and then they fly out.

But this is their mandate. Lorraine's DART focuses on observation and informatics. Lorraine is more hands-on than Connor was, which Piotr admires, and less political, which he appreciates. But this should be obvious: disaster relief, in and of itself, is less political. His working relationship with Lorraine is better than it had been with Connor. With Connor, he felt as if he were merely a set of extra limbs attached to Connor's body, that they ingested the same air, thought the same thoughts.

But with Lorraine, he feels needed. He feels he accomplishes something, even if those accomplishments are fleeting, miniscule. Lorraine trusts his work implicitly, though she occasionally peers over his shoulder to double-check his calculations. He'd never admit it to anyone—especially Rana—but he sometimes misses the adventure and the unknown that Connor fostered. But, he reminds himself, adventure is a game for the young.

Piotr boards a smaller truck with only a few pallets of sheeting and tenting. His route will stop by Ratnal on the way back to Bhuj. No one has heard from Ratnal. No calls for aid, no evacuees. The city has disappeared. Arni from the World Food Programme will travel with him. Arni has established a food distribution center in Bhuj, and if the destruction in Ratnal is as bad as feared, they will return with additional aid.

"It might be a good idea," says Arni, "to establish another distribution center here in Gandhidham. We can use those army hangars as warehouses. We can divert some food-aid flights here quite easily, don't you think?"

"We would also need to station someone here full-time," Piotr says. The age-old question: Which mouse will hang the bell around the cat's neck?

The lumbering caravan of trucks waits to exit the single navigable road. Soldiers wave them on, arms like pinwheels, but old habits die hard: drivers lean on their horns, inching right and left, gauging the available space to pass. Soldiers tap offending truck doors with batons. Many trucks have talismans dangling from their front grills: a tin eagle with its claws grasping a heart, blue-faced Vishnu holding a flute to his lips, a pair of baby shoes.

Gandhidham, Piotr decides, is a poorly planned city. It was meant to be a transportation hub linking to the port of Kandla to the south, but its design is stilted. Piotr would have formed the city as a spider: the military base as the body, the populous stretching along the legs. Each leg could feature a specialty: vegetables and fruits heading northwest; automobile parts lining the roads eastward; to the south, toward Kandla, silks and textiles. Roadside stands could buttress against actual buildings with reinforced mortar and brick. The city would creep outward. A good civil engineer could have shaped Gandhidham's soul the way Le Corbusier shaped Chandigarh's.

But Le Corbusier was no civil engineer, and Piotr is no architect.

For now, the desert lies before him, sprouting a black tail of trucks. If Piotr has erred in his calculations, he will not have to bear the brunt of that error. But second-guessing his conclusions will accomplish nothing. Worse than nothing, even: the negative impact would be even more severe. If only Stetslovich had developed a measurement for increments of need, desire, and disappointment. Piotr would plot himself onto that graph, a single point in a vast plain.

If Stetslovich's conjecture had a weakness, it was the assumption that needs and desires were separate entities, that the rational mind could distinguish one from the other. The limbic and the cortex are entwined, like lovers holding hands, forgetting where one ends and the other begins.

Piotr worked with Connor for ten years, and for that time, his occupation met his needs. But then he knew desire, a rash that delivers pleasure in the scratching. It was in Sarajevo. Connor had hired Rana as an interpreter. She spoke Arabic, Serbo-Croatian, English, Spanish, and Russian. She wore a thick skirt, with pleats as sharp and perfect as a lamp shade. Her skin was smooth and tinged with olive from her mother's side. Piotr knew he would marry her. He *knew*.

It was the way she tilted her head when she heard a certain inflection. The way her vocabulary occasionally failed her, the way she used her hands and her body to indicate the immensity of a word, its secret depths of emotion. Piotr dutifully recorded what she said, memorizing the curve of her arm, her black waves of hair. Outwardly, she seemed impassive. She translated without shuddering, without flinching. She paused before speaking, her upper lip twisting as if testing the language: *The soldiers held me down and forced me to watch them rape my wife and daughter. I begged them to kill me, but they shot me in the leg so that I could not move. When they were finished, they pushed my wife and daughter into an open ditch and covered them with dirt. They were still breathing.* She was an interlocutor, and what she said passed through her like a ghost.

On the way to Ratnal, Arni rolls down the window to circulate air. Altars, festooned with silk flowers, appear sporadically on the side of the road. Arni points out the first few, but soon grows tired. Too many gods. Someone must maintain these shrines. Someone must set offerings on the tiny pedestals.

Commerce has not abated. One passing truck is loaded with sandbags, another with corrugated cardboard tied together with twine. Two boys, no older than twelve, hold the ropes securing the cardboard. As the trucks approach each other, they threaten to run one another off the road. Both drivers honk in symphonic speech. Arni pulls his arm inside to keep it from being shorn off by this urgent delivery of cardboard.

A short time later, their truck stops.

Imagine, Stetslovich tells his class, *a bridge. Say that this bridge spans a gully carved into the earth by yearly floodwaters. The ground is soft, salt ridden. It crumbles in your hand like smoke. Say that during an earthquake, the bridge's support pillars shear away from the top load and send the traveling surface into a heap. A passenger car might be able to traverse the gully slowly. But if it's loaded down with a life's worth of possessions and a panicked family, the soft earth might swallow the tires down to the axle. Say that in addition to the misaligned chunks of pavement, there are now abandoned cars as well, stuck in the ground like the hollow shells of dead beetles. You need to cross the gully. What is the solution to this problem? You have fifteen minutes to respond.*

Connor answers: *Requisition a deployable bridge from the US military. If one isn't available within a one-day radius, purchase one from the Indian Army. Despite the overcharge, we need to establish the bridge long enough for aid to flow across and for the wounded to evacuate. After two or three days, we reposition the bridge elsewhere.*

Lorraine answers: *Getting aid to affected peoples is always our priority. We will circumvent the gully, find an area that's stable enough to support the weight of the trucks. If need be, we can lay down planks of lumber or metal sheets to provide support and traction. We can worry about the bridge's repair later.*

Babu Roshan answers: *No need to continue at all. See those cars? Strip them of parts. We can take the catalytic converters for their platinum and remove the copper wiring from its rubber. The leather from the seats, we can restitch it into coats and shoes and use the batting to stuff our own pillows.*

Rana gives no response. She cradles Katia in the crook of her arm. The question isn't worth answering.

The truck idles, and the driver, who doesn't speak English, looks to Piotr for the correct answer.

● ● ●

Lorraine once told him that he had enough experience to lead his own team. But Piotr wanted to work less in conflict zones and more in disaster relief.

"You realize," she said, "that it's no less dangerous."

Of course. But at least he wouldn't need a flak jacket. In Rwanda, for instance, armed men ran after his and Connor's vehicle, shooting in pursuit. He crouched low to the floor, and bullets pinged against the metal, cracked the back window. He and Connor had walked into gatherings of warlords where the air throbbed with anger and they were the only ones who were unarmed.

Aid workers are easy targets.

In Bosnia, he and Connor brought Rana from one refugee camp to another: Vrnograč, Miholjsko, Banja Luka, Tuzla. For six months, people pleaded to make themselves understood. An old woman pulled her hair so Piotr could see the lice crawling in the part. Men hoisted their shirts to expose their ribs and concave bellies. Rana traveled in the safety of a car, had regular meals, earned hazard pay, and young women tugged at Piotr as if to ask, *Why her? You could have any one of us. Why her?*

Occasionally, in the car, her leg brushed his. Sometimes, at the end of an interview, she'd look at him as if to ask if her work was satisfactory. Her smiles came and went like lightning.

There were the stretches of time, as long as a week, when combat paused. No guns. No mortar shells. No forced migrations. Residents of houses dotted with bullet holes traded gasoline, cigarettes, beer. Men set out tables and chairs to serve coffee to paying customers, and women sold withered carrots in the road. On those days, even if rain chilled the air, Piotr walked by Rana's side, and they ignored, momentarily, the newspapers emblazoned with ruination elsewhere.

They were in Zagreb when Piotr asked if Rana still had her passport. She clutched her chest. Yes, she said. Hidden in her brassiere. Streetcars trundled by, the Nike logo slicing through the city like a sickle. Young people chatted into cell phones the size of tea cakes. Over the course of the conflict, only a handful of rockets had been fired into Zagreb. He and Rana could have been in the commercial district of any major city. Consumer goods in the windows of every storefront: televisions, computers, cars.

He asked, did she want to stay here?

She laughed, a mirthless thing, like a cough. "I am not Croatian," she said. "I cannot live here." Indeed, Connor had pressed the State Department—in vain—to convince the new Croatian government to change its policy of return: anyone who had fled his home had only ninety days to reclaim ownership. But no one was allowed to reenter Croatia without proof of citizenship. And identity cards were only issued to those already in the country. It made Piotr's head hurt; beneath Zagreb's glittering surface was cruelty no less hard and serrated than anywhere else.

"What if," Piotr asked, "you could leave? The war, the conflict. The suffering."

She had no response. At an outdoor café, Piotr bought her a bottle of Orangina, which she held like a grenade. In the window of a Benetton store, the mannequins had their arms raised, as if surrendering. She looked at Piotr, her eyes the color of a storm.

"I tried to contact my parents in Prozor," she said. "And my neighbor told me she saw military officers sitting in folding lawn chairs outside their home. They were drinking brandy as they watched the house burn. I grew up with these people," she said. "Serbs, Croats, Muslims, Bosnians. We ate at each other's houses and played games until it was too dark to see. And now," she said, "there's nothing left."

Rana was twelve years his junior, but already bore enough sadness for three lifetimes. It hung on her bones, as inseparable from her as skin. He touched her elbow; she was cold where he was warm.

• • •

Two months before he and Connor left Bosnia, the three of them were stranded outside Sarajevo, unable to make it back into the city. The roads were blocked with rusted cargo containers, tractors, train cars. Snipers picked off those fleeing into or out of the city. They backtracked to a small guesthouse twenty miles away. They covered the windows with sheets folded over four times and pushed the mattresses to the center of the room where a stray bullet would be less likely to strike. Rana slept between them, on the rift between the mattresses.

When she left to relieve herself in the outhouse, Piotr asked Connor how they could bring her back to the United States. Surely she qualified for refugee status.

"She'd have to go through the UNHCR," Connor told him. "She's still considered an IDP."

Internally displaced person. An acronym, a chip of ice.

"The consulate in Zagreb?"

"Last I heard, their waiting list was over five thousand."

So, years, at least. He could not leave her back in Sarajevo, at the mercy of artillery shells. But if not Sarajevo, she would have to go to a camp where the roofs could not keep out the rain. He could not abandon her after she had led them past checkpoints where the guards

119

looked bored enough to kill for entertainment. After she had helped them fill notebook after notebook of testimony. She had taught him the words for "water," "shelter," and "machine gun." She'd been with them for months now— the Croat soldiers considered her a collaborator; the Muslim militias, a traitor. If they left her now, their parting would be permanent. She'd be among the wanderers, the stateless ones; those who were part of the world, but were not.

"If I married her," Piotr said, "would that change things?"

"If you married her," Connor replied, his voice growing igneous, "things would change considerably."

Piotr woke in the middle of the night, startled by far-off gunfire. She talked in her sleep, as if translating her dreams for him. He whispered to her: "I will protect you. If we run from point to point with sniper fire above us, my flak jacket will cover your head. If the NATO air strikes fail to halt the Serbian onslaught, I will smuggle you out. If a soldier with a gun asks if you are Croat, Serb, or Muslim, I will take your hand and say, 'She is American, and she is with me.'"

Further toward Ratnal, an entire village has relocated onto the road. Men squat in the driving lane. They wave their arms in wide circles, an exhausted motion that has surely been repeated over and over with no results. The driver honks, but the men don't move. He honks again, longer this time, but still they don't budge. Piotr wonders where the women are, where the children are. Something is wrong.

"Go around them," Piotr says, but even before the command leaves his mouth, men surround the cab. The driver revs the engine, as if trying to scare a flock of birds. He yells out the window, but his words drop off a cliff. He switches off the ignition, and the truck sputters still. The men hold machetes and sickles. They have checkered handkerchiefs tied over their mouths. One of them has a gun.

Piotr, Arni, and the driver exit slowly. "No sudden moves," Piotr tells Arni. They hold up their hands, palms outturned, and are ushered to the side of the road, flanked on either side. The man with the gun shifts from foot to foot. He can't be older than forty, but his skin is like shoe leather. The gun is a relic, possibly military, the metal discolored. The man holds it as if confused by its purpose. Next to Arni, another man hefts his machete loosely. It looks homemade, the metal fired in a wood pit and hammered into shape.

Others crawl in and out of the truck, removing everything: the first-aid kit, Piotr's and Arni's personal belongings, even the documents from the glove compartment. They cut the nylon straps holding the housing materials with their farming implements. The steel sheets slide off, and men below, hands raised as if in praise, catch the metal. They carry the sheets on their backs, foreheads drenched, legs shaking. One man loses his balance, and the sheet tilts until it makes contact with the ground. For a moment, Piotr does not see him as a bandit: the way his arms are spread, he could be a father pretending to be an airplane for his child. He could be adjusting the world on his shoulders.

In a way, this is their duty. They are, after all, delivering aid to those who need it most. This situation is not unheard of, and in terms of violations, this is nothing. But Piotr wonders about Ratnal, kilometers away. It has been shaken off the map. It is now a thumbprint. A smudge.

One man turns Piotr's backpack inside out. Papers scatter. Information, crucial information— plans and schemes and orders. But the man is only interested in a bag of potato chips. His cheeks bulge as he chews. How easy it would be to return with food. There's a warehouse full. They find nothing of interest in Arni's pack, but Arni clenches his jaw tight. "They're taking everything," he whispers. The men push bundles of plastic sheeting off the truck with their feet. The packets bounce as they hit the ground.

When they finish stripping the truck, the man with the gun says something to the driver. They are free to go. It's been perhaps two hours; Piotr would check his watch, but they've taken it, along with his wallet. He still feels his Walkman, though, tucked into his shirt pocket.

As they walk back toward the truck, Arni veers for his pack. He picks it off the ground and shakes it. The man with the machete shouts and points the blade like a finger. Perhaps he thinks there's a telephone in there, a two-way radio. Arni doesn't see or hear him. He brushes off his bag. And before Arni can acknowledge the shadow falling across him, the man has swung the machete.

It makes contact with Arni's face. The sound of a handclap.

Arni falls.

Piotr pushes the driver. "Truck," he yells. "Now!" Arni lies on the ground. Piotr doesn't think about the gun or where it may be aimed, because there is no flak jacket to save his life. Protective layers, careful planning—none of it saves anyone. Ever.

Blood forms on Arni's cheek. Piotr helps him to his feet. The man used the flat of the machete, but its edge has cut Arni's face. Piotr removes his shirt to staunch the bleeding. The Walkman tumbles to the ground, and Piotr stuffs it in his pants pocket. Around them, the men back away, as if startled by their own violence. The man who made the strike has dropped the machete and run. Arni is dazed; he stumbles.

"Come on," Piotr says. Arni hangs on his shoulder. The men back farther and farther away, like ripples. Piotr would say that they are safe, but all safety is transitory. He hefts Arni into the cab, then slaps the driver on the back. "Go, go!" The truck lurches but doesn't move quickly enough. Arni clutches his cheek with both hands; blood seeps through his clenched fingers. It looks as if he's juicing raspberries. "Bhuj," Piotr tells the driver, and the truck makes a wide loop to turn around, going far off the road and onto the soft ground waiting to consume them.

After Piotr joined Lorraine's team, he learned that Connor had been killed. Piotr had stopped talking to Connor before they returned from the Balkans. Their friendship ended the day he and Rana wed. They were on their last assignment, in the Krajina region. This was their last chance to marry, and Connor agreed reluctantly to witness. While Piotr's plans of marriage were still theoretical, Connor worked wholeheartedly, using his connections to secure Rana passage back to the United States with a spousal green card. But now that all that was left was the ceremony, Connor became reticent, sullen, as if they'd not been colleagues but lovers, and some lover's vow had been irrevocably breached.

They were wed in a Croatian Catholic church, because both the Orthodox church and the mosque had been burned down. The church, however, had not been immune: windows were broken, the glass swept into a corner, glittering within the debris. Birds nested in the rafters, and their wings made the sound of a book's pages being flipped. Somehow, Rana had convinced the Catholic priest to marry a lapsed Jew and a Muslim.

"You've completed your official good deed for this lifetime," Connor said. He wore his flak jacket, and its ribbons seemed ghastly, rather than cheerful. "But I suspect that you're doing this as much for yourself as you're doing it for her." Connor examined his fingernails. "Which is fine, as long as you've come to a mutually agreeable arrangement." He watched the ceremony with his arms crossed, as if resentful at the imposition on his time, and after the priest had said what he had needed to say, Connor pulled Piotr aside.

"Congratulations, I suppose," he said. Rana was crying, and the priest was comforting her. "No good deed goes unpunished."

And without knowing why, Piotr slapped him. Not hard, but hard enough to turn his head.

125

Connor brought his hand to the point of contact, openmouthed with surprise, and walked out of the church. Upon their return to the United States, Connor deployed immediately to Chechnya, and Piotr—he wondered what his options were now that he had a wife.

Connor died there, in Chechnya.

Beth told Piotr the details. Connor had been trying to broker a cease-fire between the Chechen rebels and the Russian government. For two years, he drove from Grozny to Moscow and back again, ferrying messages between low-level functionaries, notes that were little more than barbs. He must have imagined he could accomplish something, the way all aid workers do. But Connor had elevated this to a delusion: he thought he could courier away a century's worth of rancor. Or perhaps the futility of the situation was not lost on him, but in the face of doing nothing, anything seemed worthwhile.

He had grown increasingly vocal at the State Department as well, arguing that aid was not just an imperfect stopgap, but one that completely ignored the situation on the ground. He insisted on being included in policy-making meetings and, in Chechnya, gave interviews to news crews. For the BBC, he stood in the center of a razed Chechen town. Pillars of smoke rose from scorch marks on the ground. Nothing moved. Even the squirrels had abandoned the place. Two days before, Chechen rebels had abducted two Russian soldiers and had barricaded themselves in a former typewriter factory. A Russian commando force stormed the building and gunned down the rebels to retrieve their comrades. But the pallets to which their comrades had been strapped were rigged with explosives. Typewriter parts were found nearly a kilometer away: broken Cyrillic character keys, singed ribbons, words blown apart and dispersed. In response, the Russians sent troops and tanks into the nearby town, and now all that remained was a blackened crater.

"Aid without political force behind it is nothing," Connor said. He walked to a body, and the camera followed shakily, as if frightened of what it might see. The body was an old man, his face covered with soot, torso erupted with bullets. Connor removed a Band-Aid from the pocket of his flak jacket, the same one he'd worn to the Christmas party years ago, and placed it over a bullet hole. "That," he said. "That is what we're doing."

The Russian authorities found Connor's Land Rover in an open field thirty miles south of Grozny, on the outskirts of Shatoi. The car was undamaged, as if it had drifted off the road. The doors were locked, the windows rolled up.

"He knew Russian intelligence services were spreading rumors about him," Beth said. "I told him to be careful. I told him not to go back. But . . ." She sighed. Perhaps she had shut herself in Connor's office, gone through his files, his papers. Perhaps she'd found the key to his lockbox and availed herself of his secrets. So much of Connor had been confidential, and now she had to piece him back together. "You know how well Connor listens," she concluded.

Her slip into present tense. She still held out hope. It was all she could do, and in that, she was no different from Connor. Or any other aid worker.

But she was correct: Connor never listened. To anyone. Connor did only what he believed was best; anyone who did less was too timid, and anyone who did more was too reckless.

Fifty feet from the Land Rover, where the field dipped slightly and tan grass grew waist-high, they found three bodies next to each other, hands tied to feet with a single length of extension cord. They had been gagged with strips of oil-stained cloth and shot, once, in the back of the head. The exit wounds sent starbursts of blood into the grass before them.

Connor's driver. Connor's translator. And Connor's deputy. Three dead bodies from Connor's entourage. But the authorities never found Connor. They searched a two-mile radius and turned up nothing. They did discover, however, a fourth spray of blood similar to the other three and one of the ribbons Connor kept pinned to his flak jacket.

Five months after Piotr learned the circumstances of Connor's death, Beth called back.

"I'm going to Chechnya," she said. "I'm bringing back Connor's body."

Piotr tried to sway her. What they did to Connor, he said, they would not hesitate to do to her as well. Surely she had heard about the state of emergency declared by the Chechen president himself. But she was as stubborn as her husband. Their marriage must have been like two mules endlessly butting heads.

"Do you know where his body is?" he asked.

Rana must have heard him, because she came into the living room with Mikhail, then still a newborn. He lowered his voice.

"No, but I'll find him."

"Do you know where to start?"

"He spent a lot of time in Grozny. I'll begin there."

"Beth, please."

"I don't have his body. There's nothing! You don't know what it's like, having nothing." The words chafed her throat. "You don't know."

But she was wrong. He *did* know. And Rana too

must have known, because she came close, close enough for him to smell the powder on Mikhail's head. She said nothing, but hovered there, like a reminder, a memory.

"I know he's dead, Piotr. I know that. But I want to bring his body home. He deserves that much. I need your help. Maybe you can get in touch with your contacts in Chechnya. I know you and Connor worked on it before you left."

They had. But that also meant that Piotr's name was on the same lists that Connor's had been on. In the year after Connor's death, international groups pulled out of Chechnya, targeted the same way Connor had been. Indiscriminately. Ruthlessly. Russian atrocities, Chechen atrocities—there was no difference now that they all went unseen.

"Too much has changed," Piotr said. "Those contacts will be no good."

"I've got to start somewhere." He recognized the tremor in her voice. He'd heard it from women who had not drunk water in four days. Here was Beth's heart, before him, on the phone. "Come with me," she said. "Please. I can't do this alone."

In all the time he'd known her, Beth had been Connor's shadow, her personality subsumed by his. Even now, she labored to be the dutiful wife, and he understood the necessity of her journey: she, most of all, needed to bury him. He imagined her in the remains of Minutka Square, looking at street names and transliterating the Cyrillic into something recognizable. He imagined her crouching low in the backseat of a beat-up Lada Niva as it approached the border. He imagined her, a woman traveling alone, reaching out to complete strangers, Connor's ring on a gold chain around her neck, and her long, thin fingers beseeching, *Can you lend a hand, please?* But all it would take was for her to say "Grozny" instead of "Djohar" to the wrong person, and she'd be shot on the spot.

And then she unleashed her secret weapon:

"Connor would have done the same for you."

It was true: Connor would have. But here was the other truth: if he had stayed with Connor, Beth could not have asked for his help, because he would be dead. What were his obligations now? What did the living owe the dead?

Beth's breaths were the long gasps of a woman calming herself. Rana put her hand on his forearm, a light touch. He held the phone to his ear and leaned over to kiss Mikhail, who smelled of talc and laundry detergent, who seemed as small and fragile as a pressed flower.

"Beth," he said, "I have a family."

"And you think Connor doesn't?" she replied. "He still does, with or without you."

By the time Piotr arrives back in Bhuj, dusk creeps into the edges of the sky. Arni's dried blood flakes off Piotr's shirt. The driver tries to keep the steering wheel steady. He almost doesn't slow at the checkpoint, and a soldier raises his rifle, but Piotr sticks his arm out the window to wave, and the soldier lowers it.

Piotr points the driver toward the medical compound, and as he helps Arni step down from the cab, an Indian nurse rushes over. "Priority patient!" she calls out, and masked Indians swarm the truck, this time, surgical masks instead of bandannas. Arni will make his statement, and Piotr will file a report. Afterward, he can request new copies of the maps and informatics, and he can recalculate the answers to tomorrow's miseries.

But first, rest.

The medical and the aid compounds are only a few streets apart, but the distance seems immense. He weaves through makeshift camps. Religious groups, extended families, clumps of strangers huddling around communal fires. One man tries to stoke a fire with the wood of a broken table. He lights thin strips of newspaper from the near past. Movie stars. Political commentary. If only it could catch fire. The government had promised the restoration of electrical power a day after the earthquake, but it's now been four, and the darkness seems as omnipresent as before.

When he reaches his tent, Babu Roshan stands. "Very good to see you again," he says.

"I'm very tired," says Piotr.

"Certainly, certainly." He pretends as if no time has passed. "I will only take a moment."

"Please—"

"I was wondering if—"

"I don't feel like speaking—"

"I understand your fatigue—"

"No," says Piotr. "You do not."

"If you've been able to secure some housing—"

It should be funnier than it is. They should be laughing, together, at the situation.

"No," Piotr says, "we were not able to secure housing."

Babu Roshan frowns. "Nothing? I find that hard to believe."

"That is the situation."

"My friend," Babu Roshan says, "I thought that we had an *understanding*." He hangs upon the last word as if it were a threat.

"Understanding? No, understand this. There is nothing for you. You must live with what you have."

"This is unacceptable." Babu Roshan paces like an animal in a small cage. He must not be accustomed to being refused.

"I'm afraid this is how it is," Piotr says, and Babu Roshan leaves, scowling.

Finally.

Piotr reaches for his Walkman. He places it on his chest, a familiar weight, like a pacemaker.

He retrieves the cassette, which rattles noisily. There's a large crack in the face of the plastic. Three spokes of the left reel are missing, but the tape itself seems to be intact. Cosmetic damage.

Piotr lies down and closes his eyes. He sees sunlight on the machete blade. Shattered bridges. Dust plumes. His earpieces muffle the world but can't shut it out completely. Trucks come and go. Voices pass by. He wipes the corners of his eyes where moisture has accumulated. He presses "Play," and the Walkman whirs and whirs and whirs, but no music comes out.

This encounter with looters is not Piotr's first, but it is the first with an injury. When he sees Lorraine, she holds his chin, examining his face as if memorizing his features before their inevitable disfigurement. She searches for something, an indication of some sort, a message. Exactly what, he cannot tell.

"How much did we lose?" she asks.

The actual answer: probably less than what it cost to fly the team to India. But Piotr knows she's asking to see how rattled he is, to see if he still has his wits about him.

"I'm fine," he insists.

"I *want* to believe you," she says. "But there's no way that something like what happened doesn't affect you."

"It didn't happen to me."

"It doesn't have to." Lorraine frowns. "I'm glad you're all right."

Then comes the bad news: the military has instituted an escort policy. No Westerner is to leave the city limits without military accompaniment. They impose a curfew: no one is to move about after dark. Sometimes, late at night, Piotr senses figures skulking around the periphery of the aid compound, avoiding the light to escape identification. Perhaps they are soldiers on patrol, former residents retrieving personal belongings. Perhaps they are aid workers administering help. Perhaps. But he fears that they are not. Those figures are something else entirely, and their work belongs in the dark.

The aid compound itself is secure. The fire that brews the coffee is now a small bonfire, one of many dotting the city. Someone has added the morning's coffee grounds to the flame, the smoke bitter and comforting. Piotr remembers his first day of work with Lorraine's team, Rana's first day alone in their apartment. She had forgotten to turn off the coffeemaker, and the liquid in the carafe boiled into sludge. The smoke detector went off, and she called him, panicked. So much noise. So much smoke. Lorraine let him take the day off, and he returned home to open the windows and the doors, to sweep up the shards of the shattered carafe, and to comfort his wife, who still believed that no place could ever be safe.

It must be midnight now—Piotr no longer has a watch—and only a few people sit around the fire. The flames dwindle. The night air has a bracing chill, and those sitting around the fire try to bring back what warmth they have to their tents.

Ted is there, and he motions for Piotr to sit. To his left is a strapping young man, who glows on his chest and shoulders, the reflective stripes of a search-and-rescue uniform.

"This is Andy," Ted says.

"Good to meet you," Andy says. He has a strong grip, a claw. As Andy sits back, he nudges Ted in the shoulder, as if sharing a joke. In the firelight, their faces flicker, orange one moment, shadow the next. Their arms press together.

The curfew has hampered rescue efforts, Andy explains. Their best work is done at night, when everything is silent, when they can listen for signs of life. The racket during the day is too hectic. They've lodged a complaint with the military heads and hope for a quick resolution.

"But they're calling the shots," Andy says.

"Are you feeling better, Piotr?" Ted asks. Everyone asks this question, as if determined to catch him in a lie. Piotr nods, little bursts of agreement. When he returns to New York, he has resolved not to tell Rana about today. She will worry unduly. He is unharmed.

"I think it's time for me to turn in," Ted says.

"So soon?" Andy sounds disappointed.

"You, of all people, should be resting."

"Yes, Gramps," Andy says. Ted pushes him so that he leans but doesn't fall over.

Their interaction seems odd. They look at each other to shut out the world. Good. Perhaps they find some modicum of comfort, of peace.

Piotr is determined to discover the coffee brewer's identity. He has brought his pillow and blanket to the fire. He's the last one there, though he's far from the only person awake. Light seeps from beneath certain tents like a carpet. The medical area glows. Arni is there now, he imagines.

He closes his eyes and listens for footsteps. When the brewer comes, Piotr will thank him or her. Piotr remembers his mother explaining the concept of a mitzvah, a good deed for its own sake. Sometimes, selflessness seems so remote, like the light of a faraway star. Yes, Piotr does good work, but it's also profitable. Yes, he had rescued Rana, but he also desired her. There are no gifts that aren't covered in thorns.

When he wakes, the embers have died. Not even a smolder. He hears the *glug* of water pouring from a jug. The person stirs the ashes with a stick and stacks kindling into a pyramid. He positions the pot, the metal black with char. Piotr lies still, as if the brewer were a doe that would bolt if startled. Perhaps the person has already seen him. He doesn't know. And he accepts that there are things that he will never know.

The fire crackles into life. He sees clearly: legs standing next to the fire, a pair of shoes split in several places. The soles are nothing more than thin strips of rubber; the leather is polished as much as it will bear. The person waits for the water to boil. It might take an hour for that much water to heat. Dawn seems a distant promise.

It's Babu Roshan. They say nothing. The heat reaches Piotr, and the rawness of the cold peels away. Babu Roshan holds a bulging paper bag. He has defied curfew to bring them coffee. He could have been shot. Piotr doesn't know if the coffee implies an explicit exchange, a debt to be repaid at a later time, but this no longer matters. Babu Roshan pours in the coffee, dark as soil. It's an inexact science, brewing for so many people. Babu Roshan adjusts the sign about stirring up the grounds. In the last day, new languages have appeared: Russian, Arabic, Chinese.

Babu Roshan stirs with a metal ladle, which he taps against the side of the pot. He pours a paper-cupful for Piotr.

"I heard about your friend," he says.

Piotr should offer an apology. Thanks. These are small gestures, minor instances of grace. But to expect anything in return for kindness is a mistake. Back in the tent, he places the cup of coffee next to his cot, where it will grow cold by the time he wakes. This he knows—and he takes comfort in what little knowledge he can possess.

OUR LIVES IN RUINS

On this morning, the fifth since the earthquake, the dogs return. They roam in arrowhead packs, noses close to the ground, locking onto the scents that promise sustenance. They pad around the aid camp, quiet as rustling paper, and Ted imagines he's at McCarren Park. Dogs off their leashes, doing what dogs do best. There are single dogs, skittish outcasts that snap and growl and slink away. These paw at the rubbish heaped on the north side of the compound, at the open-trench latrine, and lick drops of water from the insides of discarded bottles.

On the way back from the facilities, Ted sees a dog holding a hand. More bodies are recovered than the funeral pyres can burn. When the wind carries the smoke into camp, Ted gags. Some bodies burn incompletely, and what this dog has clamped in its teeth is blackened and gnarled. It sniffs its path home, edging away when vehicles drive by and kick up veils of dust. The dog's teats hang low, brown and hard as walnuts. The tips of her fur are singed. The hand still has identifiable fingers, but it's no longer flesh. It's meat.

A passing soldier yells and cocks his rifle. A retort, a thunderous crack in the air, and the dog falls, without a yelp. The soldier grabs the dog's legs and drags her away, leaving a skid in the road like a brushstroke.

For the past four days, Ted has taken statements, transcribing stories spilling out of people into steno notebooks. The pages fill with broken words, half-formed letters, and every evening, he re-creates what he can't understand. His fingers, where he holds the pen, have bruised.

He spent yesterday afternoon in the medical tents. There, the staff maintained a fire in an old gasoline barrel, feeding it bloodied bandages, gauze, and chunks of flesh. They turned their heads when they dropped the waste in, the heat unbearable. The metal hummed as if alive.

Ted asked a battery of questions to assess the needs of the displaced. Do they have a supply of food and clean water? Sufficient shelter? Medical care? The basic necessities of life? Some complained about the inadequacy of the blankets, about the dryness of the high-energy food biscuits, about how difficult it was to balance on the crumbling edge of the latrine. But complaints meant that they were doing well enough to complain.

As he walked down the rows of cots, perspiration and rot plump in the air, people mistook him for a doctor. "I'm sorry," he repeated again and again. He remembered the story of the Agence France-Presse journalist who, during the

Rwandan atrocities, strode into a trauma center and announced, "Is there anyone here who has been raped *and* speaks French?" The injured thought he was there to help, and if he hadn't come to help, then why was he there?

Nalini, age twenty-four: My daughter, Anjali, went to school early. It was Republic Day, and her school was putting on a parade. They do it every year, and she left without breakfast. She was so excited. She would not even take an orange. I was about to scold her, but my husband said, "Nah, leave her be." She is the sun and moon to him. To the both of us. She met her friends, and the three of them skipped off toward school. I could hear them singing "Jana Gana Mana." I must have started singing myself, because Ramesh smiled as he ate his *jalub*, dipping it into his tea, a bad habit he's had for as long as we've been wed. I slapped his hand and returned to boiling the day's water. That's when it happened. I lit the stove, and the earth moved. I thought a bomb had gone off. I fell and felt my wrist crack beneath me. The food from the cupboards spilled out, and the windows shattered. I slid on the floor, and Ramesh shouted, "Get out! Get out!" So I ran. Others were running as well, pushing and shoving for the door. The old woman who lives down the hall, I saw her fall in the rush, and she did not rise. Seven of us made it out. We all lived on the first floor. The upper part of our building had caved in. I called out for Ramesh, but Ramesh never answered. I ran toward the school. I could not see anything. It was like running through a cloud. I heard screams and the sounds of buildings still falling. When I reached the school, I could not see it. I saw jumbled shoes outside where the door should have been. Shoes for tiny feet. I thought I saw Anjali's among them, her black slippers with a single flower stitched on top. But the school was no longer there. The earth moved again, and something struck me on the back of the head, and I woke here.

Nalini took a deep breath and shuddered. Her head was a globe of white cloth, wrapped diagonally across her face, one eye exposed. In the middle of her statement, she closed her eye, and Ted could not tell if she had paused or lost consciousness. She was so skinny. Her skin recited the poetry of her bones. He wanted to tuck the blanket around her to keep her from blowing away. Nurses swept down the aisle, bearing syringes. The ground upon which they walked was mottled and damp with bodily fluids. The tent seemed unfathomably deep, beds extending to the horizon, past the vanishing point. The pages of his notebook warped. The paper swallowed the tip of his pen.

But the truth is, the woman's name is not Nalini. She didn't give her name, or else she ignored his question, as if her name were unimportant. All the women to whom Ted has spoken could be Nalini—and in a way, all of them are. He could interview thousands of women, but no one cares about thousands. Even the word itself—*thousands*—is abstract. Too many zeros to be real. What does it mean, *thousands dead, thousands injured?* What does it mean to him, to anyone? But if there's one woman, a mother named Nalini—people can maybe understand that. And so what if Nalini—the woman he calls Nalini—never existed? Does this negate what Ted has written? Does this make her story any less potent?

One person's misery is not the world's, but the world's misery can be one person's.

The woman Ted called Nalini tugged his hand. "Will you find my daughter?" she asked. "Will you come back tomorrow? Promise me that you'll return."

He knew that he might never find her again. As patients recover, find loved ones, die, they disappear into the throng. He will look for her tonight—her head half swathed in gauze, the curve of her nose, the brown of her eyelids—but even if he fails, he will try to keep her alive in the pages of his notebook.

And he said to her, "I promise," as if keeping promises were the easiest thing in the world.

• • •

The uninjured live out in the open. The aftershocks have abated, but no one wants to sleep inside, no matter how sound it may be. Privacy is a quaint notion. Latrines are segregated by sex, and the women have erected a tattered set of curtains around theirs. Men urinate where they please, and it's not uncommon to see a line of them at a wall, braced against it as if holding it up. The aid camp has a tent to conceal its pit latrine, and everyone dutifully waits his turn outside. The tent flaps lash at the middle, but the breeze of a passing car sometimes spreads them apart, exuding equal parts stench and embarrassment.

Ted knows better than to breathe too deeply anywhere he goes. He carries a roll of toilet paper in his pack and a packet of tissues in his pocket. He's prepared for anything.

"You look rough around the edges," Lorraine says. The tips of her oxford shirt are tied in a knot. A clipboard full of crises juts against her hip. Random volunteer workers have begun arriving on scene, and she has her hands full trying to keep them from getting in the way and being where they shouldn't. Sometimes, she says, she just wants to slap them all.

"It usually takes me three hours just to look mediocre," Ted says. "A little rough is a blessing." What does Andy see in him? Grit and stubble. The past two nights with Andy around the fire, they've talked, mostly, but when the temperature drops low enough for his skin to prickle, Andy touches him, and it's an electric shock. The shock lingers as he tries to sleep, and sometimes in the middle of the night, while Piotr and Lorraine and he lie in their cots, Ted listens to them breathe. Lorraine reads with a tiny blue penlight; Piotr reclines with hands behind his head, glasses on his chest. Every now and then, they inhale and exhale all at the same time, an instant of synchronicity, and neither Piotr nor Lorraine notices, but in that moment, they share one body, one pneuma, one purpose.

"Is there something I can do?" he asks Lorraine. He understands why he's on observer status—this is his first time, he needs to get a feel for disaster work, watch how Lorraine and Piotr operate—but . . . But what? It's too easy to shrink, hide behind his notebook, his observer status. That's the old Ted, the one who got washed away on the Ganges nearly two years ago.

"As a matter of fact," she says, "you remember the incident with Piotr yesterday? The World Food Programme could use extra help. The military is now sending armed escorts with delivery trucks. We're not entirely happy about this—people get antsy when they see soldiers."

Stefan from UNDAC comes up to them. He

taps Lorraine's forearm and kisses her cheeks. His features seem to have been passed down through German aristocracy. He hands her a sheaf of papers, whispers in her ear, then strides off. His khakis seem immune to wrinkles. He walks as if he owns the ground before him.

"He's got a great ass," Lorraine says.

Ted coughs.

"Don't pretend you weren't looking. You'd think for a guy in his fifties, it'd be saggy, but it's amazingly firm."

"Amazingly?"

"Like cantaloupes."

"I don't remember reading this in the annual report."

"This is a high-stress job, and when people work in close proximity—what do you expect? It's emergency sex. All the aid workers sleep with one another."

"Even Catholic Charities?"

"*Especially* Catholic Charities!"

"You mean," Lorraine adds, "that you haven't slept with that search-and-rescue guy?"

"No," Ted says. The possibility hasn't crossed his mind. Andy's body against his. His salty lips.

"I'm surprised. He seems full of spunk."

Ted can't say anything that won't sound filthy.

"If you let it," she says, "this job will break your heart every second of every day. You have to have a way to pull yourself together." She glances at her clipboard. "And, Ted," she says, "be careful, OK?"

He promises that he will be careful, but careful about what, he isn't sure.

Once, while walking through Gramercy Park, Lorraine told him that there were two types of aid workers. The first type, she said, were running toward something. "Like God or whatever." She flicked her hand, shooing away a fly. "It doesn't have to be God. They're trying to better themselves." She took out a cigarette and tapped it against the pack. The sides of her index and middle fingers had callused to accommodate the butt. "The missionary types last forever because they see it as their life's calling."

She gave him the number of her therapist.

"Don't worry. I don't get a discount for referrals."

"Are you sure you don't need this card?" he asked.

"I've got him on speed dial," she replied.

"The other type of aid worker," she continued, "goes into aid work because they're running away from something."

A line of cabs wiggled down the street like an eel. The city was a Möbius strip, a never-ending loop.

"What type are you?" she asked.

After a pause, Ted replied. "I guess I'm running

away." Should he have felt some sort of relief? Because he didn't. "How about you?"

She gave him a cockeyed glance. "What do you think?"

Irina, Arni's deputy, has been in charge of the warehouse since Arni was medevaced out. She's kept distribution flowing, but Arni's replacement hasn't been able to secure a flight from Delhi, and she hasn't had time to coordinate outlying delivery routes. Piotr consults maps stretched out across a pallet of water bottles, and Irina nods, as if understanding what she must do. Ted moves to look, but Piotr holds up a finger: *Wait.*

Ted sits on a sack of rice. The grains shift under him, and he sinks into it. Waiting is part of his job description. He waited until Lorraine felt he was ready, and then again for an appropriate opportunity. What sort of person waits for disaster to strike?

The last one hit in November. The sky was the color of metal shavings. He'd spent the morning familiarizing himself with reports. Eight hundred dead from flooding in Mozambique. Honduran and Nicaraguan victims from Hurricane Mitch: eleven thousand. İzmit earthquake in Turkey: fourteen thousand, with informal reports of up to forty thousand. These numbers came from annual reports, eyewitness accounts, estimates from the field, and when he got home, one more:

a message from Dr. Mark, John's boyfriend. John was dead. He died two days ago, and he was sorry that he'd only gotten around to calling him now. The memorial service would be—shit, there was the other line. Sorry. He'd call back. John was dead, and Ted had fallen to third day's notice. He was beneath call-waiting. He hated that Dr. Mark got to be the tragic one, the noble one. Ted picked up the receiver and started to dial John's number. He wanted to say, *You'll never believe what I just heard,* but on the fourth digit, Ted stared at the telephone as if nothing good had ever come from it. He tried to throw it across the room, but the jack kept it from going too far, and the base jerked back and landed on its side like an injured animal. The handset cracked but didn't break. Ted could feel himself breathing heavily, as if he were angry, but about what, he didn't know. Maybe it wasn't anger. A sliver of plastic from the phone lay on the floor. What kept the world from crumbling every second of every day?

He picked the phone back up and clamped it in his hand, until it was almost one piece again. He dialed John's number again and, this time, left his own message: "Is there something I can do?"

Piotr wants him to do reconnaissance. "With all the volunteers coming in," he says, "we can't put them at risk." Ted will pave the way for others.

But it also means he is expendable. He has trouble imagining Piotr herding volunteers.

"A soldier will accompany you," Piotr says, "but your own safety is paramount. If anything looks strange, leave immediately. I will be on the delivery truck. You can contact me with this." He hands Ted a CB radio the size of a briefcase. Dust has accumulated between the knobs.

Ted picks up the mic. "Smokey," he says, "this is Bandit. Come in, over." His throat makes the sound of static. Piotr stares. "I've actually never used one of these."

"Here," Piotr says, and he flicks a switch. Little green and red indicator lights that look like broken specks of candy blip on. Piotr shows him a button on the side of the mic. "Press this, speak, then let go. We will be on channel seventeen."

Ted looks at the radio. He turns it on its side, then back again. All the indicators are Cyrillic. Russian hand-me-downs. This place is the world's largest Goodwill.

"The channel knob is here," Piotr says. "It has been set. Incoming volume is here, and that's outgoing volume."

"What's the range on this?"

"Four miles maybe. The military wants satellite-phone traffic to a minimum, so this is our backup. Radio if you feel something is amiss," Piotr says. "Use your discretion."

Whatever he can do, Ted supposes. He picks

151

up the mic and pushes the button. "Roger that." But before he can say, *Over and out,* a squeal of feedback pierces the air. That noise is his voice, distorted, deafening.

This work requires a certain amount of duplicity. Knowing to whom to speak and the right tone of voice with which to speak. Piotr cajoles so softly that following his suggestions feels like a compliment. Lorraine, on the other hand, blusters: she's a metal wedge; complications split in two when she presses into them.

As Ted tries to secure a driver from the motor pool, he wishes he had their skills. He holds Piotr's map. A loop of cities to the northeast of Bhuj is highlighted in blue. "Food distribution," Ted says to the soldier guarding the lot. "I need a car."

The lot lies at the far end of the air force base. From here, the jets look like tents, their fumes flowing in on hot breezes. A gas tanker is parked at the end of the lot like a bulwark, and military vehicles—Jeeps, Land Rovers, light trucks—line up with their engines running. Vaporized petroleum settles into Ted's throat, makes it difficult to speak.

A scrapyard has built up around the motor pool, though Ted can't distinguish between functioning and nonfunctioning. The military has commandeered most working vehicles.

Only soldiers drive. Some cars are obviously destroyed: skulls caved in, as if crushed beneath a building. Dark fluids leak onto the ground. Gas tank covers gape open, contents siphoned away. Army mechanics, their uniforms with a camouflage pattern of grease, salvage what they can. Little bits of machinery like still-vital organs. Cars that look perfectly drivable have their hoods propped open, revealing nothing but emptiness inside.

"I'm with USAID." He pulls his ID card from his wallet. The soldier seems unimpressed. Lorraine, he imagines, would simply barge in and demand a car. Piotr would find the soldier's superior and convince him to release one. This is a test.

Ted points into the lot. Then to himself. He follows the soldier's eyes to make sure he's been understood. Good. He traces the blue-inked path for the soldier, who gives a small nod and shrugs, disinterested. Still good, though. Ted's wallet is still out, and he opens the fold to show the bills inside. Mostly ones, worn and faded, no more than thirty dollars, tops, but the soldier beckons Ted with his finger and leads him to an unlocked car, the keys in the ignition. He's never heard of this brand: a Maruti 800, blue like the color one associates with amateur paintings of the ocean. Spots of rust dot the doors and the wheel wells. The inside smells of hot vinyl, hot enough to sear the skin off your thighs. He rolls down the passenger-side window while the soldier yells something, and other soldiers, napping in the shade between cars, rise and brush themselves off. They move cars out of the way, like parking valets. When the soldier returns and knocks on the door, he looks around, as if checking if anyone is watching. He slides his hand in the window, palm up. A low five. Ted tells himself, *Don't do anything stupid,* but the rest of him has already handed over the money.

Past the old fort walls of Bhuj, Bhid Gate, one of five ancient entryways to the city, lies toppled. The bricks from the top of the gate—a jaw with punched-out teeth—have fallen onto the auto rickshaws below. A drink cart, with a row of smashed-open bottles of colored syrups, thrums with flies. Signs were painted on the brick surface, but these have long flaked off. The bright-yellow Vodafone announcement is as obsolete as the gate itself. A faded poster announces "Rahul!"

At the gate, men stand upon a scaffold of wooden poles lashed together with rough brown rope. With hammers and chisels, they chip at the gate's surface. One concentrates on a frieze of elephants, legs and trunks raised as if dancing, the larger ones cradling the smaller ones with their feet. The stone is orange, as if rubbed with

154

rust. Another man carries a lotus the size of a bowling ball up a metal ramp into a tractor trailer.

For a moment, Ted thinks that they're clearing rubble. But that's not what they're doing at all.

One day, he will see these pieces pried off Bhid Gate again. He'll be walking through SoHo, on his way to brunch, or to exchange his current cell phone for a newer model. And in a storefront that he never looks into because he feels inadequate every time he sees something that he can never have, he'll see that lotus, or those elephants, still entwined, abandoned by the herd. They will have outrageous prices: Chinese and Japanese antiques have peaked, Africa hasn't yet made a comeback, and India is definitely on the way up. The provenance will be incorrect. Reclaimed from a temple to be demolished in Amritsar. Right. *Who's your buyer?* he'll demand, and the owner of the gallery (called the Mehta Collection or Vijayarajji Antiques) will assure him that these pieces are, indeed, authentic. The owner, a middle-aged white man, will be dressed in a linen kurta with gold embroidery along the hem. His collar will be splayed to show his tanned, sagging skin and white wisps of chest hair. Ted imagines Bhuj as he has never seen it: where his eyes are drawn to every surface, where goddesses carved into the walls are an act of devotion, where mortar is set properly and never crumbles, where children chase each other rather than lie in cots with bloody stumps. And he will push the pieces—these *trophies*—to the ground. He'll grind them beneath his feet, return them to the city to which they belong: the destroyed city, the unseen city.

No one should own that stuff, right, John?

Abso-fucking-lutely.

Ted feels like a tourist. That's what seasoned aid workers call people who pop in and out of disaster areas. Disaster relief as an ego stroke. Lorraine should add them to her list of types of aid workers—the passers-through to go along with the running-aways and the running-towards.

Isn't aid work supposed *to make you feel better?*

Not if you're doing it right, she says.

Lorraine had come to USAID after a stint with International Orthodox Christian Charities. "That's what you get for being raised Greek," she said. She had been in Cambodia, on an agricultural project, when, about fifty feet behind her, a roaming herd of cattle trod onto an unexploded land mine. When she woke up, the doctors were still picking shrapnel out of her back.

Sometimes, in the office, when she reaches for a binder on a high shelf, her shirt rides up, and Ted sees the scars, pale puckers of skin.

"I couldn't do this just to make my parents proud," she told him. "I needed to do this for myself."

When Ted first started training with USAID, he imagined himself in front of television cameras, handing a housing kit to a grateful family. The camera would zoom in on the beads of sweat on his face as he helped a dust-ravaged wife set up the family tent. She would marvel at the new pots, the tin of cooking oil, the blankets encased in Mylar. *Here, the American government delivers sorely needed aid to the residents of Lodai, a small town in the devastated Gujarat region.* The chyron would identify him as "Ted Armstrong, USAID worker." *The United States is committed to helping those in need around the world,* he would say, the rest of his spiel cut off in the interest of time. The narrator would deliver inspirational words, accompanied by cuts to scenes shot earlier in the day (a young Oxfam worker's blond hair falling across the face of a bottle-feeding infant, uniformed men with Union Jack patches on their shoulders, grunting as they clear away rubble) and give information on how to contribute.

But the reality? Stuck behind camels.

The soldier drifts to a stop, laying on the horn. The herd, an undulation of tan fur, obstructs the road. They graze at bits of scrub poking out of the ground, buckteeth working like a pestle. A young boy wearing a white turban keeps them in line by flicking a cane of frayed bamboo. He skips behind them, zigzagging across the road. The car pulls parallel to the boy, who looks at Ted. Ted wills his mouth into a smile. The boy stares at him, hard. *What is this Westerner doing here? Go home,* ferengi, *go home.*

The soldier tries to find a path through, but the camels refuse to give way. Such awkward beasts, all sinew and muscle. As the driver honks, a relentless noise, they saunter off the road. Ted, still looking at the boy, distends his jaw and shifts it laterally, the best imitation of a camel he's ever done, down to the ridiculous scruff on his chin. But the car has already moved on, and the boy is far past laughing.

Ted consults the map. It's useless. A fourth-generation photocopy. The roads are so faint they may as well not exist. Town and village names are broken, no longer words, but mere indications, suggestions of place. Nagor, Raydhanpur, Boladi, Lodai, Jhuran, Jawaharnagar. Ted tries to estimate how far they've gone with the scale indicator at the bottom of the map, but as he looks for the road signs and markers, he realizes that they're written in Gujarati. Even the numerals are different: loops and squiggles. Ciphers.

He leans to the driver. "Do you know where we are?"

The driver shakes his head, a dismissal. *Don't bother me.*

In the distance, Ted sees a handful of peaked roofs. "Is this Lodai?" he asks. On the map, the word "Lodai" is larger than the other towns, but smaller than Bhuj. Font size as an approximation of population. He's lost any sense of scale, of distance. "Turn here," he says, pointing. "Here."

The washboard road leads toward the roofs. The car grinds out a herald of dust. Maybe the villagers use this as an early warning system. *Here we come,* the dust says. *We are almost at your doorstep.*

But as they approach, Ted sees that this isn't a town, not in any proper sense. It's an outpost, so small that Ted isn't sure it even has a name. Six mud huts, arranged in a semicircle; between the third and fourth huts, a canopy of palm fronds, propped by bamboo poles; in the center, a rectangular water tank that has cracked, leaching its contents into the sand. Three of the huts have collapsed. Half the village! But to say that this place was destroyed is to assume that it had existed in the first place. If Ted gives it a name, will it concretize? Two elderly men sit in the shade of the fronds. Where are the other people who live here? Are they waiting on the road to ambush passersby? Are these the men who attacked Arni yesterday?

"Do you need water?" Ted asks.

One man holds up his hands, palms out, and shakes them. His fingers are callused and white at the knuckles, like rings of alabaster. He points at the tank.

"We don't have concrete. We can't fix the tank. Rice," Ted says. "We can bring you rice." Six huts, Ted notes. Six households. Six food packets. Ted looks at the soldier, hoping that he will translate. But that's not in his job description. Maybe everyone else is searching for food and water and whatever else they need to survive.

How *do* they survive here? They are on the very edge of desolation itself: the Great Rann, the unforgiving desert, which, even now, Ted feels caked onto his skin. These people have made peace with the Rann, eked out an existence the earthquake could not decimate. They have retrieved their belongings from the rubble. Already, they have patched cracks in the standing huts with dried patties of cow dung. One is missing its thatch roof, but the hot season is still months away. Bamboo poles mark where a new hut will stand.

"If anyone is injured," Ted says, "we can transport them." One man has a long scrape down the length of his arm, but it has already scabbed over. Ted sees bruises, dark inkblots beneath the skin, but no broken limbs, no gaping wounds. Mud hurts, but does not maim; mud injures, but does not kill; mud crushes, but does not obliterate.

"I'll be back," Ted says. "I promise." He sees himself returning with food and water and building materials. He sees the gratitude on their faces, these old men who will remember him, recognize what he is delivering. He makes promises because he wants the pleasure of fulfilling them. *You're not doing it right,* he hears Lorraine say. *You're being selfish,* John says. But this is all Ted knows how to do. He doesn't know the name of this place. He doesn't even know where he is.

Ted hadn't taken this job in order to impress John, though John *had* been impressed. *You're actually doing something less evil?* Ted had taken the job because—because he wanted a change, he supposes—though anyone could have said the same. One woman he trained with had been the VP for finance at an international bank. Another had dropped out of his anthropology PhD. They were all running away.

But those two knew what they were doing. The woman wanted to work specifically in development, the failed PhD in the preservation of cultural heritages. When someone asked Ted what his focus would be, he answered, "Everything." This was part of his new life, after all. More willingness to fight. For what? For *everything*.

Maybe that's why Lorraine had taken him onto her team. DART members, she said, need to be jacks-of-all-trades. One minute you're restoring the power grid, the next you're negotiating food aid. Oh, sure, she and Piotr had their specialties—his was logistics, hers volunteer coordination—but flexibility was more important.

"I don't have any specialties," Ted told her.

"You will," she said.

And why did he choose aid work as his new career, his new life? Oh, that's right—the sins. According to some Eastern religions, the good acts you perform in this life determine how you will be reborn in your next life. Bad deeds in past life need to be reconciled in your current life. Based on that metric, Ted's way behind. He hasn't even begun to atone for the things he's done in *this* life. People always claim to have been Napoléon, Genghis Khan, and Cleopatra in past lives, but no one wants to have been the chambermaid, the stable hand, the street whore. No one wants to be the drug rep, the Chelsea boy, the yuppie. But everyone wants to be reborn.

Lodai lies up ahead, an outcropping of concrete homes, or, at least, objects in the shape of homes. Who knows what they are now. As Ted leans forward to look, a jolt shakes him, and he smacks his forehead against the windshield. The car swerves, and from beneath them, there's a thrumming sound. The soldier curses. He turns the wheel, but the car doesn't respond. They veer across the road, off it, and toward a shallow ditch, and although Ted knows that he'll be OK, that the car won't flip over, seeing the cleft in the ground, his breath hiccups, and he puts his arms out to brace himself. His legs tense.

The car eases into the ditch, pauses, and rolls backward, like it's rocking Ted to sleep.

The front passenger-side tire is flat. No surprise: it's almost bald, a flat loop of rubber. The soldier curses in a tone that transcends language. "Is there a spare?" Ted asks. But the trunk is empty, nothing in the indentation where the spare belongs. He wonders if it was sold long ago by its owner, or if the army appropriated it. Not that it matters. He takes the CB from the car and pats the hood, as if thanking it for its service, and when the soldier looks at him oddly, he kicks the flat, because he doesn't want to look like he's *not* angry. But in the catalog of things that have gone wrong in his life, this is minor.

Back about a hundred feet, Ted finds the culprit: a crack in the road. One edge of the blacktop rises three inches higher than the other. The split spans the width of the roadway and into the landscape itself. Is this how much the earth has moved? Three inches along a vertical plane: enough to explode a tire, enough to flatten a house, enough to kill thousands. Such a small distance. An index finger. He's always imagined earthquakes to be huge things—the ground opens up and swallows people whole, the land cracks like arctic ice, and, in between the floes, one can stare straight into the center of the earth. But it's a tiny thing. And Ted, himself, is a tiny thing. One tiny thing responds to another.

The road into Lodai serpentines up an incline, a treeless route into a treeless town, as if the land is too dry for anything green. At its base, where the town starts, piles of stones rise. This must be where the residents dump their debris. Scraps of cloth and broken chunks of plastic peek from between the rocks. Wires, twigs. The piles look like cairns, ritualistic.

Ted walks to the sandy center of town. A concrete water tank sits there, half-full. The water is cool on his fingertips, and he dabs a few drops on the back of his neck. Most of the one-story houses are intact. More, actually, than he had expected.

Two children watch from a doorway, a boy and a girl in white pajamas with sleeves that extend to their knuckles. They're bleary, in that half space after a nap. Farther in the house, he sees a floor mat, upon which ten other people sleep. Everyone escapes the hot part of the day. Only the foolish are up and about—mad dogs and Americans.

He kneels. "Hi," he says. "I'm here to help." The children giggle and run away.

The noon sun fills the air with static and silence. Ted runs through the CB channels, a squawk as he switches from one to another. "Hello? Hello?" He doesn't expect an answer. Lorraine and Piotr have surely forgotten him for now. In a few hours, they may start to worry, but at this moment, no one thinks about him, no one remembers him.

The road ends in a klatch of homes at the top of the hill, along with a pea-green mosque. Turmeric dots speckle the mosque's side, but on closer inspection, they're handprints—fingers spread as if climbing up the wall. Just past the mosque, the road he came in on comes into view, a black line bisecting the desert's body, the occasional vehicle creeping across it like an insect through fur. Maybe CB reception is better here.

Even after other villagers rouse, they take little notice of his presence. He's an oddity, an obstacle. Women chop thorny shrubs with adzes, striking the stems until they splinter. Older boys stack the dry branches, gray and speckled like granite. Two teenage girls carry metal jugs to and from the water tank, the jugs in a column four high, a doughnut of cloth cushioning their skulls from the weight. They walk quick and steady.

How have they recovered so quickly? Is it a matter of chores? Of survival? Maybe grief is a luxury, an indulgence. Maybe it's a flavor on the tongue, one that alters the taste of everything. Maybe this is the remedy for grief: to be forgotten, and to forget.

Just—not yet. OK, John? Not yet.

By two, he hasn't made contact. The soldier dozes in the shade of the mosque, his rifle pointing straight into the air. Ted uses his hand as a visor, but the brightness weighs on his brow like a stone. The road sears his retinas. The desert consumes the horizon.

Ted follows a footpath between two houses to a courtyard. On the ground are trapezoidal pyramids, so white that they look new. Some are adorned with a single vermillion dot on the side, others with painted tridents. This must be a graveyard. So unlike Bhuj: no mounds of corpses, no ever-burning pyres. No stench that sinks into your clothes, waiting to stifle you.

Someone shouts—an elderly woman reclining beneath a corrugated tin roof weighted with rocks to keep the wind from blowing it away. The waves of tin are rusted, and sun angles through the jagged holes. With one hand, she fans herself with a palm frond, and with the other, she waves, as if scratching the air: *Come here.*

As Ted approaches, she points at her feet, then

his. Oh—shoes. When he steps onto the tiles, the cool bites through his socks, a relief he hadn't imagined possible. She sits cross-legged. Around her left ankle, she wears gold bangles as thin as string. She smooths her sari against her legs. The cloth is worn, the color of adobe. She smacks her lips to moisten her mouth. Her gray hair is tied in a bun and secured with blue thread. She is all knots.

She pats the ground next to her. *Sit. Stay out of trouble.*

Ted hears the motorcycles puttering before he sees them, a rumble like an oncoming headache. The men returning. He moves to rise, but the old woman puts a hand on his shoulder. *Stay put.* On one cycle, four men squeeze together like plywood. Flatbed carts with ragged and splintered rails are hitched to two of the motorcycles.

Once parked, the men convene around an older man in a white robe. He has a shaggy salt-and-pepper beard, and his hair has the same raspy texture as his beard. Around his neck, a cinnabar necklace, the beads as big as dried dates. The elderly woman calls out, and he comes over to them. He says something to Ted. They shake. This is their common language: their hands. He says something to the other men, and they laugh. Ted, the butt of a joke. The elder has dark, bony spurs at his ankles, as if they had once been broken. He speaks as if Ted can understand him completely.

He points to the ground, then the sky, and then, with an open palm, sweeps the air. *Ted, meet world.*

He tugs Ted toward a two-story structure. The door has a medallion in the shape of a rising sun. Maybe a setting sun. Atop the door is a frieze adorned with small carvings: rosettes in interlocking patterns. How many New Yorkers would pay thousands in order to turn that piece into an objet d'art? How many would praise its authenticity, its spirituality? But it belongs *here,* Ted thinks, where it has meaning, even if that meaning is lost on Ted—or maybe especially since that meaning is lost.

Before entering, the elder rings a bell dangling above the doorway. Inside, it's cool: quiet shade, a hint of incense. On the second floor is a long concrete bin topped with what looks like marble. But it's not marble—it's a layer of ash. From his robes, the elder retrieves a photograph, rolled and gray at the edges, with folds that cut through the image like lightning. Four figures, sun bleached into sepia. The elder points to one of the men, then himself. In the picture, he has his arm around two young boys. He puts a fingertip over the face of the boy to his right. He dips his finger in the ash, and then touches his forehead, his tongue, his neck.

. . .

The men gather beneath the shelter for tea. They invite the soldier. The glass cups from which they drink are as small as mice, and flecked with paint from decorations long chipped off. To the right, the women huddle around a shallow pit fire. The burning branches hiss and pop, and the smoke smells sweet, like acacia. A branch occasionally curls out of the pit, a Hindi character written in flame. A young girl squooshes a blob of brown dough between her fingers. Other women toss the dough until it flattens and slap it onto a metal sheet laid over the fire. The old woman fans the flames with her frond, her hand tracing a figure eight. They must have a store of food for contingencies—earthquakes, droughts, wayward white men. The women laugh among themselves, conspiring the way only women can.

The elder male slides a cup toward Ted. Ted shakes his head, but the elder says something, his head wobbling from side to side, and points to the cup, as if delivering an order. The foam on the water's surface swirls and clashes. That's all he needs. To get seriously ill in India. Again. The aid trucks have chlorine tablets for water purification. Who knows what might be festering in the tank?

Still. It's only tea. It's been boiled. Ted takes a sip. The liquid is hot. The astringency turns taut on his tongue, and a leaf gets caught between his upper lip and gums.

The old woman brings the bread on a dented tin platter. The bread is almost lavender, dotted with grain. The men take one and close their eyes, mumbling a prayer before ripping it with their fingers. The old woman doesn't give Ted a chance to refuse and plops a piece into his hands. It's as warm as skin. Only after all the men have been served does the elder take his portion. The old woman returns to Ted and, from the folds of her sari, produces a red onion the size of a baby's fist. With one swift karate chop, she splits it in two, sending forth a spray of milky fluid. The papery skin crinkles away, and with a paring knife, she cuts the stem end of a shriveled lime and squeezes it onto the onion. The bright tang of the juice, the spiciness of the onion, the earthiness of the millet, slightly sweet, slightly ashen.

The men eat in silence, as if food were a blessing that should never be interrupted.

The women clear the dishes and sweep with straw brooms, the swish of bristles against the tile like a mother quieting her baby. Only after their chores do the women eat, and this bothers Ted, though he's in no position to do anything about it. He feels he should be more grateful. These people have just fed him when they have precious little themselves.

After the sun peaks, the men resume clearing rubble. They use anything with wheels—old carts, bicycles, suitcases—to roll rocks to the bottom of the hill. Ted tries to help. Ted strains with a stone he can barely lift, looking for guidance where to put it. A man on a motorcycle waves at him to put it down, his hand flapping as if spanking a child. He points Ted back beneath the shelter, where the old woman hobbles next to him. Her face is a dried apricot, her smile the pitting incision. She has no teeth. On her feet, she has calluses as hard as leather where her skin meets the straps of her sandals.

Ted nods, and she nods back. Does she merely mimic his motion, or does the nod have a universal meaning? How many men in this village are her sons and grandsons? How many daughters and daughters-in-law have learned how to make chapati by her hands?

"I'm sorry," he tells her, "that I can't do more."

He can barely hear her reply, her voice a murmur deep within her throat. The unfamiliar syllables and phonemes fail to process in his weak, limited brain. Her words are acrobats, bending and twisting. But he listens anyway. She tells him about the quality of the dust from one season to the next: how she can taste the monsoon air, the oncoming whirlwinds. She tells him about the joy of serving water to thirsty strangers. She says that she has lived her life, and that it has been a good one, and that she has no regrets about how she has lived it. She tells him that the world that he has pulled away from now pulls him back, and he should neither resist nor meekly accept it. His life is still his, after all, and he should do with it what he pleases. She laughs, the only sound he understands clearly, and she pats his knee as if he were her son, her laziest son, her most self-indulgent son, but her son nonetheless, and she rises, her joints creaking, to bring him another cup of tea.

It's nearly five when he finally makes contact with Piotr. Ted is glad to hear his voice.

"Is this where you've been hiding?" Piotr asks.

"My car broke down," Ted replies. "Long story."

There's a pause. Then Piotr says, "Lorraine has a present for you."

When Piotr and the aid truck arrives, the sun hangs low in the sky, the land awash in light as if it were cast in bronze. Piotr hops out of the cab, and Ted asks, "So, where's this present?" and Piotr gestures behind him. A Jeep full of teenagers drives up. They're dressed in shorts and T-shirts with Scripture quotes.

"They're all yours," Piotr says.

Ted gives the orders—"I want three people each unloading the housing kits. Carry it by the ropes. You don't want to rip holes in someone's roof. Offer one per family."

The villagers look at the housing kits, canvas-wrapped cubes. Everyone recognizes the bags of rice, but these things—what could they be? Two female volunteers pass out boxes of canned goods. There better be can openers in there too.

Ted offers two village girls wobbly plastic bladders of water. "So you don't have to carry so much every day," he says. They wear shawls in colors that defy the desert—the green of new shoots, the blue of the deepest part of the ocean. The shawls have tiny mirrors embroidered into them, flashes of brightness. Gold earrings the shape of peacock feathers rest on their shoulders.

The girls each peel off a bag of water. The vinyl sounds as if it's ripping. They turn to leave.

"No, wait," he says. "These are for you. Take them." He pushes the packets toward them.

The girls hold up what they have. The water sloshes like it's alive.

They don't understand. "It's all for you," he says, but the girls nod and walk away, and Ted can't believe how beautiful they are, and how stupid he is, and how this has probably always been the case.

Ted rides back with the volunteers. He thought he'd be grateful to hear English again, but . . . The volunteers, from Patrick Henry College, had been doing a winter study abroad in Delhi, and when they heard about the earthquake, they just *had* to come and help. They're so chirpy that Ted wants to plug his ears.

"It was a calling," says one girl, her hair in a long, blond ponytail. Others jabber in agreement.

"We didn't even have to talk our faculty sponsor into it," says a young man, who should have been tanning himself on a beach. "But he was thinking the same thing."

"We were totally of one mind about this."

Everyone nods so vigorously that Ted imagines their heads snapping off in unison.

They ask him about doing this for a living, about what he's seen, and when he answers that he's new to the job himself, they don't seem disappointed. In fact, they press him harder: Why *this* line of work? What about it? Did he have a calling? A stroke of divine inspiration? Ted wants to answer *yes* but can't bring himself to believe that God has killed thousands—maimed thousands more—just to make him a better person.

Night settles in, and soldiers, hands on rifle butts, remind everyone of curfew. He asks Lorraine if she sicced the evangelical group on him. "It wasn't me," she replies. She looks heavenward. "It was God's plan." At the volunteers' behest, he meets their faculty sponsor, Mr. Meyer, a jovial bag of pastry dough.

174

"I'm glad you were able to give my kids some direction," he says. "I wouldn't let them out on their own, but I know they were in good hands." There are fifteen students total. They compare little gifts that they were given: A twig sculpture. A string bracelet. A marble. Others have cameras with irrefutable proof of their good deeds. "Will you be able to work with them tomorrow?" Mr. Meyer asks, but Ted shakes his head no. *I go where I'm needed most.*

The last bits of sunlight lie low on the horizon, seeping into the earth. Cooking fires have started again. Farther on, the ever-present glow from the medical tents.

The medical tents at night seem somehow more dire. As people sleep, they appear dead. The pain, localized in their bodies during the day, becomes unmoored, diffuses in the air. He can smell it.

It's difficult to tell one person from another. All their faces are carved out of darkness. Many are not asleep at all, but have fallen into an open-eyed stupor. Morphine is in short supply. One man, hunched into an egg, stares at something directly across from him, clasping his hands to his lower lip. Missing limbs, extra limbs: a man with an amputation below the knee, an old woman with splints made from tree branches. Limbs that jut out as if suddenly vestigial. Limbs materialize out of nowhere to beg for help. Ted feels as if his

175

own limbs could abandon him at any second and reattach themselves to new bodies. *Here, take my hand. Here, have a foot.* He almost wishes it would happen.

Ted isn't sure who recognizes whom first. It's a shared moment, instantaneous, like a lightbulb burning through its filament. Had Ted seen him first, he might have sneaked away, shielding his face behind his hand. But their eyes meet, and Ted seizes. It *is* him—Ted would recognize him anywhere. He wears sky-blue surgical scrubs and a face mask around his throat, and he's a few pounds heavier, but it's him nonetheless. His voice still has a baritone singsong: "You are the last person I expected to encounter here."

Ted feels something rise inside him, and he knows exactly what it is: his past life, the one he thought he'd left behind, incomplete, in India two years ago. There it is, crowding out his current life, bringing with it a long ledger of errors and grievances to rectify. His past life jumps in his mouth, leaving him dumbstruck. His past life stands before him, with that wry smile, concentrated on the right side of the face, and his current life manages to croak out, finally, "It's nice to see you again, Dev."

RELIEF

PILGRIMS TO AN UNFAMILIAR GOD

1999

I. Love during the Plague Years

Ted's taxi had waited at the light for no longer than ten seconds when the little girl approached. Ann was dozing. The plane ride had been rough on her. They had expected a car to pick them up, but the line of chauffeurs outside the gate held up everyone's names but theirs. So while Ann watched the luggage, Ted searched for a cab. The drivers auctioned themselves off; they'd show him four sites, no, five sites, six sites and a place to watch the beautiful sunset. And even after he'd secured a ride for what he considered a good price, other cabbies accosted him, trying to undercut the winning driver. They grabbed his bags, then Ann's bags, and the driver shooed them away with a harsh word. Ted felt as though he were being led by a ring through his nose.

And now, this little girl. She rapped on the window. He rolled it down, and her left hand darted in, palm up. Her ragged dress had smears of dirt and grease. It looked as if it had never been white. Her hair was a bundle of sticks. She couldn't have been older than ten but already had thick calluses on her brown-skinned hands. Ted knew he'd encounter poverty, and every guidebook he'd consulted insisted that he resist the urge to give to beggars. A coldhearted assessment, but not without reason.

Ted shook his head. "Sorry."

Her hand remained. The audacity of desperation. Ted smiled in what he thought was a sympathetic way. The girl smiled back.

"I don't have anything," he said.

The light turned, and the entire automotive mass inched forward in unison. The driver revved the engine until the brakes smoked. As the taxi moved, the girl balled her right hand. Her fist seemed as small as a crab apple, yet it landed solidly on Ted's cheekbone, with the sound of someone popping an inflated plastic bag. The taxi pulled away before he could react. The girl was swallowed by the metal swell of traffic.

"Jesus Christ! Did you see that?"

"See what?" Ann asked.

"I just got punched." The strike had been surprisingly strong. Ann clutched her handbag between her legs. "She's long gone," Ted said.

"A woman? You got punched by a woman?"

"A girl. Maybe twelve?"

Ann closed her eyes again.

Ted rolled the window up and tapped the

laminated paper sign informing riders about the AC surcharge. The driver pushed a button, and the green AC light came on, but the cold air sputtering from the vents dissipated long before Ted felt it. He leaned between the driver's and passenger's seats, trying to catch what little comfort there was.

He tilted his face into the rearview mirror, the taxi's most useless appendage. A bruise blossomed on his cheek. The sun was setting, the sky a dark roil of haze and pollution. It burned orange, smoking hot. The taxi whipped around traffic circles and barreled into fractional openings between other vehicles. The driver asked Ann if she wanted to buy jewelry, silk textiles, perfume, spices, and, hearing no response, halfheartedly indicated the Parliament building, the India Gate, the Red Fort—ornate shapes in the half-light. But all Ted saw was people: every available inch occupied by humanity, with the occasional head of cattle wandering into the road.

Ted liked telling the story of the little girl. It was, after all, his first experience in India. But by the end of the conference, he had grown tired of it. When he and Ann hobnobbed with other drug reps or took a prospective doctor client out to dinner, she said, "Tell them the story," and he did. But the story was the outline around which

181

Ann composed her pitch. Ann talked about that moment as if she'd been awake in the taxi. Ted didn't mind her co-opting his story; he welcomed it; they were a team, after all, and this was their charm offensive. But with each telling, the story grew more distant, downgraded from *event* to *occurrence* to *anecdote*.

The bruise, however, refused to fade. Even five days later, its center was dark purple and, at its edges, gangrenous green yellow. "That means it's healing," Ann said. She applied a thick daub of foundation, blending it with a wedge-shaped sponge. "Not an exact match," she said, "but it'll do."

For the last five mornings, this was their ritual. Before coffee, before manning the booth: makeup. But on this morning, with the light peering in on either side of the thick curtain, Ted couldn't quite remember where he was. India, he remembered: New Delhi, the conference. It was almost seven—he'd overslept—and in an hour he and Ann needed to be down at their booth for the final day. As Ted roused, he knew his bruise was visible. During the night, the makeup smeared onto the sheets, the pillowcases.

Dev stared at Ted's face.

"What happened?" He traced a finger along Ted's cheek, as if measuring the bruise.

So Ted told the story again. Not in an attempt to entertain or with an end purpose, but because

Dev had asked. Dev listened with a curious smile, a smile that maybe cheered on the girl as much as it empathized with Ted. The right side of Dev's mouth curled like a question mark, and as Dev spoke, Ted gripped the edge of the mattress and tugged at the seam of the sheet. Ted looked into Dev's face, his gaze, the dark intensity of his smile. "This is India," Dev said. He nodded, bringing the subject to a close.

He should have hated Dev. Or, rather, continued to hate Dev with the blind intensity reserved for strangers. He knew of Dev long before he'd met him—Dev was, after all, a rising star. The brash director of HIV Services at New Delhi General Hospital. The patent scofflaw. Dev's clinic was one of the major distribution centers of Triacept, and even though the WTO, pending a final decision, had put a stay on its distribution, Dev's clinic, Ted had heard, still prescribed it. Dev had testified before the WTO panel about Triacept's necessity in combating HIV. He didn't deny that Triacept was three protease inhibitors—Crixevir, Advantis, and Relevir, all unlicensed—in a single capsule. His testimony sidestepped intellectual property issues to focus on the imperative for poorer nations to treat HIV infections cheaply and effectively. But surely he knew that without proper distribution and rigorous oversight and follow-up, the risk of developing resistant strains was too high. Had he considered the possibilities of adverse reactions from the combination? The WTO's ruling would come soon, but Ted knew that they—the drug companies—were in the right.

The HIV Treatment Conference was a minor conference. It didn't bring in heads of state, like the International AIDS Conference, but attracted ministers of health at least. Ted and Ann had a clear goal: twenty-five names for the physician-outreach team, with at least twelve teaching physicians, since MD/PhDs were much more effective for speaking engagements.

Dev would never sign up for physician out-reach—the self-righteous types never did—but Ted sneaked into Dev's session nonetheless. The face of the enemy had a roundness to it, a soft, malleable handsomeness. Dev's stomach overhung his belt, as if it were trying to hold back middle age. He wore a suit but no tie, and his collar revealed a V of flesh. His cuff links glinted gold. Ted should have hidden his Avartis name tag, because Dev's eyes glanced down, a tiny change of focus: he'd been discovered.

"My friends," Dev said. "Thank you for coming."

The speech was like innumerable others he'd heard at innumerable conferences: *Observable results. Research methodology. Statistical deviations.* But the room fell into rapt attention;

there were none of the typical conference whispers, shuffles of paper, furtive pager checks. Dev sat as if he had a metal rod instead of a spinal cord. Ted took note of the physicians around him, possible candidates for outreach, and suddenly felt an intense weight on his chest, as if someone were sitting on it. Dev was looking at him. Dev paused, midsentence, and for an instant, it felt as though they were alone in that room, the two of them locked in silent combat. Dev looked down at his papers. He'd lost his place, and in that pause, Ted made a break for it. Dev had regained his composure, resumed his talk, and Ted caught his eye. Dev smirked: *I know what you're doing.*

Ted walked back to the Avartis booth, where Ann furtively flipped through her Fodor's. Static electricity crackled beneath his feet.

"What's that grin about?" she asked. "Did you sign up someone big?"

"If only," he replied. He felt light-headed, full of helium. "It's strange being here. In a foreign country."

"You live in Chelsea. That's its own foreign country. Homostonia."

"At least the natives are friendlier."

"Fewer assaults from eight-year-old girls?"

"For instance."

Ted peeked at what Ann was reading: the restaurant listings. "Going out for dinner?"

"Thinking about it," she said. "By the way, someone asked for you. John someone."

"John." Ted wondered aloud. It was poor form to forget a contact. He tried to remember the people he'd met thus far, flipped through the business cards he'd received. "John," Ted said again, trying out the name on different faces he knew. He paced the booth, as if it were a cage.

"Bald. Muscular."

He cycled to the John he knew the best.

"No way. What's he doing here? It's been *six* years."

"I kind of suspected that it might have been *that* John," Ann said. "Want to hunker down in avoidance mode?"

Ted polished fingerprints off the plastic Crixevir model. It was the size of a newborn. People couldn't help but shake it or stroke its shiny surface. How many people in the world were, at this moment, swallowing this pill? Was John on Crixevir? Could he feel it in his bloodstream, like electric sparks, like hope? Was his body fat peeling away from his face and buttocks and repositing itself on his abdomen?

"Well," Ted said, "if it happens, it happens."

"Ken and Jill have invited us out to drinks," Ann said.

"Ken?"

"From Glaxo Wellcome."

"Oh, right."

186

"And Jill from—"

"I know," Ted said.

When Ann said, *Ken and Jill have invited us,* she meant, *Ken and Jill invited me, and you are free to accompany me.* He had an attenuated relationship with the other drug reps. Ann was the public face of the Crixevir team, with her broad, brassy personality that people, particularly gay men, loved in small, controlled doses. She went to short-lived SoHo clubs in abandoned storefronts. Ted was an afterthought, an appendage. He'd watched Ann, in her business pantsuit, dance in high heels with men that wouldn't have given him the time of day. "But that's why we make a killer team," Ann had said. "I lure them with my boobs and bullshit, and then you nail them with sincerity. You actually believe what you say about Crixevir."

"Tell them I'm sorry," he said. "There's some stuff I need to do."

"Stuff," Ann said. She fanned brochures across the table. "You know, for a gay guy, you're kind of a downer."

"Tell me about it," he replied.

Ted made the walk of shame from Dev's room to his own. Shirt untucked, hair at odd angles. The hotel staff didn't notice; their invisibility was a paid-for privilege. An unfamiliar satisfaction settled onto Ted's chest: he remembered Dev's heft pressing against him, how solid he felt, like a dam. When Dev left the bed, the sheets ballooned, and a chill swept in the vacated space. "Did you know," Dev said, rooting on the floor for his underwear, "that you smile in your sleep?" Ted touched the corners of his mouth, as if double-checking. Dev had an outpost of hair on the small of his back, right above his buttocks. "A curious thing," Dev said. He went to shower, and Ted retrieved his clothes: boxers beside the bed; pants collapsed at the foot, socks scrunched up inside the legs; shirt balled up near the window.

By the time Dev emerged from the bathroom, drying his hair, a towel cinched around his waist, Ted had dressed. Dev squirted sweet-smelling coconut oil into his hands and slicked back his hair, taming the unruly curls beneath his fingers. Dev approached Ted, arms raised as if for an embrace, but instead smeared the excess oil onto Ted's face.

Ted could smell it now as he entered his own room. Could he keep this experience for himself? Not as a story, but as something vital. A moment that brought continuous pleasure. While he'd lived with John, he'd lived in the future, always wondering what was going to happen. After John, he lived in the past, remembering what life with John had been like. The present eluded him, evanescent as the scent of coconuts wafting by.

As he showered, he rubbed the tender spot

along his collarbone, where Dev had scored his skin with stubble. It felt like a sunburn. As he was about to go downstairs, Ann knocked on their adjoining door. But it wasn't really Ann; it was a hideous replica of her in a hotel robe. She had the pallor of bread; she sweat and shivered simultaneously, hair plastered against her skull.

"What happened to you?" Ted asked.

"To *me?*" she said. "What happened to *you?*"

"I was out."

"I hope you at least sealed the deal," she said. "I've been vomiting my brains out."

"I guess I'm breaking down the booth alone?"

"Stupid Ken. Wanted 'the real India.' He got us food off a street cart. He's twice as bad off." Ann burped, and the sourness spilled into the room. "I asked room service for Pepto-Bismol, but they couldn't understand me. Do you have anything?"

"I think I've got a dose or two of Cipro."

"Cipro? Shit, you play rough, don't you?" She slipped the whole bottle into her pocket. "Details later," she said, "when they won't make me barf."

Details, then:

Dev rapped the side of the Avartis booth, saying, "You know, it's generally considered rude to leave in the middle of a person's presentation." Ted apologized, and Dev said, "It's quite all right." Free for dinner? Yes.

At dinner, Ted started his pitch: "Avartis is

189

looking for key opinion leaders to represent us," and Dev sighed. Must you?

Second tack: "This summer, we're convening an informational session at Lake Como. In Italy. We can arrange a speaking engagement—"

Dev interrupted. "Will you go? To Lake Como, that is," and Ted replied, "I wish I could—" and Dev said, "Then, no.

"You can't hope to sway me," Dev continued, "especially since Triacept is so effective. Which you would have known if you'd stayed for my entire presentation."

Ted countered: "But what if the WTO rules against Triacept?" and Dev said, "They won't." Ted pressed: "But what if they do?" And Dev said, "If they do, I will be too busy with dying patients to come to Lake Como."

Other doctors and drug reps mingled seamlessly. They laughed at one another's jokes, threw their heads back without disturbing their cocktails.

"I see I've upset you," Dev said.

Ted insisted, "No."

Dev continued, "You're not the first to approach me. The other reps. So full of bonhomie. I turned them down too, but they smile through their rejection. I can see you take it personally."

Ted said, "I don't," and Dev said, "You do."

"I'm not Avartis," Ted said.

"But you *are* Crixevir," Dev replied.

These, of course, weren't the details that Ann wanted. So instead:

Dev asked Ted to come to his room after dinner. Further conversation, maybe a nightcap, a more personal excoriation of Avartis. Dev closed the door and latched the privacy lock. "Make yourself comfortable," he said. From Dev's window, sickly yellow letters floated in midair: Shangri-la. Adventurers for centuries had searched for Shangri-la, and all Ted had to do was walk across the street.

"How do you find India?" Dev asked. He hung his jacket, the metal hangers clinking like chimes. He unbuttoned his shirt, unearthing a black morass of hair above the curve of his undershirt.

"Being here feels a little strange," Ted said.

"The culture shock can be quite extreme."

"No, not that," Ted said. "I actually haven't been outside the hotel yet."

"You haven't? Poor thing." He patted Ted's head and kept his hand there. Ted felt his scalp prickle beneath Dev's touch.

"I don't mind," Ted said, leaning back. Dev's hand was a cradle. "I like being here." The sentence hung on his tongue; it was a sentiment he hadn't thought through. What did it mean to be *here?* Not just in Dev's room, not just in India, but present in his own body? His body responded to Dev's advances, but Ted could not locate himself in it. He felt like a machine. A machine hidden among other machines.

Dev extended a hand, and Ted took it. Years of syringe pressing and prescription writing had left calluses on Dev's thumb and index fingers. Dev caressed his face. *I'm calling to you,* the flesh said. *Here you are.*

Dev unbuckled his belt and let his trousers drop. His belly puckered over the elastic of his briefs, and the cotton ribbing was stretched so that it looked striped. Thick ringlets of hair covered his upper thighs. Ted pressed his face against Dev's right thigh, buried his nose in the intersection of cloth and skin. He wrapped his arms around Dev's legs, and Dev fell backward onto the bed.

"My shoes." Dev laughed. "I've still got my shoes on."

Ted helped him out of his shoes, which Dev took to the closet. Ted undressed, and Dev lay back in bed, watching. "I like your body," Dev said. "I like your skin." Ted joined Dev in bed, and Dev clutched him, and Ted knew that he was *here,* if for no other reason than Dev was holding him down.

Coconut. Dev smelled of coconut. Ted wondered if he had a distinct smell, and if he did, if it was external or intrinsic, an inescapable aspect of himself. John always smelled voltaic, the static of his Lycra bike shorts. Ted sniffed his wrist. Soap, laundry detergent—but nothing that he could identify as uniquely *Ted*. Maybe his mistake was assuming that there was a unique Ted to begin with.

Six days ago, Ted had arrived to a blank hall with tables skirted in white. Then, one by one, flags unfurled, claiming terra incognita in the name of Merck, SmithKline Beecham, Glaxo Wellcome. Now those banners were rolled up, the land returned to its native state, no worse for the wear. A few conversations lingered, but these dwindled, as if the exhibition hall had run out of breath.

Ted collapsed the Crixevir booth into two knee-high cardboard boxes and a duffel bag. Not much, but still burdensome. Maybe Ann and Dev were right. Maybe he was inextricable from Crixevir. Once, at the manufacturing plant in North Carolina, he stood in sterile blue bootees and watched the purple-and-white pills spill from the mouth of a machine. They clattered onto the conveyor belt, rat-a-tat, a barrage of BB pellets. He smelled their sweetness. He thought at first that it was the sucrose coating—sugar to mask the medicine— but it wasn't that. It took a while for him to identify the smell. Benzene. Maybe that's what he smelled like.

And then, John simply said, "Ted."

● ● ●

Jesus. John.

Ted's instinct was to shake hands, a neutral gesture, friendly and meaningless, but his hand stopped mid-dart, as if it were an animal realizing it was trapped. John leaned forward for a hug. For six years, they'd assiduously avoided each other, and for six years, Ted had imagined the course of John's illness. Sometimes his own cruelty frightened him. He imagined John a corpse, cheeks sunken in to reveal the skull underneath, arms dry and brittle. John's cycling-hardened legs desiccated and withered. Ted told himself that he would not recognize John when he saw him, and that that would make it easy not to remember how much he had once loved him.

Ted broke away from the hug. "How are you?" he asked.

"Do you really have time for the answer?" John replied. He was taking a triple cocktail therapy of protease inhibitors, including Crixevir. His viral load was near undetectable, and his T-cell counts had never been better. But the benefits package he got from working for the International Alliance against AIDS still left him with a crushing pharmaceutical co-pay.

"You want to know what's ironic?" John asked. "After bitching you out for working for a reactionary, profiteering conglomerate—which it still is, don't get me wrong—I shack up with someone who works for a Catholic organization. Mark Rifkin. Maybe you've heard of him."

John. So coy. Of course Ted had heard of Mark Rifkin. Rifkin had put St. Anthony's Medical Center on the map. What was once a small Catholic clinic had, in ten years' time, become a full-fledged research facility. Avartis had paid well for the privilege of doing clinical trials for Crixevir at St. Anthony's. Rifkin spoke across the country—across the world—for different companies, and Ann had tentatively recruited him to speak for Avartis too. The other reps swarmed Rifkin. He handed out business cards like papal blessings. He was preternaturally handsome, the type of handsomeness that didn't trigger desire as much as shame: shame at one's own mediocrity, at one's own shortcomings. John hadn't come to gloat—that was an incidental benefit.

"I'm happy for you," Ted said.

"Thanks."

"You look good."

"What you're actually saying," John said, "is that I look fat. Otherwise you would have said that I look great."

"You look great."

"Much better," John said. "Where's your partner?"

"Oh, my work keeps me too busy," Ted said, and it took him a moment to realize that John had meant "partner" in a different sense. "Oh,

Ann. She caught a stomach bug. She's laid up in her room."

"That's unfortunate," John said. "About Ann." His tone shifted. "Didn't I tell you this job would eat you alive?"

"I don't remember that."

"Sounds like something I would have said. And it's true, isn't it?"

"It's not bad. I make a good living. I travel."

"I used to think that Avartis was killing me for a few bucks," John said. "I know better now. I know Avartis is trying to save my life. Still for a few bucks, though." He put his hands on his hips. His biceps bulged beneath his T-shirt. It was a folly to have a ridiculously good-looking boyfriend. Unless you were obscenely rich. Or ridiculously good-looking yourself.

"But you know what sucks?" John continued. "I have to rely on Mark for my meds. I can't afford them on my salary. He pays for them out of pocket."

"There's a gay guy on Avartis's board of directors," Ted said. "We have a pretty good partner benefit package."

"If I were still with you," John said, "you'd probably be dead by now."

Ted couldn't respond.

"We would have strangled each other. Besides," John said, "if Mark knew that you were hitting on me, he'd strangle you himself."

"I didn't mean it like that," Ted said. "I've met someone. A doctor. Here at the conference."

"Do you mean that he's *here* at the conference or that you *met* him at the conference?"

"Kind of both?"

"That's pretty shameless, don't you think? Hitting on someone at an AIDS conference?" John threw his hands back. "Not that I'm judging. What's his name?"

"Dev."

"And he's based in?"

"Delhi General."

"I see." John folded his hands, his preparation for lecture mode. "Don't take this the wrong way. It's been six years, but that doesn't mean I don't still care. I *do* care. But in a different way now. You understand?"

Ted understood.

"Mark used to ask what you were like, and I said you were like a stuck door. It takes an incredible amount of effort to open you up, but once you're open, you're completely open until someone slams you shut. And then someone has to make the effort to open you up again. This was what it was like when we were together. It's my fault you slammed shut. I'm sorry I broke up with you so abruptly. I really am. I did it, and then didn't stay around to help open you up just a little so that someone else could get their foot in. I get the sense that you've opened the door again, and that's great, but I don't want it to get slammed so hard that no one can open it."

"Is this how it's going to be?" Ted asked. "Every time we meet, you're going to chew me out about my life?"

"Basically," John said.

"Then, here." Ted took out a business card. Printed there, an undeniable confirmation of his identity: his name, the word "Crixevir," the Avartis logo. The smell of benzene clung to it.

John and Mark left together. Two gorgeous men, John's hand on Mark's shoulder, tugging at him to share a secret. He wanted to be happy for John—he really did—but all he could think was, *That should have been me.* He was six years too late. Maybe eight years. Ten. He had done just enough, and it wasn't enough. John's illness had descended into their lives, and Ted had made room for it. He had accommodated it. The battle was futile, but maybe he could have done more.

He asked Ann, "Do you think I'm closed off?"

She looked pale, sleep deprived, but better. "Never really thought about it. You're shy. Not 'closed.' Safe, maybe. You're not a bank vault."

"Still throwing up?"

"Haven't eaten anything since last night. Nothing to throw up. I think your Cipro did the trick. I could eat a horse right now."

"There's time to call room service." Ted was

packed, ready for the flight home. "What do you mean, 'safe'?"

"It's not a bad thing. I mean, if I'd gone through what you did with John, I'd probably be boring too."

"Great," Ted said. "I've become a boring, middle-aged gay man."

"Thirty-two isn't middle-aged. Not unless you're gay," she said. "Oh, wait—"

"Do you think," he asked, "we're doing something good?"

Ted had never considered himself as someone who promoted *a drug;* he promoted *Crixevir,* which, at this moment, kept John and countless others alive. Why, then, did this feel insufficient? Why was it not *enough?*

"Don't even ask the question," Ann replied. "Otherwise, you're in for a world of disappointment."

Ann called room service for tea. The waiter brought it in on a silver tray. He laid the cups in front of them and poured the tea in a single, unbroken stream. He asked, "Sugar?" and Ann said yes, and Ted said no, and the man stirred a spoonful into Ann's cup. She downed the last Cipro pill. Ciprofloxacin. A runaway hit for Bayer. It would retain its patent for another six years or so, Ted guessed. When Crixevir's patent expired, would its reps still insist that doctors use the original product, rather than a generic formulation? Would he still defend Crixevir fervently if, for instance, the WTO ruled against Avartis?

Ann picked up a biscuit from the saucer. "These," she said, "are the best things ever. I'm so hungry I'd even risk eating on the street again." She bit the cookie in half. "Can you tell what's in it?"

Ted chewed. "Cardamom."

"When I get back to New York, I'm going to buy a pound of this stuff."

Ah, yes. Tomorrow they would head back to New York. Ann, presumably, to roll in a bed of cardamom pods. But Ted's life was inertial. He couldn't move forward because everything else moved at an even faster rate. Catching up wasn't the painful part; the painful part was knowing that he had missed something, possibly something important, and by missing it, he would never know what that something was.

The decision, then, seemed simple:

"I think I'm going to stay awhile," he said. "I'm postponing my flight back."

"Seriously?"

"I missed out on so much. It'll be like a vacation."

"*Like* a vacation? Is this about the guy you hooked up with last night?"

"I wouldn't say he *isn't* part of it."

"That's so sweet," she said. She thumped her

chest. "I think I feel cardamom coming back up. You know that Avartis won't spring for extra time in Le Méridien."

"There are other hotels. This hotel—it's not really part of Delhi. It's not the real India."

"The *real* India," Ann said. "Look what it did to me. Look what it did to you." She brushed her finger against his bruise.

"At the very least, I want to see the Taj Mahal."

"You know that's not actually in New Delhi, right? It's like a day trip away."

"Oh," he said. "I didn't."

She handed him her Fodor's. "Forget what I said about you being shy," she said. "But at least stay safe."

Safe. The endless variations of the word. Ann meant it in regard to his physical well-being, but to a gay man, it held another meaning altogether. Maybe Ann meant it both ways. But he knew *safe* as much as anyone should. Last night, nothing had even approached DEFCON 5 unsafe. Nothing in the past six years had. He had told the few post-John men with whom he'd grown physically familiar that he'd once had an HIV-positive boyfriend, and for most, no further explanation was necessary for why their intimacy never progressed beyond a certain point. But one, whom he'd dated several weeks, challenged him. "That's in the past," he said. "We can play safe.

If you don't like it, just say so. Don't use your ex as a crutch." And Ted told him that he liked it but wasn't comfortable with it. He wasn't ready. And the guy said, "See? Just say what you mean," and dumped Ted soon afterward.

But John was not a crutch. He was a first love and had therefore taken on mythic stature. They had met their senior year of college, both of them in the generation for which HIV was not a surprise, but for which it was an unfolding mystery. In high school, he'd hear one thing, and then its exact opposite. Wear gloves, don't wear gloves. Kiss. Don't kiss. Beware of mosquitoes and toilet seats.

At that age, it was easy to believe in things, like *forever* and *The One*.

What had happened last night simply felt *right*. He couldn't explain it better than that. At one point, he woke to find Dev's head resting on his upper arm. There was no lost circulation, no tickling of fine hairs. His arm didn't tire or cramp. It was meant to support the weight of Dev's head, as if the muscles and ligaments had been preparing for this moment. Maybe this too was a permutation of *safe*.

As he walked to Dev's room, he thought about sightseeing. What were those places the cabbie mentioned on the drive into town? He could consult the Fodor's or, better yet, ask Dev. Dev could show him the hidden byways of Delhi:

sights that couldn't be captured with a camera or with a story. The secret heart of Delhi itself. Ted kept thinking about what John had said. A closed door! What was this, then, if he wasn't throwing himself open to adventure? With his own doctor, as influential in Delhi as anyone could be.

He knocked on Dev's door, his hand shaking. Dev called, "Just a second." Did Avartis have a Delhi branch? If they didn't, how difficult would it be to find a position here? How quickly could he learn Hindi?

Dev opened the door twice: once to see who it was; then again, closing it quickly behind Ted. He laid his head on Ted's shoulder, and again, it felt *right*.

"All packed?" Dev asked.

"I hate the last day of conferences. I always feel like I haven't done enough."

"But you have. Correct?"

"I just *feel* that I haven't."

"What you feel, what you feel," Dev repeated. He had his hands on Ted's waist.

"Listen," Ted said. "I've decided to stay a few extra days in Delhi. Maybe a week—"

"You're staying. Ah—"

This wasn't the reaction he had expected. "Is this a problem?"

"Not at all. There's much to see. It is a beautiful city. You'll have a wonderful time."

Maybe John was right after all: Ted felt a door

shutting—Pandora's box had loosed its anxieties into the world and now closed on the only thing left inside. *I'm so stupid.*

"Tomorrow, I am traveling to Benares," Dev said. "I'm conducting clinical trials there."

"Benares?"

"Also known as Varanasi."

"Will you be gone long?"

"It's an overnight train ride. I'll be gone for at least five days." There was no reason to doubt Dev was telling the truth. He still had time to uncancel his flight, to return to New York with his tail between his legs. It had only been one night, after all. The gay equivalent to a handshake.

"I see I've disappointed you," Dev said.

"No," Ted said. "It's OK." This was the benefit of being safe: he didn't open himself up to humiliation. The world loved risk takers. *Man hikes across Antarctica. Girl flies around the world in a hot air balloon. Man falls for Indian doctor, wishes for a different life.* But the rest of the world consisted of the shy, the safe, the stuck. If Ted had spun an alternative life out of a single evening, then it was his own fault that he was let down by it.

"I should let you pack, then," Ted said.

"Wait." Dev spoke very slowly. "You could—accompany me. To Benares."

"It's all right," Ted said.

"No," Dev said. "I would like you to come.

Come see India outside this hotel. Outside of Delhi." Dev smiled, though it seemed unsteady. Was Dev merely being polite? Was Ted supposed to insist that he didn't want to go, even though he wanted to go so much? But even more, he wanted for Dev to want him to go. It was difficult for Ted not to pitch forward into the future, not to fall back into the past. What did it mean to live in the present moment?

"I'd like to go," Ted said. "With you."

"Get your belongings," Dev said. "Spend the night with me. Tomorrow we travel."

The present was a precarious balance, a toehold at the peak of a mountain. But Ted closed his eyes and stepped forward anyway.

II. The Shiv Ganga Express

The next morning, Ted felt the first twinge of pain at the Delhi train station. Dev had gone to get a first-class car with air-conditioning, and when Ted suggested that they take what the locals take, Dev replied, "Even the locals take first class. Anything more authentic would suffocate you." It would only take a few minutes, Dev said.

The lines before the ticket booths folded back upon themselves until the station was a solid flume of people. Families spread blankets on the ground and slept on plastic bags stuffed with more plastic bags. People stepped over splayed arms as if they were spills. Men squatted with their backs against the marble columns. There was squawking like a large flock of birds, and people before the teller window fanned out their money, preening. The teller, her hair in a neat bun, tapped the keyboard, unperturbed.

Ted saw other tourists, young, adventurous ones, who carried their entire lives on their backs: bedrolls, water bottles, sneakers dangling by their shoelaces. They seemed jocular and carefree, unbathed, hair pulled back in bandannas, living as if the world had been created for their exploration. They made Ted feel very, very old.

An Indian fellow came up to Ted. "Where are you going?" he asked.

"Varanasi."

He took Ted's elbow. "Come."

"I'm waiting for my friend."

"Your friend is there," he said.

Ted felt his stomach clench, as if someone had jabbed him. "Come," the man said again. He took both his bag and Dev's—an ant carrying ten times his own body weight. The man pulled Ted to the entrance of the train station, into the sunlight and the noise of Delhi. Ted couldn't see the pavement for all the vehicles. The city beckoned—*Come, come*—and out there, Dev was waiting.

"Take auto rickshaw to tourist bureau," the man said. "Pay no more than ten rupees for ride. Hurry, before the office closes!" The driver started his engine. A hot blast of exhaust blew up Ted's pant leg.

But he heard Dev calling. Dev sprinted toward them, yelling, and the man dropped the bags with a thud and fled into the station. The rickshaw driver started to speak, but Dev cut him off with a curt word.

"I leave you alone for five minutes," Dev said, "and you start following strange men. Is this what I should expect?"

"The man said he was taking me to you." The pain in Ted's stomach subsided, though a jagged remnant was lodged deep within. "I thought you'd sent him." Ted felt disoriented. North, south, west: these had no meaning. Every direction he turned was an unknown and unknowable place. A city he had hidden from for a week. A labyrinthine train station where people waited to lead him astray.

"Come," said Dev. He clapped Ted on the back. "Our train will be boarding soon." *Come*—people told him to come, and he did. He excelled at following instructions. He had done so at work, he had done so with John, and now he did so with Dev. As long as he followed instructions, nothing that went wrong was his fault. *The instructions said*... There was safety in not having to decide. He followed Dev into the shade of the station, up metal staircases, around other passengers.

An automated female voice announced incomprehensible comings and goings on the platforms, and afterward, a grandiose jingle rang through the station, as if each announcement were an accomplishment. Dev glanced behind him every so often to make sure Ted was there, and Ted nodded: *Yes. I'm coming.*

His nausea intensified as the train approached. He felt the train before he saw it: the engine's surge of heat, the smell of grease and ozone, the metal screech of the brakes. Bodies pressed against him: women with armpit stains on their saris, men for whom personal space was a foreign concept, squealing children. The nausea, sudden and forceful as a punch, swept him. He balled his fists, put one into his mouth. Sweat broke out along his forehead. He tasted bile and bit his knuckles until the urge to vomit passed. He wiped his forehead with his shirtsleeve.

It was just after six in the evening, and the sky glowed radioactive. The heat was a monstrous weight. The awnings of the station and the concrete around the tracks shined white-hot. Ted shielded his eyes.

When the train stopped, people swarmed the doors, like an ocean siphoned into a funnel. "We're farther up," Dev said. The third-class cars had no windows, only gaps through which people stretched their arms, as though they were oaring the train forward.

Ted walked slowly, to not upset his stomach further. The crowd flowed around him. Ted imagined tripping, getting crushed in the undertow. He'd heard about stampedes at Indian train stations, the deaths by trampling. He didn't want to lose sight of Dev. He'd be stuck. Lost.

Dev waited on the edge of the platform, taking his hand out of his pocket to check the time. He waved the tickets in the air.

"I'm not feeling so well," Ted said.

"Once you're out of the heat, you will feel better."

"My stomach," Ted said. He placed his hand over the approximate discomfort.

"We will be there soon."

In the train's passageway, an old woman nudged him with her cane. Not rudely, he was just in the way.

When Dev mentioned "first class," Ted had expected a private berth. But the compartment looked like a college dorm, one bunk atop another. A family of four occupied the bunks on the right side. Two kids dangled from the top, and the father had plugged a miniature fan into the wall socket above the window.

"I thought you got a private compartment," Ted said.

"Private," Dev said, as if the word didn't exist.

He sat on the bottom bunk, occupied with his luggage.

The father nodded at Ted. The fan oscillated, left, right, back again.

"This is first class?"

"The individual compartments were sold," Dev said. "You should consider yourself lucky to have even this."

Lucky. Ted nodded back.

Dev asked, "Do you need help climbing up?"

Ted shook his head. The Navajo pattern of the upholstery transfixed him; he stared, trying to discover its repetitions, its interlocking scheme.

The door slid open. *Another* passenger? No: the man held up a metal bucket of bottled waters. Dev spoke, and the man left.

The windows had two tints: One offered the world in amber, a layer of condensation making everything indistinct. The other was the world in gray; it was already dusk, and Ted couldn't tell if the world had indeed grown dark or if the window provided its own darkness. The platform was gray; the dented metal chests on a pulley, waiting to be loaded, were gray.

The train pulled forward, a hiccup, and men rushed alongside, as if they were late.

Ted unfastened the privacy curtain bunched against the wall.

"Not yet," said Dev.

The red curtain had a design of crescents

and swirls. Ted thought of cranes in flight. The emergency stop cord was wrapped in red velvet the same color, as if begging to be touched, pulled.

The door slid open again. This man had butcher paper–wrapped bundles under his arms. He placed one on each bunk. A set of sheets and a thin, fibrous blanket.

"Chai?" the man asked. The family said no. Dev said no too.

"I'll take one," Ted said.

Ted couldn't sit upright. His head hit the ceiling, and he kept his neck bent. Hunched over, his stomach didn't bother him as much. Dev was reading a medical paper from the conference. Ted untied his shoelaces, and his shoes landed with a thunk on the ground. Dev looked up, annoyed. The young boy across from him giggled. Ted pulled off his socks with some difficulty—damp, clingy—and laid them across the bed to dry.

The door again. A gray-haired bellman came in. He surveyed the cabin and approached Ted. He nudged Ted's shoes under Dev's bunk and took off his slippers. He unfolded the sheets from their bundle. Standing on Dev's seat, he tucked the sheets tight. He picked up and quickly put down Ted's socks, holding up his hands: *Sorry*.

The other side of Delhi presented itself: a burned-out house, black with soot; buildings only half-constructed, abandoned after two walls out of four. The city was a facade, a soundstage: from one side, it seemed solid, real, alive; from the other, it was propped up with bamboo poles. Concrete had broken off into crags; rusted rebar jutted out of abandoned projects. An unfinished city.

The bellman returned with a brown plastic tray. On it was a yellow thermos the size of a beer bottle. The chai. The warmth of the cinnamon lingered on his tongue, but the sugar soured his mouth. The chai formed a skin, as if trying to heal over a wound. He screwed the thermos closed and set it by his pillow. He would rest, and when he woke, he'd feel better. He'd sleep it off.

Dev had stopped reading; chin on hand, he leaned into the window, as if trading secrets with his reflection. Outside, young boys in a dirt field played gully cricket. They'd built a wicket out of concrete blocks; the ball was a tennis ball, the bat a polished stick. Ted imagined Dev as one of the boys.

No. If anything, Dev would have played at a private school with its own pitch. Dev, wearing crisp whites and bat in hand; Dev, winding his arm in a wide circle to bowl; Dev, catching a fly ball with his bare hands and running into a scrum with his teammates.

Ted folded his hands against his stomach. Dev stood, and for an instant, Ted thought that Dev was checking on him, but instead, he clicked the lock for the berth door, secured the privacy curtain around them, and resumed staring out the window.

Wrong again. Dev wouldn't have been playing cricket at all. He'd have been sitting under the shade of a tree, a book in his lap, the wind carrying cheers and the crack of ball against wood to him. He'd look up at his mates, and they'd wave for him to join, and he'd shake his head no. *Come play, come play,* they'd say, and he'd stay where he was, content with his current position.

Three hours in, Ted woke, aware of a distant growl, like the snore of a great beast. The rhythm of the wheels on the rails. Through the gap in the curtain, he saw the woman across from him curled toward the wall, while her husband massaged a cream into his face. Dev dozed with a pencil in his fingers, a medical journal open in his lap. Ted's stomachache hadn't abated. He swallowed three times in quick succession, trying to clear bile, but couldn't produce enough saliva to wash the bitter taste away.

The man with the face cream closed his curtain.

Near the door, there was a stack of TV dinner–sized trays, smeared with red and brown. Crumpled balls of foil lay on top. The smell of the food lingered: ginger, some sort of curry.

He had slept through dinner. Maybe the pain he felt was hunger. Was there a way to distinguish different types of pain?

He climbed down the metal rungs on the wall and sat next to Dev. Even that small effort produced sweat all over his body. Dev had his feet propped on his suitcase. His lap was a valley into which Ted wanted to fall. Just for a moment. The heat on the train was unbearable, and Dev's neck—dark, shaved smooth—would be cool to the touch. Ted's body buckled. His head rested on Dev's shoulder.

Ted expected a nudge, maybe a quick jerk, but the force of the push: Ted's body flailed, and his head knocked against the bedpost. It wasn't painful—not compared with his stomachache—but Ted made no effort to right himself. He had deserved it: it was a mistake, but he couldn't help himself.

"Not when we're in public," Dev whispered.

The reality of the train rushed back: the woman murmured to her husband, a Bollywood song seeped through the Walkman the kids on the top bunk shared. Dev sat ramrod straight, hands on thighs. Would he stay in that position for the entire trip?

After a few minutes of silence, Ted asked, "Where are we?"

"We are going," said Dev, head resolutely straight, "to Varanasi."

• • •

Ted knew Varanasi only as a dot along the Ganges, hiding in the creases of the guidebook's foldout map. For every promise of beauty, Fodor's warned, there was an equally dire promise of wily pickpockets, of contaminated water, of dangers so wide-ranging it was a wonder anyone ever left home. Every year in Varanasi, it read, two or three tourists disappeared. Some dropped out of society, cutting ties with their previous lives for a more enlightened existence. The others—simply disappeared.

The pain had condensed from a diffuse queasiness to a sharp stab.

"A few more hours," Dev said. "Get some rest."

Ted was ready, to some extent, to deal with traveler's diarrhea. He'd brought salt tablets and Cipro, though Ann had depleted the latter. He had planned against what he could expect. One or two days of loose bowels was a small price to pay for traveling abroad. But now, he felt cheated. He'd skipped so much: the Red Fort, Humayun's Tomb, the bazaars and spice markets, crowds so vast that Ann could only describe them by holding her arms out, as if embracing the world. He hadn't seen the Taj Mahal. People would be horrified to learn that he'd been to India and not gone to the Taj Mahal.

"Do you think it may be motion sickness?"

"I don't know," Ted said. The cramp throbbed, radiated. "I just wish it weren't so *far*."

"Less far now."

"Why Varanasi?" Ted asked. "Why so far from Delhi?"

"Everyone should see Varanasi," Dev said. "It is one of India's holiest cities."

"I didn't know you were devout."

"Me? No, not me. It's just superstition." Dev crossed his arms. "My wife, she likes to have a bottle of Ganga water on hand when she cooks." He removed an empty plastic bottle from his bag. "I take it back to the lab, centrifuge it to remove sediment, and irradiate it. Perfectly safe."

"Your wife?"

"Yes," Dev said.

"I didn't know you were married."

"I told you." Hesitation crept into Dev's voice, a birdlike quiver.

"I'd remember something like that," Ted said. He felt like throwing up, the acid gurgling in his throat, sourness in his mouth. "Does she know about you?"

Outside, the darkness gave no indication of movement: no blurred lights, no stationary objects rushing by. Travel was a suspension, a held breath, the transition between one state of being and another. The centrifugal force pulled at his bones, but the distance between him and his destination only seemed to increase, as if this trip wasn't a movement *toward* but a movement *away*. Dev's voice, when it came, came from this ever-further place.

"She entered the marriage with her eyes open," Dev said—a radio transmission plucked from the ether.

When the feeling overcame him, Ted tore back the curtain, bolted out of the cabin, and ran the length of the car. The restroom was at the far end. His body clenched: it was a race. Could he find the lock on the door? Could he undo his belt buckle and pants? The split second before his haunches landed on the toilet seat, he felt—not relief, really, because pain followed the length of all thirty-feet worth of intestines—but release. Explosive release, the type that made Ted feel ashamed that he could not control his own body, that his own body could rebel.

There were things that, later, he was thankful for: that the bathroom was unoccupied, that its stainless steel walls gave the appearance of being sanitary, that it had a Western-style toilet instead of a squat one. Squat toilets unbalanced him, and the guidebook said that oftentimes, squat toilets were nothing more than a hole in the floor. Indeed, as Ted sat, warm puffs of air greeted him, the rhythm of train ties. He felt wheels beneath him, their terrible friction against the rails.

And after this first wave passed—his bowels

once again clenched, agitated—he realized that in his rush, he had forgotten tissues. There were no towels, no toilet paper, nothing for him to banish the filth between his legs, clinging to his skin. Stickiness. All the things you feel when you think you're dying.

Pants around ankles, he waddled to the sink, cupped a handful of water, and waddled back. He rinsed himself as best he could, forcing himself to look away from his hand, as if seeing uncleanliness was admitting to its existence. He brushed droplets of water off his buttocks, down his thighs. He didn't want it to soak through his boxers and spot his trousers.

There was a time, when he was still with John, that he both anticipated and feared John's decline. He, one day, would have to bathe John. He could do it, he knew, but he also knew that he could not *not* do it. These were the lies of love: that it was not disgusting, that it could transcend illness, that it could be more than an unending series of obligations.

When did he and John have "The Conversation"? It must have been when they moved in together. The Conversation was the formalization of his commitment, both verbal and mental. If Ted had to divide his life into a series of *befores* and *afters,* this would have been the first schism. *The news.* Ted still didn't know what to call it. *The information.* The more he stuck a name to it, the more it peeled away. What do you call something that changes your life? Maybe it was ridiculous to even try to name it. By naming it, maybe he could put limits on it. Give it boundaries. A specific meaning. But—The Conversation would do.

He frequently wondered how often John had had The Conversation with others. If it was John's method of scaring people off, of testing them. Because that's what it felt like: a test. One of many for Ted to take.

Ted even remembered his first *actual* test, taken in February, after he and John had been together for five months. They'd always been scrupulously careful. Well, maybe not *scrupulous*—but cautious. The clinic had the whiteness of a blizzard, and the nurses shuffled papers like they were made of snow. Everyone sat in a hush. They were assigned numbers—blood drawn today, and in a week or so, the results. Ted said he could have gotten the test at the NYU health center, but John insisted no. "There's a difference," he said, "between *confidential* and *anonymous* testing."

"I don't see the difference."

"It's not a difference you *see*," John said. "It's one you *live*."

When it was Ted's turn, a middle-aged woman with sandy-blond curls pulled on latex gloves with a single snap. "I need to ask you a few questions for research," she said. "Your responses will be completely anonymous, so I'd like you to be honest." She ran through the battery of questions with a strict efficiency, but Ted couldn't answer without tittering like a schoolgirl. Never had he had to think so much about sex before: what, with whom, how many times.

Ted rolled up his sleeve. The nurse tied a strip of rubber tubing above his elbow. "First time?" she asked.

"How can you tell?"

"You're shaking so much I can barely get this knotted. If you don't hold still, your arm is going to look like a sheet of stamps." She held his arm, gentle, firm. The latex pulled his hairs. "Easy, easy."

"You've done this a lot?"

"Oh, honey," she said, "you have no idea." The needle entered his skin. The slow trickle of blood in the vial looked so dark, so thick, he didn't think it was blood at all. More like the sludge that came out of the faucet first thing in the morning. "It's better if you don't look," she said.

A week later, Ted told himself that he wasn't worried, that he knew everything would be fine—but he couldn't be sure. Back in the clinic, he saw a Hispanic couple, the girl with one hand in her boyfriend's, the other on her belly, her face awash with worry. A sullen young man in an army jacket stitched together with safety pins refused to pull in his legs as Ted walked by. They prayed for the same diagnosis in silence, in unison.

But Ted was alone for his moment of panic. The nurse, the same one who had drawn his blood two weeks ago, came in and sat across from him, her face set and serious, her eyes betraying no sign of good news. "Let me tell you a few things about HIV," she said, and Ted thought, *Oh, God, no*. But then he realized: this was an informational spiel. There was genius to the timing: if the talk had come after a yes, he would have been too devastated to listen; if it had come after a no, he wouldn't have cared. This was the secret of communication: give the information *you* want the person to hear before telling them the information *they* want to hear.

"Now," she said, "about you and your boy-friend. This is going to be complicated for the both of you, but not impossible. I've known many successful positive-negative couples." She made it sound as if they were a battery. "It's important that you not be afraid."

Afraid. No, not afraid. More like numb. In stasis. Given over to inertia.

"I want you," she said, "to get tested every six months."

So—The Conversation must have taken place before then, obviously. But the fact that he couldn't recall the exact date bothered him. It was something he swore he'd never forget, and now, he'd forgotten it. John *must* have told him, maybe as early as their third or fourth date, when they first undressed in each other's presence, Ted unwilling to relinquish his undershirt and boxers, ashamed of his doughy skin, his undefined form, and John, with a serious expression on his face— serious?—maybe resigned. Maybe he'd grown familiar with rejection and fear and wanted to get it over with. Or maybe it was even later still, after Ted had grown accustomed to the excitement of walking to John's apartment, and to the marbled strength of John's thighs, and to the silly bombast of John's pronouncements. Maybe John told him late enough for Ted to harbor a secret grudge— *Why did you wait until I couldn't pull away?*—and that was the first crack that would eventually split them apart. Ted couldn't remember. But he knew that The Conversation must have happened, because Ted made his choice, and in this way, The Conversation wasn't important. Not compared with everything that followed.

"I feel like I'm going to die," Ted said to Dev.

"Dehydration has made you delirious. Drink some of your chai." Dev fetched the thermos from the upper bunk. Ted pushed it aside. "At least drink some water. You feel weak because you haven't taken in any calories. Here." Dev reached under the seat and brought out a tray, still covered in foil. He peeled back the foil. A pool of water had formed on the surface of the chicken.

"I can't."

"Something bland. Some bread." Dev ripped off a chunk of naan, and Ted chewed until it was paste in his mouth.

"Swallow," Dev said.

"Too dry."

Dev unscrewed the cap on the thermos and poured a cup. Still warm.

"Can I ask a favor?" Ted said.

"For what?"

"I need a prescription. For Triacept," Ted said. "It's not for me. I met a friend at the conference . . . I hadn't seen him for years."

Dev laughed, a sound so startling Ted realized that he'd never heard it before. A snicker, yes; an amused chuckle, yes; but never laughter.

"You want *me* to write *you* a prescription for Triacept."

"It's not for me," Ted repeated. "John—before Crixevir, he wasted away to almost nothing. I took care of him. He's alive today. I want to help him."

Dev wiped the corners of his eyes. "Do you not see the irony? In what you're asking?"

Ted, for a third and final time, said, "It's not for me."

He and John were together for four and a half years. Ted wished that he could say those were happy years, because if they were happy, then it would never have ended. But he couldn't say they were *unhappy,* either. They were just there, like a bedsheet tossed in the air. While it was airborne, the cloth stretched out forever, billowing like a parachute, and when it landed, he could see how rippled and crooked it was, and how it came to an end, right at the hem.

John opted not to take AZT, because he was asymptomatic. "If things get worse," he said, "I'll think about it then." *If,* not *when:* a practical consideration. AZT's price had come down, but it was still out of reach, a sum that made student loans seem like pocket change. Most people their age saved for vacations or bigger apartments, but Ted knew his life would be dedicated to medication.

That meant keeping their lives afloat. Normal. Maybe that was the problem. Ted wanted them to be normal. They could have gone on that way, not comfortable, but . . . living. They weren't "normal," of course, not in the way Ted had imagined normality to be. They had so long ago diverged from normality that Ted could see neither where they had been nor where they were going. They lumbered on. People told Ted, *Don't blame yourself. Your relationship was a unique circumstance.* But circumstances didn't negate Ted's desire. John's face had a righteousness, like he was a preacher in a past life. When his stubble grew out, or when the hair poked its way back through his scalp, he projected a magnetic force, drawing even faraway objects into his orbit. He was lean and muscular from cycling. Not the hard chunks of overexercise but something taut and sinewy—something supple.

But desire alone couldn't override Ted's fear. Once, they attended a nonpenetrative eroticism workshop at the Gay and Lesbian Community Center. A small, bearded man who looked like he should have been selling apples conducted it. There were exercise mats along the floor. He and John were the only couple who weren't middle-aged.

The leader asked people—only if they felt comfortable—to take off their shirts, and Ted saw how some men were little more than rib cages on spines. One had dark lesions dotting his body, as if his skin had burned away. That, Ted knew, would be John someday. But the man's boyfriend held him and caressed his skin, on the verge of crying. Beyond the illness, there was an aching love, a heartbreaking tenderness. That, Ted hoped, would be him someday.

The workshop was mostly holding exercises: Ted behind John, then the other way around. Ted closed his eyes and waited to feel John's fingers skating along the curves of his body. They worked with differing sensations: hot breath on skin, and the cool moisture left behind. Ted ran his chin up the side of John's torso, coming to rest with his nose buried in John's armpit, a secret nook. But—as wonderful as all that was—it wasn't the same. It didn't feel as *close*.

They walked home from the workshop, passing by the Chelsea Piers. The piers jutted into the river like legs. They had missed the heyday of the piers' mass debauchery by almost two decades, but that didn't mean that there wasn't cruising going on. Each time they passed a good-looking man, John stole a glance. Ted asked, "Am I cuter than him?" and John replied, "Yes. Much cuter." The lie made Ted feel better, nevertheless.

Then, John stopped. "Look," he said.

At first, Ted thought John was indicating the sky, the stars barely visible against the city's electric thrum. Cloud edges glowed neon. But John pointed toward a balcony six stories up, a cocktail party, figures in elegant silhouette. Music tumbled over the edge, where it mixed with the general cacophony: thunderous rhythms from tiny cars held together with duct tape and Bondo, the pound of the joggers' feet, the susurrus of the river. On the balcony, a woman stood with her hands dangling over the railing. Her wineglass threatened to crash onto their heads. She looked utterly bored, utterly beautiful. John leaned in close and whispered, "I wonder if that woman is happy up there." If Ted had answered what he really felt, he would have said, *Yes*. But he knew that this wasn't what John wanted to hear. "She looks miserable," he said, and John pulled him close. Sweat sparkled along John's collarbone like a necklace. Ted caught the eye of the woman on the balcony. She reared back as if she'd been insulted and walked inside.

Over the next two hours, Ted went to the bathroom four more times, each an episode of abject shame. He had evacuated his bowels but continued to feel more coming out of him. His internal organs had liquefied. He contended with the metal toilet seat, with the bathroom that shook like the inside of a throat, with a packet of tissue clutched in his hand as he braced himself between the sink and the wall.

But the fourth time, something within him let loose, like air rushing out of a balloon, and he pressed his hand to his stomach to make sure he was intact. What came out of him no longer had the consistency of diarrhea or water, but of something in between. Against his better judgment—against his will—he looked into the toilet. There, among the specks and chunks of shit, were tarry streaks that he knew were blood. And even worse, a viscous liquid, discolored, foamy, a substance he didn't know that his body could produce.

He had hoped that whatever it was within him

was being flushed out, that each evacuation cleansed him. But this wasn't in fact true. He was getting worse. Here was the proof.

"Dev," he said, "something's wrong." Dev had turned to the wall, a huddled mass, the shape of him familiar, the bulk of him not. Ted felt dizzy, and he reached out to shake that mass, afraid to arouse Dev's ire, but more afraid of not knowing what was happening inside him at that very moment.

Ted could pinpoint the moment things changed between John and him. It was shortly before they broke up, though to say they "broke up" suggested that they had spoken face-to-face about their relationship, its direction, its downward spiral. That some mutual decision had been come to, agreed upon. No. John had cleared out all his belongings one day while Ted was at work, and Ted came home to find a John-shaped vacancy in his life.

But the shift happened before then, when John decided to shave his head. To make himself more aerodynamic, he said. It was August. He'd keep cool that way, he said. Afterward, his head reminded Ted of an orange, the skin pitted with tiny pockmarks from the razor. Ted ran his hands over John's scalp, mapping out the nicks, the dry spots, the small patches of fuzz. They went to the makeup counter at Macy's, and Ted filled his palms with lotion from the testers and, once out of the store, poured the lotion in an empty shampoo bottle. He scraped his hand against the mouth of the bottle, and whatever was left between his fingers, he rubbed into John's scalp. The scents mixed together—ylang-ylang, lemon verbena, orchid.

John said, "I smell like a tampon."

"With your bald head," Ted said, "you look like one too."

He replied, "I guess that'd make you the string."

After he'd showered off the scent, he yelled for Ted to come into the bathroom. There, nude, the steam enrobing him, John pointed at his back.

"What is this?" he said.

It could have been a hickey. A rash scratched raw. A bruise from a punch. But Ted knew what it was and what it wasn't. It was the first dark spot, an unmistakable sign that John's luck had collapsed.

"This is a fucking genocide," John said, the ire reddening his face. "We're dying here." He brought home information from the ACT UP treatment committee, and Ted spent hours reading *Lancet* and *JAMA* articles until he believed that he could understand the arcane language of illness. John said as long as he stayed asymptomatic, he could take interferon for his Kaposi's sarcoma. The single splotch on his back. The black hole.

But the interferon treatments left him lethargic and sluggish.

Ted kept this deep within him—but he wondered if it would have been easier if he were HIV positive too. Maybe then he could feel what John felt. Their combined fury would leave scorch marks on the street. People would have to shade their eyes when they passed. But the truth was, if Ted became positive, John would have never forgiven himself. *I didn't go through shit,* he would say, *so that you could go through the exact same shit.*

For the weeks immediately following John's departure, Ted thought, *If I forgive him, he'll come back. I just have to forgive him, and it'll work.* And Ted forgave and forgave and forgave. And it didn't work. John didn't return. And every day, Ted discovered a new disappearance: a shirt here, a tchotchke there. Imperceptible bits. Ted would look at the nightstand and notice a circle outlined in the dust, and he'd have to think about what had been there and what was now missing.

After the pity came the anger. Ted couldn't wait to call John a coward, a fraud, a bastard, right to his face. He hated feeling like he'd never love someone so intensely, so urgently again. It was easy to remember love. To memorialize it. He slipped into it like an old T-shirt and thought, *This had been new once. This had been beautiful.* It wasn't the memory that hurt; it was the distance between the present and that memory. Once, he dreamed that he and John were sleeping in bunk beds, and in the dark, John had climbed down to join him. Their skin was bathed in shadow, and they tumbled to the floor. Ted saw them clearly, as if he were a third person in the room, and he couldn't tell which one was him and which was John. They were rolled together, whole. When he woke, he felt warm and content, luxuriating in that feeling. And then he realized that it was the worst dream he'd ever had.

But their paths never crossed, and after a while, Ted had made the distinction in his life: *before John/after John.* Ted ran into mutual friends, mostly those who fell more on the John spectrum than on the Ted, and one told him, "You know the real reason, don't you? He left you because he thought it'd be easier." Easier for John? Sure. He could once again engage in intimacy without fear, cross infection aside.

"No," the friend said. "Easier for *you.* In case, you know . . ."

It wasn't easier. Ted hired on at Avartis and moved to Chelsea, overlooking the piers. He went on failed dates. He wondered, sometimes, if John had started taking AZT or the regimen of newer ddI drugs. When he was offered the lead on Crixevir, he wondered if John had taken part in the clinical trials, one of the corpses—cheeks sunken in to reveal the bone underneath, arms dry and brittle—who made a Lazarus-like recovery. Every so often, he glanced through the obituaries in *LGNY*, looking for John's name. He was out there, somewhere. Or if he had died, he was one of the thousands of anonymous ones.

When the weather turned warm, Ted went onto his balcony. The sound of the river was like pleasant company. He watched the people below him, hoping to catch a glimpse, maybe, of John's bike racing down the street. He often saw couples walking hand in hand. Occasionally, they saw him too, and he imagined one telling the other, *Look. I wonder if that man is happy up there.* And after a pause, the other would answer, *He looks miserable.*

Dev asked Ted to lie as still as he could. Ted's instinct was to coil up, but he did as Dev asked. Dev checked the curtain twice.

"See if you can identify exactly where the pain is coming from," Dev said. He pressed his fingertips against Ted's abdomen, a pressure so faint that it could have been rain.

"There," said Ted when Dev had reached his upper left abdomen. "Right there." Dev pushed a little harder. Ted gasped, but Dev continued his inch-by-inch inventory of Ted's stomach.

Sunrise bled into the sky. Shapes moved against the horizon. Dev left to wash his hands, and Ted put his own hands on his stomach. What did Dev discover that he could not? Could Dev read skin the way the blind read braille? Ted looked at the sunlight without sun. What did Dev keep saying? That's right: *We will be there before you know it.*

At some point, he must have fallen asleep, an uneasy sleep full of twinges and cramps. He could no longer sustain both consciousness and illness. And in this sleep, he heard, as if in the distance, children babbling, luggage being shifted, yawning from mouths unknown. Dev asked, "Are you able to get up?" and Ted swung his feet onto the floor. He looked for his bag, but Dev said, "I've got it."

Off the train, the full force of morning hit him, like epilepsy: the overwhelming light, the inability to take it all in. He realized how strange it was not to be moving, how each stage of travel required its own adjustment. People avoided him, even those desperately selling him something. He had the aura of contagion.

Dev summoned a taxi. Dev knew where they were going, Ted told himself. But this was less reassuring than it might have been a day earlier. There was too much everything, everywhere. When they reached the hotel, Dev argued with the man behind the desk while a boy, probably the man's son, led Ted to his room. The interior was dark and cool, and the boy turned on the light, but Ted quickly flicked it off again. Two twin beds, on opposite sides of the room. The morning through the curtains made the room glow blue. Ted collapsed onto the nearest bed.

Nausea and fatigue blurred distinctions of time: a second-long ache stretched out over a minute, and a minute of rest reduced to a blink. Wood scraped along the floor. Ted tried not to take heed of the movement around him. He had stopped thinking of this as a *vacation;* it was now something to survive.

Dev sat beside Ted. Rustling sheets, squeaking bedsprings, untying shoes. He could feel Dev gauging if he was awake or not. Dev whispered, "Lift your head," and pulled the pillow from beneath Ted's head. He supported it with his hand until he had slid his own legs beneath. "Relax," Dev said, and he stroked Ted's hair, fingers tracing a line across Ted's forehead, along his temple, coming to rest behind his ear, Dev murmuring, all the while, "Poor thing. Poor thing."

III. Fire Ceremonies

Ted slept through his first day in Varanasi. Sickness cast a haze over the room; he felt like an insect, held fast in amber. He was dimly aware of the world outside: occupants in other rooms discussing plans and adventures, footsteps trundling away, a radio playing incomprehensible ragas. In Le Méridien, he could shut everything out; the only sounds he heard were the ones he made. But the outside encroached here. Not unwelcome, merely unexpected.

Then, sometime during the afternoon, the air conditioner sputtered off. It clanked and regurgitated internal fluids, and the wall shuddered from its exertion. The ceiling fan slowed and, off balance, shook in its socket. It could come loose and crush him. Decapitate him. The breeze died. No radios, no televisions. The alarm clock plugged into the wall had shut off. The world was still, and Ted lay, aware of its stillness. The air. The noise. His own breaths, growing very, very calm.

Dev returned that evening. By then, the air-conditioning and ceiling fan had resumed, and the alarm clock blinked red midnight. Dev pushed the beds together again. He felt Ted's forehead with the back of his hand, the way a mother might, and took a bottle of water from his bag. He reached into his jacket pocket.

"This," he said, holding up a small white pill, "is an antidiarrheal." Ted hadn't realized how dry his mouth was, the way his lips stuck together, gummy. "This one," Dev continued, holding a second pill, "is a salt tablet to help you retain water." Ted expected the harsh burn of table salt, but it left only a tingle on his tongue. "And finally, this," he said, "is for what ails you."

"It's huge," Ted said. Something you would give a horse. It wasn't a pill at all, but a capsule: inside, thousands of tiny dots, which, for some reason, reminded Ted of bullets. Or of Crixevir.

"Open wide."

The capsule did not go down easily, but Dev massaged Ted's throat, and even after he had swallowed it, it felt stuck in his craw.

"Here," Dev said, tucking his fingers under Ted's side. "Lie on your stomach."

"Does it disperse the drugs faster?" Ted asked. Something to do with body weight, maybe. The gentle pressure on the digestive tract.

"When I was young," Dev said, "whenever I had a tummy ache, my father told me to lie on my stomach."

Dev lay next to Ted, an arm draped across Ted's back.

"Feel better?" Dev asked.

"Not yet," Ted said.

"You will," Dev said, rubbing his nose against Ted's neck. "You will."

By the next morning, there was still pain, but this was familiar pain—hunger. Familiar and bone deep. His insides rumbled like a herd of mice. Dev was already separating the beds.

"You're a miracle worker," Ted said.

Dev turned, as if surprised to hear another voice. "You're awake."

Ted arched his back. How good it felt to stretch the skin on his stomach. "What did you give me? Cipro?"

"Diloxanide furoate."

"Don't know that one."

"I wouldn't expect you to," Dev said. "It's banned in the United States. Carcinogenic in high concentrations, but the best and quickest treatment for your condition."

"My condition?"

"Amoebas," Dev said. He placed the pill bottle on the nightstand. "You must take another dose in two days."

Just the thought made him feel unclean, contaminated. "Are you sure?"

"Quite sure. I tested a sample at the lab yesterday."

"A sample?"

"You know," Dev said quickly. He trailed off, but pulled the sheet from its tuck. Ted no longer had anything to hide. Dev knew him inside and out. The intimate secrets of his body, revealed.

"Thank you," Ted replied, more a reflex than actual thanks.

"I need to go to the clinic today, so I must leave you," Dev said. "You should explore, if you feel well enough. I asked the desk clerk to bring breakfast."

"You didn't have to do that."

"When we arrived yesterday, the clerk thought

237

I was your driver. He demanded that I rent servant's quarters for myself."

"I guess you showed him."

"As a matter of fact," Dev said, "I did."

Ted ate toast and jam—the jam jar giving a satisfying, hermetically sealed pop as he opened it—in bed. He showered and dressed. The leather chairs and high-count sheets in Le Méridien couldn't compete with the simple luxury of clean clothes.

The desk clerk, a mustachioed, obsequious man, gave Ted a poorly photocopied map that had been folded in fourths. A business card was stapled to the corner. This wasn't a hotel; it was a *guesthouse*.

The clerk traced the path to the Ganges.

"You are here," he said. "Assi Ghat." He pointed at a dot on the map and another farther up, where the page creased to a point. "North. Burning ghats. No pictures."

"How far should I go?"

The man shrugged. "Until you turn back."

The Ganges didn't give off the gentle roar of a seaside, but a constant lapping, like an unquenchable thirst. But even before he saw the water, children accosted him. One girl, no older than eight, clutched a basket filled with bowls made from leaves. Each bowl had a tea light surrounded by pink flower petals. Ted shook his head. She followed barefoot, as if tethered to him.

The river appeared: as wide, at least, as a highway, and moving just as fast. The dun-colored water reflected the sun in wave glints. This was Hinduism's holiest river, the Great Mother. Should he have felt more respect, more reverence?

This was not the river's failing, of course, but his own. Along the ghats, the steps down to the river, was a life he could not understand. Strange symbols, strange movements. A woman, a sari draped over her head like a shawl, circled a large ficus tree with a piece of red string, tied it off, and smeared turmeric onto the trunk. These things had meaning—the number of times she walked around the tree, the color of the string, the amount of turmeric in her hand. If he could understand those meanings, then maybe he could understand his own.

A cluster of children followed him, both boys and girls, each offering something: guided tour, boat ride, silk, chai, flowers. One made a cigarette gesture: *You want kush?* Ted pretended to hear none of it, and when one child tired, disappearing into the crowds along the ghats, another took her place. Ted watched their fists suspiciously.

Knee-deep in the river, two women washed laundry. They stood before tilted slabs of rock and twisted the cloth until it was a thick rope. With a single movement, they raised the cloth above their heads and slapped it against the rock.

Their smacks echoed in the air. An explosion of soap, a corona of suds. A teenage girl spread them to dry, and like that, the stone steps took on color, patches of lavender, blue, ocher. Bedsheets, school uniforms.

A boy pulled his shirttail. "Mister, where you from?" When Ted didn't answer, he tugged again. "Mister. Hey."

Teenage boys bobbed in the water like seals. This boy should have been with them, stripped to his underwear, diving in. Around him: snorting water buffaloes, tourists and their endlessly clicking cameras, the chirp of mynah birds on the water buffaloes' backs, the scamper of golden monkeys along the tops of walls. Near the bank, a man rose from the water, flapping his arms to frighten a stray dog nosing at his robes. His white beard dripped onto his chest, and once out of the river, he rooted in his clothes until he found something for the dog to eat.

The boy should have been in this cacophony of joy. Not bothering Ted. *"Parlez-vous Français?"* the boy asked. *"Habla Español?"* The faster Ted walked, the faster he pursued. Smoke rose up ahead. A burning ghat. "Please," the boy said. "Come see beautiful silks. Best in all Benares."

On the steps overlooking the cremation platform, everything here was the color of ash: the steps, the stones, the ground. Logs were stacked in pyramids, waiting for bodies. The boy sat next to Ted. Near them, an old woman fought the tide of dirt and goat droppings with a straw broom.

The wood smoke had a bittersweet underpinning, which Ted recognized instinctually as burned flesh. On the bank, a man in white walked clockwise three times around an unlit pyre. Was that the direction the universe turned? It meant something, the same way that it meant something that the man didn't cry, the way he walked with his back straight. The body on the pyre was shrouded in white cloth.

"Four thousand rupees to burn a body," the boy said. "English?" Ted shook his head. "Understand," he said. He kept saying this—"understand." It wasn't a question—*Do you understand?*—but a command—*You* must *understand.*

The man lit the end of a long stick; the tip fanned out like a webbed foot. He dropped it and stepped back from the heat. The pyre didn't catch, but attendants stoked the fire. The cloth burned away first. Then, after a few minutes, the flesh had blackened and peeled away, and yellowish fat dripped down, making the flame burn hotter, a more vivid orange, the color of the holy men's robes.

Ted felt the heat on his face. The world smoldered.

"Body with good karma," the boy said. "Burns faster."

If a body with good karma burned quickly, how long would it take Ted to turn to ash? Hours—days—a never-ending flame? Who would circle his body, and who would pour ghee onto the fire? Who would watch him bubble and combust until what was left of him could be scooped into someone's hands? He had never considered his own loneliness before—it had always been there, this estrangement—but now he realized he had no one to mourn him. How close had he come to death, with John, with amoebas? He felt it close by, licking his skin, not with cold, but with heat.

He watched the fire for what seemed like hours. The logs shed white, flaky ash. Except for the dark-skinned attendants, he and the boy were the only witnesses. Was he intruding on someone's private grief? The center of the pyre had collapsed, and the head and legs stuck out like branches. One of the attendants took a large pole and pushed those into the fire, sprinkling sawdust in. Soon, bones and kindling were indistinguishable, and finally, only cinders remained.

The boy held out his hand. "Donation for burning," he said. "Good karma."

Ted said, "Zidovudine? Didanosine tenofovir disoproxil, fumarate."

The boy said, "Mister? Please?"

Ted responded, "Saquinavir—emtricitabine aldesleukin."

Gobbledygook: a formulary of AIDS drugs. He didn't want the boy hounding him in any language whatsoever. He wanted to make it clear that there would be no communication whatsoever—no way for them to connect.

But the boy would not relent, even as Ted walked away. Among the other sounds—parakeets squawking from holes in the walls, cheers and yelps from bathers in the river—the boy called, the same three words, "please," "mister," and "understand," in infinite variation, as if uttering the correct combination might make Ted a better person.

Dev returned, late in the afternoon. In the room, he kissed Ted on the lips.

"Come," he said. "Let's take a boat ride. All the tourists do." He said "tourists" as if it were slanderous.

"What's wrong with being a tourist?"

"Nothing," Dev replied. He brushed Ted's cheek with the back of his fingers. "My little tourist. Let's take a boat."

Dev chatted first with a middle-aged boatman. An amiable bargaining session, Ted thought, though he probably would have assented to whatever price. It was not that he didn't know he was being ripped off, but what seemed like an astronomical sum—*hundreds* of rupees—was no more than a few dollars. But the boatman said something wrong, and Dev said, "Let's go." Ted thought this was part of the strategy: walk off and let the boatman follow. But even as the boatman counteroffered, Dev ignored him.

"What was that all about?"

"He assumed I was your tour guide," Dev said. "He said to charge you four thousand rupees and we would share the money afterward."

"Is that a bad price?"

Dev flagged another boatman. He couldn't have been older than fourteen. His skin was sun dark. The joints of his hands were thick and callused, like wood burls.

"He's too young," Ted said, but it was too late. Dev had made the deal. It didn't, however, stop others from calling, "Sir, boat?"

The boy laid down a plank for them to cross to his boat. Puddles pooled on its bottom. The boy pointed to where they should sit and unroped his boat from its brothers. Other young boatmen slept like lumps of laundry, absenting themselves from the unceasing racket: innumerable boys serving innumerable tourists, a supply and demand of which Ted was now a part.

"How much?" Ted asked.

Dev spread his legs to rest his feet on dry spots. The boy took the oars.

"How much do I owe you?"

"Don't insult me," Dev said. "You are my guest."

The boy rowed without gloves, and his arms quivered as if the weight were almost too much to bear. When Dev wasn't looking, he'd slip the boy a tip.

"What's your name?"

The boy looked at Dev, as if asking permission to speak. "Arun," he said.

Arun, then. Arun would get a *big* tip.

Arun rowed north, announcing the names of the ghats: Bachhraj, Panchkot, Shivala. Huge murals on the walls: blue-skinned gods in repose, a red-lettered exhortation to "Please Do Sri Ram Jay Ram Jay Ram / Jay Ram Ram Jay Ram Ram" against a yellow background. At the top of the steps sat a clump of saffron-turbaned men, three of them naked and white from head to ankles with ash. No doubt holy. What would it take to reach the state of being heedless to the world? To have nothing—not even clothes? No attachments whatsoever.

Dev took in everything with a bemused smile.

"Some of those men look Caucasian," Ted said.

"Sadhus," Dev said. "Holy men are called sadhus. And there may be some Caucasians among the sadhus."

"Interesting."

"Not particularly," Dev said. "Westerners put a spiritual gloss on their charas smoking. But what they do is drop out of society, abdicate their responsibilities. They appear as Shaiva sadhus but are little more than beggars. They cannot find themselves at home, and therefore think they can find themselves in Hinduism, Jainism. I did my residency in New York and could have stayed in the States if I wanted. But India is my home."

Dev uncapped a plastic bottle and dipped it into the Ganges, and for a second, Ted didn't understand why. Then he remembered: *the wife.*

"How's the water?" he asked. He tried to keep his voice light, playful.

Dev screwed the cap back on. "See for yourself." What Dev had in the bottle was almost clear. It looked almost clean.

Ted dipped his hand into the river. It was warm.

"I pray you don't have cuts or open sores on your hand," Dev said.

"Nope."

"I would advise against putting that hand near your eyes or mouth. All the sewers in the Old City drain into the Ganges. And factories upriver deposit heavy metals and toxic chemicals. The water is nearly anoxic. It's driven the Ganges dolphin into near extinction. They are so rare that it's considered good luck to see one."

And yet, none of this stopped the bathers. Women washed themselves fully clothed. They splashed the tops of their heads and let it run down their faces. They didn't fear the water. They had a spiritual and physical fortitude that Ted did not. Dev had called him a *tourist.* Not exact, but not incorrect, either. He was more than a tourist, less than a pilgrim. He thought again about calling Avartis to see if they had an India branch. Or better yet, once the WTO ruled in favor of India, he could come to work with the manufacturer of Triacept. The WTO ruling would embolden other countries—Brazil, Thailand, the African nations—to produce their own generics. India could be a hub, a major exporter of Triacept. Their factories were already in production; it'd be a matter of ramping up production, marketing worldwide. That was where Ted could come in.

Ted's life stretched before him—not the one he was living, but the one he *could* be living. He and Dev, living in a modest New Delhi apartment. He saw it as clearly as he could see Dev sitting across from him, Dev and his curious smile, the one Ted could not decipher. He saw a lifetime of smiles, and he saw himself peeling away their mysteries, one by one. The nuances, the permutations: the position of his lips, where his eyes focused, how his cheeks puffed. He saw himself waking to that smile every morning and forecasting, from it, the course of the day.

The sun was low, hanging just above the scalloped temple spires and the flat roofs of the guesthouses. The city looked as if it were built of pink stone. Religious chants collided midair with Bollywood rock songs as each balcony provided its own sound track. The ancient world and the modern, simultaneous. Everything here was a contradiction.

Ahead in the river, something bobbed, breaking the surface as if gasping for breath. Arun batted it away with an oar.

"Body," Arun said. He grinned, as if he'd just played a prank.

"The poor cannot afford cremation," Dev said. "So they cast bodies into the water. The situation deteriorated to where the government released snapping turtles into the Ganges to devour the corpses. But the turtles couldn't survive in the water, and when the dead turtles washed up downstream, the poor villagers ate them. Those villagers too grew sick and died, and their bodies were released into the Ganges. And so the great wheel turns."

Ted wanted to lay his hand on Dev's, to remind Dev that he was there. To share pleasure was also to share burdens. But not with Arun looking on. Other boats floated by, ones carrying a single Western tourist and longer ones with Indian women who lined up on the rim like macaws. A motorized boat, lit up like a dinner cruise. Everywhere: witnesses.

Dev fiddled, absentmindedly, with the cap of the Ganges water bottle. Ted could not imagine Dev's wife—she was hazy, featureless. How could he compete with an unknown force? He was the *other woman*. Maybe Ted could have his own apartment for Dev to come and go as he pleased. Maybe—

Ridiculous, he could hear Dev saying. It was ridiculous to live in the future; it was ridiculous even to try to guess at it.

An encompassing quiet overtook the area. The river reclaimed its voice, its sloshing, its pull and tow. Another blackout. Dev reclined, fingers laced behind his head, the water bottle forgotten for now. From the shore, disappointed shouts, though people didn't panic or cease their activity. This was a way of life.

"Burning ghat," Arun said.

This was the second ghat, the larger. Manikarnika. At the other, Harishchandra, there had only been one or two bodies burning at a time. Here, Ted counted at least seven, with room for more. The hillside was blackened, as if it could not eat enough wood. Logs were stacked twenty to thirty feet high, balanced precariously, and some had spilled down haphazardly, until the land looked striated, scarred. At the river, boats brought more logs, and men in dirty T-shirts carried logs atop their heads, threading past the bodies that had just been bathed in the river and past the burning bodies. Colorful, noisy processions brought new bodies covered in marigold garlands and orange cloth.

Arun spoke. "He wants to know," Dev said, "if you know how this ghat got its name." Arun, giddy as if telling a joke, blurted it out. One day, Shiva and his wife, Parvati, were sitting by a water tank when one of Parvati's earrings fell in. Shiva dug in the ground until a deep well had formed.

"*Mani* means jewel," Dev said, "and *karnika* means well."

If Dev were to drop, say, his wedding ring into the river, how far could Ted dive before he ran out of breath, before he was carried away by the current? Would Dev notice him slipping into the water?

A man waded in the water near the base of the ghat. He held a large pan.

"What's he doing?" Ted asked.

Dev transferred the question to Arun.

"He's looking for jewelry or gold teeth that may have been in the ashes," Dev said. "He feels for them with his feet."

"Hard way to make a living."

"There are worse ways," Dev said. "He could be a pharmaceutical-company lackey." Again, that smile.

The sun had now set, and Arun rowed them back the way they had come.

"Here's what I wanted you to see," Dev said.

"What am I looking at?"

"Ganga Aarti," Arun said.

A jumble of boats had gathered around Dashashwamedh Ghat, and Arun jockeyed for position. Along the steps, two older women laid out leaf bowls. Five platforms stuck out from the steps like diving boards, and a young priest sat on each. Each wore a yellow cloth draped over his hip and left shoulder.

Ted couldn't pinpoint the exact moment when darkness took over. Maybe it had always been waiting, and he hadn't noticed its presence. Up where the ghat became an alley into the Old City, streetlights flickered on, and the area took on the color of an apricot. The women who had set out the bowls now lit them. Dots of flame.

The priests stood with their implements of prayer: a conch shell, a round censer, a silver six-tiered tray, a lamp with a fanned cobra head, a silver handbell that they rang in time to the chant coming over the loudspeaker. The speaker was broken, all hiss and feedback. The sound hurt Ted's ears. Arun sang along.

"What's the ceremony for?"

"It's an offering to the Ganges," Dev said.

"And the fire?"

"An offering to the fire god, I suppose."

"You don't know?"

Dev shrugged. "What is there to know?"

Another boat pulled up beside theirs. The mother grappled their boat with a hook, and the daughter held up a flower bowl. Their boat was filled with these bowls, along with other sundries: garlands, potato chips, and foil packets of fennel seeds. Before Dev could shoo them off, Ted said, "I'll take one."

"Good karma," the girl said. "You pray and set on water." She lit the candle in the bowl. "You pray for wife, yes?"

Dev probably thought this fatuous, a waste of money. Ted thought about John, who was probably already back in New York with Dr. Mark. A prayer for John, then.

The girl handed him another bowl. "Parents."

OK, his parents. The bowls didn't float far. The boats around them had formed a blockade of calm water.

She handed him a third bowl. "Parents."

"You already gave me one for my parents."

"*One* parent. For the other."

"That will do—" Dev said.

Ted interrupted him: "Last one."

"One hundred," the girl said. Ted fished out a hundred-rupee bill, and the girl said, "Each."

"Outrageous," Dev said. "Let me teach you a magic word. *Nahi*." Long *a*, short *i*. "It means no," he said.

Arun had stopped singing. He hollered to other boat rowers, none of them, it seemed, older than sixteen.

The candle in the bowl was a tea light with an improvised twine wick. The candle tin was battered. Maybe after the ceremony, the mother and daughter collected the spent tins to reuse.

Dev gave the girl a bill—Ted couldn't see the denomination—and they rowed to the next boat. Other tourists, other opportunities.

The priests held their tiered lamps aloft, each tier, a ring of fire. People clapped to the drumming droning from the speakers. The priests drew circles in the air with the lamps, in all four directions. A summoning, an invocation to the divine: *Let your presence be known.* There were other lights too: camera flashes from other boats and from along the ghat. Brief moments of brightness, like silver coins flipping.

Ted set this third bowl in the water, and it caught the current. For himself and Dev. The black river in ceaseless movement, and atop, this tiny light, a small prayer in a wide, engulfing world.

The ceremony had ended, though the lamps still smoked. And all of a sudden, rush hour on the Ganges. An outboard motor roared into life; Ted was surprised to see that boat filled not with Western tourists, but Indian ones. Another sales boat came by. A boy held out videotapes and CDs of the Ganga Aarti. "Souvenirs," he called.

Ted said, *"Nahi."*

Back at the guesthouse, Dev asked, "Did you enjoy your ride?"

Ted unbuttoned Dev's shirt and hung it. "I did."

"I hoped you might." Dev removed his shoes

and tucked his socks into them. He fell onto the bed. "I am exhausted."

"You've had quite the day." This emulation of home life, of stability, it had an expiration date. Ted laid his face on Dev's shoulder, the warmth of it. Coconut. He thought about the Ganga Aarti. Ephemeral fires, perpetual water. He had *liked* it, he could *appreciate* it, but he could not *understand* it. The priests had made fire dance. Within Ted was another heat, a different spinning fire. Dev could *like* it, could *appreciate* it, but could he *understand* it?

"It's a custom," Dev said, "for pilgrims to Benares to leave something behind. A symbol of freeing yourself of earthly matters."

"Are you leaving something?"

"Yes," Dev said.

"What?"

Dev rooted on the floor. Everything could be left behind, everything forgotten. "I'm leaving behind," Dev said, "a sock," and threw it at Ted's face.

Ted mock winced and tucked the still-warm sock under his pillow.

"It's mine now."

"What do you intend to give up?" Dev asked.

"I don't know. I'm not sure I have anything."

"Liar." Dev hovered over Ted and slowly lowered himself. "You have everything." Ted remembered the Ganga Aarti again: as the priests waved their tiered lamps aloft, the individual flames coalesced into a cone of fire. Dev's body touched his. What fantastic heat! Dev chanted in Ted's ear—*lovely, beautiful*—a rhythmic blessing, and the bed frame rang as it struck the wall. Praise be to the fire and to the river. To the night and the sky.

The next day, Dev said that he'd be back in the early afternoon, that they'd do something interesting that evening, and that Ted should stay out of trouble. Saying that, of course, made Ted *want* to get into trouble, but what sort? Certainly not trouble with a capital *T*, like hashish, or stolen antiquities, or prostitutes. But a more manageable trouble that didn't require bravery or planning. Like wandering down an unknown alleyway, or refusing to pay attention, or simply being in the way. In any case, Ted was unlikely to get into any trouble whatsoever.

In fact, he found the streets of the Old City to be a warren, the roads twisting upon themselves, branching out, stopping altogether. He consulted the map, but few of the streets had markers, and he oftentimes had to walk until he saw a shop awning with the street name. Signs with Roman lettering lured him back to the ghats, to another guesthouse, to a restaurant or bakery. Merchants beckoned from their doorways, holding spools of silk in their arms.

This place could not cooperate with the modern world. Power cables and telephone lines were strewn overhead, tangled around one another like strangling ivy. The buildings were weighted with age, their fronts wrinkled and sagging. Litter lined the road, bridging the broken paving stones. Even the dust seemed dingier.

If only that were the worst of it.

Cows sauntered in the road, giving way for nothing and occasionally letting loose a fire hose of piss. He could at least avoid the huge cow patties, visible at twenty paces. More insidious were dog droppings, lumps that made him rear back. And then there were droppings of more indeterminate origin, most likely human. But occasionally among the dirt and shit and commerce, a temple, a painted facade, an altar to a many-armed god. Leaping tigers in plaster. A family of rhesus monkeys groomed each other and observed Ted warily.

The crowds in the commercial area of Dashashwamedh weren't more extreme than anything he'd seen in Times Square, but he felt more vulnerable. No one had qualms about jostling him or yanking his elbow or staring at him with no other purpose than to stare. He wasn't being singled out; other tourists were eyed and cajoled with the same intensity. A phalanx of auto rickshaws idled near the road. They snapped to attention when Ted approached. They offered destinations—*Train station? Golden Temple? Burning ghat?*—but Ted already knew where he was going: back home to wait for Dev.

But by five, Dev hadn't returned. By seven, Ted began to worry. Maybe worry was too strong. *Increased concern.* It was probably nothing. In research, things piling on top of things was common. The clinical trials for Crixevir were delayed, first by worries about the sample size, then the controversy over double-blinds, and then issues of how to select the appropriate population. Like he said, things on top of things.

Eight o'clock. Then nine. Restaurants were closing. The Ganga Aarti was nothing but smoke. Life retreated indoors.

Maybe Dev had gotten lost. Or stuck in traffic. He should have been here by now.

It wasn't until after ten that Dev returned. Ted was ready to chide him, but Dev looked grim.

"Congratulations," Dev said.

"For what?"

"You don't know."

"No," Ted said. "I've been waiting here."

Dev smiled. Not amusement—chagrin. Had Ted done something?

"You haven't heard."

"No. Tell me."

Dev threw his hands in the air. "You won. The WTO issued its ruling on Triacept."

Ted had forgotten all about that. This room in

Varanasi had seemed so far removed from that life. Ted had almost willed it out of existence. And yet—here it came: one earth crashing into another.

He asked anyhow. "How did they rule?"

"We must stop manufacturing and distributing Triacept immediately. No appeal." It hurt to see how much this hurt Dev, how his voice trembled, how he couldn't even look at Ted. "If we do not comply, the US can impose trade sanctions on Indian pharmaceuticals."

"I'm sorry," said Ted.

"No. No pity for me. If you must feel sorry, feel sorry for all the people this affects. Feel sorry for my patients who will die. For their families. Your precious copyrights have been protected. Well done."

"Why are you blaming me?"

"I need to fly back to Delhi. I need to assess treatment plans and options."

"I'm not part of the legal team. I didn't argue the case."

Dev's eyes narrowed. "You work for Avartis."

"In marketing."

"*Marketing!* Do you see how much worse that is?"

"I do outreach, go to conferences," Ted said. How small his words seemed, how small his accomplishments.

"Yes," Dev said. "You do *so* much."

"But it's something, isn't it? The more people who know about Crixevir, the better. It saves *lives*."

"And you think this makes you a better person. You say you try to help. But what have you *done?*"

"What do you expect me to do, then?"

"You want me to tell you what to do." Dev shook his head.

"I haven't made things worse."

"But neither have you made things better."

An emptiness opened inside him. A hole. It felt like nothing—like less than nothing. He wasn't a light in the darkness—he *was* the darkness.

"Tell me. What should I do?"

"My friend, I am not the one you should be asking."

And in that void, something else crept in. Something Ted knew that he shouldn't have allowed but that was impossible to keep out. Later, Ted would replay this moment, trying new scenarios, different approaches. Maybe he could have changed the outcome; maybe an infinity of futures with Dev would have still been within reach. But what he said was irrevocable.

A mistake, a terrible mistake:

"*Friend?* Does your *wife* know that you're with a *friend* right now?"

And it was done.

"That," Dev said, "is my burden."

259

"Why am I even here?" Ted asked.

"You wanted to come."

Dev had misunderstood the question. Ted hadn't meant *Why am I here* with you? but *Why am I here* on earth?

This reckoning had been coming—days away, Ted thought, hours, minutes—but not so soon.

Ted took Dev's hand. Dev tried to shake him off, but Ted held it tight. He pulled Dev down onto the twin bed, where they lay together. Ted could swear that their hearts synchronized, that when Dev's pulse throbbed, his own neck responded, his own wrists. Silly, wasn't it? He could hear Dev's anger in his breathing, as if he were hyperventilating. Dev's chest thrummed against his back. Dev's hard-on pressed the back of his leg. Ted touched it; it was real. This wasn't love, of course; this couldn't move to New York with him; this couldn't consolidate households and talk, tentatively, about adopting; this couldn't grow old together and find quiet comfort in afternoon tea and crossword puzzles. This wouldn't turn around one day and say, *It was worth it. Every single moment.* This was one thing, and one thing only, and Ted got on his hands and knees. Dev said, "I don't have any condoms," and Ted said, "I don't care." This approached, slathered in coconut oil. This caused pain and fear. This gave pleasure, a mechanical kind, varying in tempo and intensity. This was undignified. This raised a sweat. This caused them to moan, not loud enough for the people next door to hear, but loud enough to remind themselves of their own presence. This made Ted hold his breath to keep from crying. This was not the answer, but this was all that Ted could offer. This brought release and, with it, a numbness, a vacuum where once something had been. This was all. This was it.

Dev went to the bathroom to shower. The water sounded as if it were sizzling. Ted stayed stomach down on the mattress. The sheets were soaked and, in the air-conditioning, freezing cold. Ted pulled the top sheet across his body. The water ran for ages, and Ted imagined Dev furiously scrubbing off every remnant of Ted. But Ted had Dev inside him. He would never rid himself of Dev.

Dev finished. A puff of steam entered the room. The light in the bathroom turned off. Ted lay there, arms and hands under his body, conserving heat. From the other side of the room, Dev's bedsprings creaked, and Ted lay there, and thought, now it was his turn, his turn to shower, his turn to be clean, his turn—

Ted woke before dawn, disturbed by dreams. Dreams of water, dreams of tides, dreams in which he was held down and drowned. The top sheet had knotted around his legs, and his arm was outstretched, as if bracing for—for—? He was still on his stomach, still a little sore. It took a few minutes to clear the daze from his mind. Day hadn't broken, but he heard children in the street, the burble of the river not thirty steps away. He smelled the stink of life even a closed window could not keep out.

He looked at Dev's bed, empty; his bags, gone; Dev, himself, gone. He'd left wordlessly, and now, Ted couldn't remember the tune of the song that Dev hummed while shaving. He couldn't remember if the hairs on Dev's chest twisted to the left or the right. Dev left him, even now.

Things took on an automatic simplicity: shower, shampoo, plastic bag to quarantine dirty clothes from clean ones. He found Dev's sock under his pillow, the one Dev had thrown at him, and stuffed it in his pocket. He opened the drawers, searching for other errant articles of clothing, and was disappointed to find not a copy of the Bhagavad Gita, but another goddamn Gideon Bible.

At some point, he'd go to the train station and find a ride back to Delhi. And from Delhi, home.

Ted buried his face in Dev's pillow and, for a moment, inhaled a ghostly coconut.

At the hotel desk, the clerk said, "Sir, sir," and handed Ted an envelope with the flap tucked in.

Ted was tempted to throw it away, to never read it, but what if it was an apology? *Dear Ted, I'm sorry that I have to leave . . .* The scrap of paper inside was thin, ready to crumble in his fingertips. A prescription for Triacept. Five hundred units, a year and a half's worth. The authorization signature was illegible. He compared the name printed at the top of the sheet—Dr. Devander Khanna—to the scrawl below. No resemblance whatsoever.

There was probably only a short window in which he could fill the prescription, before word of the ruling had disseminated. But he had time, just as, later, he had time to stare at the schedule in Varanasi Junction and to dismiss the hustlers trying to sell him a space in a retiring room with a magic word: *nahi.*

The sun rose above the east side of the river, the barren side, the side with ramshackle huts that no one noticed. Was the Ganges less holy on that bank?

A raging chasm, an unbreachable gulf.

This early, the Ganges was a different river. No crowds. Only the devout: a woman shaving her head with a straight razor; a gaggle of youngsters waddling by in duckling-white robes; a young man carrying his mother in his arms, dipping her in the water, and bringing her back up the steps. A man, chest-deep, filled and emptied a silver chalice. His long white beard floated in the water like cotton. These silent acts of devotion.

Ted threw Dev's sock as far as he could into the river.

You left something behind in Varanasi, Ted told Dev. *Two things, as a matter of fact.*

And what will you leave behind?

I don't know.

You do *know.*

The sun gathered strength. Flashes of heat skimmed off the water.

You know, Dev said, *but you're afraid.*

I'm not afraid, Ted insisted. *OK, maybe a little.*

Let go, Dev said.

Ted stepped in. The water came to his ankle. He couldn't see his foot. Pilgrims bathed in the Ganges to circumvent the cycle of rebirth. They would no longer need a physical body. Their souls rose directly to heaven. Even one drop, carried by the wind a thousand miles, was enough to purify someone.

If I do this, will you forgive me?

It is not a matter of forgiveness, Dev said.

Ted waded in waist-high. The ground shifted beneath his feet; his shoes felt as if they were coming loose. The sun pricked the crown of his head, the skin on his arms.

God, he prayed, *or gods, whichever the case may be, I offer you my old life, slightly used,*

*slightly worse for the wear. Its quotient of good
deeds to bad deeds is running less than half-and-
half, which is why I give it to you now. I want to
ascend. Not all the way to heaven, but to a place
with a little less suffering, a little less sadness.
I want to be the one who reduces that suffering,
that sadness. I want—*

Dev interrupted: *It is not a matter of want.*

You're right.

I will be, Ted continued, *a better person.*

He stretched his arms hallelujah wide. And
though the reasons why he shouldn't were
many—E. coli, dysentery, cholera, hepatitis—he
fell backward anyhow. The baptism was quick,
warm, uneventful. He shook the water out of
his hair and wiped it from his eyes. He still had
Dev's pill, a dose that both healed and poisoned.
In that respect, it was indistinguishable from the
Ganges.

Let go, Dev said, and Ted let go. Dev was
gone. John was gone. The silt lodged beneath his
fingernails was gone. He let go of what he saw
around him and what he would never understand.
He let go of his clothes and his job, his career
and his expense account. He let go of Ann, who'd
be fine without him. He let go of his Chelsea
apartment and its high ceilings, its proximity to
the trappings of his old life. He let go of the past
and the future, of sad memories and unrealized
possibilities alike. All gone. He let go: good-

265

bye, good-bye, good-bye. A dam broke, and a flood washed the old Ted away. The river took him northbound, where he would mingle with the ashes of loved ones already freed from their bodies.

RECOVERY

VARIETIES OF HUNGER

Here's the problem with food distribution in Bhuj:

Muslims don't eat pork.

Hindus don't eat beef, and a large number of Hindus are vegetarian.

Jains don't eat meat of any kind, including fish or eggs. As well, no honey, no figs, no butter. Orthodox Jains also abstain from root vegetables, and the monks who believe in nonviolence—ahimsa—extend this to all living creatures. They cover their mouths with cloth to avoid inhaling mosquitoes or gnats and sweep the path in front of them as they walk to clear ants that might be crushed by their footsteps.

"Wait," says Irina. "There's more."

The monks don't eat from sunset to sunrise, as this is when bacteria flourish. No food that's been left out overnight. Onion and garlic inflame the senses and increase sexual desire, so nix those too. Finally, there's something about mixing raw grains with raw yogurt or milk, but Irina isn't exactly sure what that's about.

"Do we need to follow these strictures?" Ted asks.

Irina grabs her ponytail by its root and shifts it over to her left shoulder. Her nose is as sharp as a milk carton spout. "Obviously," she says, "getting food into people's mouths is our primary responsibility. But there's no difference between someone starving because they don't have food available and someone starving because they are unable to eat the food they have."

Last week, this warehouse stored ammunition. The smell of gunpowder lingers, and the floor is black with tire treads. Fuel canisters line the walls, draped with sand camouflage tarps, their rotund bodies on the verge of exploding. All it would take is a spark. A match.

Irina doesn't know how long the World Food Programme can store supplies here—over three hundred metric tons of food have passed through—but she hopes that they can establish a semipermanent facility. "At least until the emergency has passed," she says.

But who knows when that will be?

Irina shrugs. "Better to ask God than me."

She takes Ted on a tour. Grains here, prepackaged ready-to-eat meals here, perishables here. Ted tries to commit the layout to memory. He feels likes a new employee at a supermarket. The floor near the entrance is treacherous with spilled grain. People skid and leave streaks. All this food—enough to slide in—and so much hunger everywhere else.

"Most of the immediate need has passed," Irina

says, "so we're transitioning from high-energy biscuits and BP-5s toward food baskets. Use your judgment."

His judgment. Oh boy. Yesterday, several trucks repeated their routes, delivering to villages that had already received aid bundles. Some dumped the food on the side of the road: rice spilling out of burlap sacks; pallets of water bottles, full of brightness, covered beneath sand. This is now his problem.

"In the city itself, people have gotten accustomed to the distribution points," Irina continues. "You shouldn't have any trouble."

"What sorts of trouble?"

"Crowds," she says. "Riots." She wipes a lock of blond hair off her face and tucks it behind her ear. "The ordinary."

Trucks back up to wooden ramps set at the entrance, and workers wheel crates onto them. The engines' rumbles bounce off the walls. A den of lions.

"Shall I go with the deliveries?" Ted asks.

"Only if you want."

His palm smells like diesel, and his knuckles are creased with grime. His fingernails are the longest he's ever let them grow, and they're gray from quick to tip. He wouldn't eat with these hands, much less pass out food with them.

Irina gives Ted a map of Bhuj, highlighted in different colors. Piotr's handiwork. Colored pathways circle in on themselves. Large dots are distribution points for the various religions and sects centered around temples. People flee toward what they know, toward community.

"But if they're starving—" Ted continues, "*really* starving—can't they compromise?"

She puts a hand on Ted's shoulder. "Have you ever gone hungry?" she asks.

She doesn't challenge; she doesn't mock.

The trucks delivering to the religious centers, she says, handle themselves. These centers are accustomed to preparing food for festivals, holidays, and weddings. Even with damaged infrastructure, they persist. Monks minister to the injured and the bereft. From the folds of their longhis, they offer fruit, prayer beads, bandages. The elderly Sisters of Charity, stooped and frail in their gray habits, clear rubble away brick by brick.

What is it about religion that brings about such devotion? When he was young, Ted watched the news footage from the shelters around the city every Thanksgiving. A cramped cafeteria, homeless men wearing stocking caps and thin polyester jackets. Families from deep in Westchester County came to help— tall teenage boys in basketball jerseys, ladling mashed potatoes from heating trays; young girls with glittery eye shadow, passing out slices of pumpkin pie; their parents beaming with benevolence. They spoke the language of evangelism—the day's blessing, the grace of God—and their recipients responded in kind: *Thank you, Jesus.* Ted's parents never made him do anything of the sort, but there was always the implication: *There but for the grace of God goes* you.

Ted tries to remember what he ate this morning—coffee and a high-energy biscuit that crumbled in his mouth like sand. He has to cinch the waist of his pants with a safety pin, lest it slide off his hips. If he fasts, does this prove moral rectitude? Willingness to sacrifice?

"Oh!" Irina says. "I almost forgot. Hindu Vaishnavites don't eat root vegetables, either."

The trick to food-basket distribution, Irina says, is to give only to the women. These baskets are designed to last a family group several days. The World Food Programme learned this the hard way: in Somalia, when they gave men the food baskets, the men traded them for munitions. Giving the baskets to the women means better chance of the food being eaten.

The term "family group," though, seems nebulous. Ted understands the "family" part—but "group"? Does a group include uncles and cousins? As he saw in Lodai yesterday, it's not uncommon for the entire passel of relatives to live like geese in a pen. Do grandparents count, or do they warrant their own basket? It's not much, these baskets: flour or rice, chickpeas or lentils, a bottle of vegetable oil fortified with vitamins A and D, sugar, iodized salt.

Though the WFP prefers to purchase food locally, Irina explains, sometimes bulk donations from corporations arrive. For instance, two days ago, a crate arrived with incomprehensible stenciling on it, consonants jumbled together the way only Scandinavians can manage. No one knows what's in it. Arni had secured it, but now he's gone, and nobody can translate the export label.

Ted gets a crowbar. "Let's see."

Inside: boxes. And inside the boxes: cans. Ted hopes that the label will yield answers, but no: it's a cartoon penguin holding a broom, like a Christmas card. Stupid Scandinavians. He scans the ingredients for a cognate—*vatten, vetemjöl, nöttalg*—and after that fails, he looks at the nutritional information. Whatever this is, it has a lot of calories: two hundred kilocalories per one hundred grams and nine grams of *fett*.

Irina hooks her knuckle under the tab and pulls back the top. A thin layer of aspic makes the whatever-it-is sparkle.

"Looks like Spam," Ted says, though the color—akin to raspberry mousse—is too dark. The contents smell almost metallic, like a rubbed penny.

Ted and Irina look at each other. It's a dare.

"You first," he says.

"Not on your life."

"That's what I'm afraid of."

"Rock paper scissors, then."

Her paper covers his rock.

"Here goes," Ted says. He dips his finger through the aspic. The texture is solid, like bologna. He scrapes a bit with his fingernail and brings it to his mouth.

"And?"

"It doesn't taste like anything."

"Maybe you need a bigger piece." Irina finds a spoon. "Ready?"

"Ready."

They both chew thoughtfully.

"Salty," she says.

There's a creaminess, a layer of fat on his tongue. Nothing like Spam. Spam-based meals were a short-lived experiment from his mother. It was a cost-cutting measure, something she'd found a coupon for. She fried slices of it one morning along with the eggs, and since Ted had to finish his plate before he was allowed to watch cartoons, he had a few bites before discarding the rest beneath the browned, crisp edges of egg. His father pushed his plate away with a firm "You know, the bacon was just fine."

"I can't think of any religions that would allow this," Ted says.

• • •

The first distribution point is in front of the Bhuj jail. The jail has cracked like a nut. The heavy door lies on its hinges, and the walls have split, but—truth be told—this was not a high-security facility. The criminals and militants now sift their way through the general populace. Earthquake as amnesty. Ted isn't worried. Not really.

The afternoon sun has flensed away the night's cool. In the lot, women wait for the truck to pull up. A mother with two young children stretches her sari across the back of their heads to shield them from the sun. The only man present helps an elderly woman; she holds his forearm and rests her weight on him. As the truck arrives, those who have been reclining stand, and others appear from beneath the shade of nearby doorways and tents. They shift left and right, like commuters trying to position themselves to exactly where the subway door opens. The soldiers hop off the back, guns slung on their shoulders, and bark a few words. This is a familiar drill. There are blankets on the ground. People have waited here all night. Maybe this is home.

Ted hands a basket to a young woman—maybe twenty. Her head is draped with a tan scarf that sparkles in the sun. She turns the basket over in her hands. It rattles and sloshes. She pierces the cellophane with her fingernail and holds up the vegetable oil to the sun, and it glows like honey.

The recipient of the basket announces something—an aside to a friend—but it's overheard, and excitement runs through the crowd, and then there are hands everywhere. The crowd swells and surges forth; the soldiers bristle. The trucks rocks gently.

Ted sees an elderly woman. Her arm is bent at the elbow, an open hand close to her breast, as though beseeching. *If I can get something to her,* he thinks, *it'll be OK.* No one pushes her aside—that he sees, at least—but she falls farther and farther behind, her small hand, a bird's claw, disappearing beneath the others.

"One at a time," Ted says. How do you say *one per family group* in Hindi? The crowd clumps around the truck, and hands reach for the still-sealed baskets. He understands now why some aid workers dump and run. It's not the violence—it's the claustrophobia. The bodies press against him, the static of their clothes against his.

A boy, maybe twelve, stands in the shade of the truck. He wears a T-shirt announcing "San Diego Padres, 1998 World Series Winner." The cloth is so thin that Ted can see the boy's ribs underneath. "Hello," Ted says. The boy cups his hands. Ted speaks slowly: "Your mother?"

But it's useless. So far, Ted has only learned

the word for water: *pani*. He's heard *earthquake* referred to in three different ways: *bhukampa*, *lodai*, *gadgadati*. How is he supposed to help anyone if he can't understand what they need?

Well, Irina never said "only give food to women" was a hard-and-fast rule, and if one can't be flexible during an emergency, then when can one? Ted roots in the piles of plastic wrap. It's like swimming in spiderwebs. He hands the boy a basket. Does he even know how to prepare food? Ted watches him leave. He'll have to learn.

At the next distribution point, Ted sees the boy again. Same dirty face, same T-shirt. Maybe the Padres sent boxes of these shirts to India when they lost the World Series that year. The crowd here is larger, more unruly. One soldier no longer looks to see who receives the food; he hands it out so quickly he might as well be flinging it.

Ted stands straight. His bones hum. He holds a breath and lets it leak through his nostrils. He is a conduit, a funnel through which food flows, and it's up to him to pace distribution. OK, then.

He puts a hand on the soldier's back, who stops, paralyzed. Ted nods, and the soldier slows his pace to something more fluid, more natural. And Ted watches the hands take the baskets. One second, empty; the next, full; and then finally, clasped together for a split second, a gesture of thanks.

The boy beckons Ted, waving with his hand, asking him to follow. The boy judges him; he's not trying hard enough or fast enough.

Ted nudges the soldier. "What does that boy want?" he asks.

The soldier asks, listens. "His father can't move. He needs to bring enough food for them to survive."

"Does his father need medical attention? Is he badly hurt? Tell him—" Ted doesn't know what to say. "How much food does he need?"

"He says they haven't eaten for several days."

Bloodshot eyes. The boy's skin looks like it's melting off the bone.

"OK," says Ted. The boy is probably telling the truth. Probably. Ted takes a food basket under each arm and jumps off. Ted has a moment of misgiving, a regret so strong that he has to stamp it out like a burning match.

"Lead the way," he tells the boy, and off they go.

The city is a maze, and following the boy this deep into it is a mistake. Even with Irina's map, he can't figure it out. He notes landmarks: the refugee tents at the Dwarkadish temple, a hygiene poster glued to the wall of the Decent Public School.

279

Why are you following him? Lorraine asks. *There are thousands like him.*

He needs my help.

Lorraine's experience has tempered and sharpened her. When she encounters a problem, she cuts through it: *I don't care; just get it done.* Ted, on the other hand, hammers at the problem until he's dented and bruised.

The boy hops over splintered chunks of timber with the precision of a cat. The afternoon brings haze, a heaviness in the air like paste.

His family has no access to food, Ted replies. *He needs food.*

Thousands, Lorraine insists.

Maybe Ted has a self-destructive streak, like a snake waiting patiently underfoot. He should have asked a soldier to accompany him. John used to tell him that spontaneity was not his strong suit, that his sudden impulses always ended badly. "Every time you do something by the seat of your pants," John said, "you live to regret it." But that, Ted figures, is his normal state of being: he lives and he regrets, so therefore he will always live to regret.

"How much farther is it?" Ted asks.

The boy calls out, "*Challo, challo,*" and Ted *challo*es. Ted checks the sun, as if to determine how many hours lie between him and curfew. If Piotr were out all night, Lorraine wouldn't worry, but with him—?

I'm not a child, he says.
Then stop acting like one, she replies.

The boy leads Ted into a fortified courtyard, walled off from the rest of the city. This place could be a medieval European fortress, built from buff-colored stone. A vertical crack runs up the side of a clock tower. The hands on the clocks have frozen at different times; one is missing its hands altogether. On the south face, the hours from four to six have fallen out.

Ted looks for a campfire, a lean-to, some indication of life, but finds instead marble pillars shaking off their Corinthian entablatures, slabs of cornices from overhead. He looks behind him—the keystones in the arched passageway he passed beneath have slipped. A tremor could trap him here.

To his left is a wooden sign on stilts that says "Aina Mahal Museum." One of its supports has shattered, and the arrow points toward the sky. Along the ground, broken statuary. Torsos dancing despite missing heads and limbs—a chorus line of amputees. He remembers his parents taking him to a fair when he was twelve, where he bought a ticket for the Krazy Kastle. After the out-of-proportion room and the glow-in-the-dark room was a room where everything was upside down. A chandelier stuck upright out of the floor like a

281

crystal stalagmite, and overhead was a fully set Thanksgiving meal: a turkey, a bowl of peas, mashed potatoes. Right now, he feels the same discombobulation.

Ted's instinct is to retreat. He should leave the baskets and go back.

The boy chatters to a man in a doorway, half-hidden in the shade. Ted had mistaken him for a statue. The man—nearly bald, slim, with features as jagged as rock—rises in a swift movement. He holds a pistol.

"Karsan," the man says in crisp, accented English. "You've brought a friend."

The man introduces himself as Prasant, the curator of the Aina Mahal.

"I apologize for the brusque reception," he says. The nosepieces of his glasses form red craters on either side of his nose. Flecks of dry skin curl off his lips. "I've been on guard since the earthquake. Karsan has been kind enough to fetch me food so that I don't have to leave the grounds."

"Is he your son?"

"No," Prasant says. "He's the son of one of my guards." Karsan picks off the plastic seal of a water bottle and hands it to Prasant, who sips just enough to wet his mouth. "His father has been—lost—these last few days."

Ted eyes the pistol.

"It's an antique," Prasant says. "If I tried to shoot, it would most likely explode in my hand. It's not even loaded." Prasant holds the gun for Ted to inspect, but Ted waves his hand no. "I have it to deter looters."

"Here too?"

"They send scouts. The antique dealers from Delhi and Mumbai were prowling around like dogs. I have to sit watch." He points behind him, to a building with a shattered stairway. "Whatever remains, I protect."

"How much damage has there been?"

"I don't know," Prasant says. He chokes, as if out of breath. "I don't know."

The men carrying away pieces of Bhid Gate yesterday. Ted remembers his uselessness—not in doing good, but in preventing evil.

"I cannot guard this place by myself," Prasant says. His hand strangles the gun. "I'm too old to keep all the jackals from the door."

"Your other workers?"

Prasant holds his hand out, as if introducing Ted to his staff.

"I'll try to get someone," Ted says. "The army—"

"The army. They see everything and do nothing. Soldiers come by, poke in their heads, and move on. They wait so that they can loot this place themselves. If it weren't for Karsan, I would have starved to death."

Ted imagines Prasant's corpse propped against the doorway, withered in the sun. A guardian even after death.

"Prasant, this place is unstable. If there's another strong aftershock, it could come down on your head. It's not worth your life."

"The food you brought," he says. "It will keep me."

"What about Karsan?"

"Where can he go? He is my son now," Prasant says, and Karsan, as if understanding, smiles.

And Ted remembers, once again, the fair: burning machine grease and boiled hot dogs and the flattened grass underfoot. He remembers his father pulling him aside after he had filled up on funnel cakes and boardwalk fries, how he felt as though he himself had been deep-fried. He remembers how night had just fallen, and the lights on the rides came on, the bulbs streaking the sky like fireworks. His mother stood against a metal fence, smoothing out her dress, and his father bent to one knee. "There's something we'd like to tell you," he said. Ted was old enough to know that something important was happening, but not old enough to guess what it could have been. "Your mother and I, we love you very much," his father said, "and we will always love you. We love you enough so's to not keep secrets from you, and we hope that you won't keep secrets from us." His father looked at his mother, who nodded, and Ted felt the oil from the funnel cake creep into his esophagus, burning its way up. "We've both decided that you're old enough now to understand," his father continued, "and you deserve to know." His father grasped his hands, as if to hold him in place. "You're adopted," he said.

His mother chimed in, "We love you, and we'll always be your parents, no matter what," and his father nodded, and Ted knew enough to hug them both, and afterward, he pointed to the Ferris wheel, the unblinking, neon eye, and said, "I want to go." Ted endured the slow, silent revolutions. The wheel convulsed, disgorging passengers in a clatter of metal. As their car dangled at the apex and a new family far below them entered, Ted tugged the sleeve of his mother's dress and cried into it, and by the time it was their turn to exit, he had finished.

Ted unfolds the map and shows it to Prasant. "Here are some camps. They're close by." He taps the Swaminarayan temple, the Ram Dhun temple—both aid hubs. Prasant looks at Ted: *You're telling* me *where the temples in* my *city are?*

"If you keep ants away from food," Prasant says, "they never find it. But once they discover it, they descend like a swarm."

Ted sucks his lips inside his mouth and bites

them closed. He can't win this battle. "You don't have to be alone," he says.

Prasant replies, "I'm not alone." He crosses the gun across his chest. His eyes focus on the horizon. "This is why I must stay."

Ted makes his way back, reading the street names painted on the sides of still-standing houses. He makes good headway until he hits a section of town where no houses stand.

This must be Soniwad.

Everything here seems removed from its original context: a tire inside a bathtub, a motorcycle under a heap of bricks, a green plastic pail filled with dust. North, he knows, is the direction to the police grounds. But he needs to hurry—the sun has almost set. Shadows grow teeth. Soniwad almost looks too dense to pass through, a field of stones overgrown onto the streets. Two men on the side of the road scavenge wood. They carry table legs and window frames. When they see him, they eye him, as if gauging whether or not they could take him in a fight. After he passes, they root around again, shifting rock, breaking glass.

Farther ahead, two other men rummage through the rubble. They've got metal detectors strapped around their waists. Rescue workers with newly arrived high-tech equipment, maybe. Ted waves—maybe Andy is with them—when he notices that they're dressed in civilian clothes. No protective gear, no reflective stripes. One of the men registers something, and they dig. The man holds up the discovery, and it glints in the light. He tosses it aside.

Strange.

They parse the land. Finally, one uncovers something that excites them both. They tug at it. It's stuck in the ground like a tree stump. Ted shivers.

"Hey—" he says. "Hey!"

They can't hear him through their headphones. Ted stumbles toward them, and once they catch sight of him, they run in the other direction. He'll never catch them. Metal bars poke out like thorny tetanus-tipped weeds. The men split up and disappear.

Ted huffs, out of breath. His ankles ache. He stands, bowlegged, on two chunks of stone. Metal detectors? The ground is disturbed with their footprints, and he searches for what they were tampering with.

It's an arm.

A woman's arm, white with dust. It juts from beneath the large slab of stone. Around the woman's wrist are gold bangles as thin as hairs.

"Bastards," he yells. He hurls a rock in the direction they ran. "You fucking bastards!" But what can he do? As soon as he leaves, they'll come back. The metal detectors will sniff out the scent of the gold. It will be weeks before the bulldozers arrive to shift her into a final, indigent burial. And he's not Prasant. He can't sit here indefinitely to guard this woman's arm.

The bracelets cut into her skin. Her skin is bloated and splotched. He can smell her—probably not her alone. This is a neighborhood of baked, rotting flesh.

How long have those men been looting, corpse-robbing? They looked well fed, well equipped. Probably aren't even from this area. He stares at the woman's arm, the fine black hairs, the purpling beneath her fingernails. She's been forgotten. Maybe her whole family's dead. Maybe they're waiting for her to show up.

What was that Prasant said? Karsan's father was *lost*. This woman is *lost*. Like so many others. He doesn't know what street he's on, what address this could have been. This street is *lost;* this neighborhood is *lost*. Does it matter, then, if she has jewelry or not? Why intervene now? Why stop these men and not the two from twenty minutes earlier? Better to live and let live than be *lost*.

Still. They can't get away with this.

He wants to pelt them with stones. He wants to dig a deep trap and cover it with twigs so that they tumble in when they approach. All the fancy locating equipment in the world wouldn't be able to find them.

He wants, he wants, he wants. But all he does is delay the inevitable.

No sign of them. Of anyone.

The woman's skin is cool to the touch, taut and malleable like a water balloon. He holds the bracelets with two fingers of his right hand and, with his left, squeezes her skin enough to inch them forward. They catch the knuckle of her middle finger, but he coaxes the metal over, and the bracelets slide off.

There are seven altogether, and—what did he just do? He's just as bad as they are. Worse, even. He did it to *thwart* them. An act of pettiness to what end? The woman's arm is bare and dark. It lies on the ground like the cut end of a worm.

He slips the bangles into his pocket. He breaks into a run. When he's far enough, he fishes them out and hurls them into the ruins of Soniwad. They spin and shine in the air, like pieces of the sun falling to the earth, and when they land, they hardly make a noise, a *tink, tink, tink* you'd only hear if you were listening—and then they're gone.

When he arrives back at camp, Lorraine asks, "How was your adventure?"

Ted can't begin to respond.

She busies herself with her clipboard. "You're very popular today."

Ted shakes off his stupor, like a swimmer coming up for a breath. The woman's arm holds him underwater.

"Irina stopped by to make sure you got back OK. She said she was a little worried when she heard you'd gone off on your own." Lorraine drums her fingers against the clipboard. "I told her you're not the reckless type. Right?"

"Right."

"She left you a gift." Lorraine hands him a cardboard box. "Careful, it's kind of heavy."

"What's in it?"

"Heck if I know."

When Ted opens it, he recognizes the cans— the Swedish mystery meat from this morning.

Lorraine picks one up. "Weird."

"Wait till you see what's inside."

"I'd rather not know."

Something in his pocket feels odd.

Lorraine brings him a Styrofoam tub. "One of the ladies from Oxfam cooked this up. I have no idea how. They're genius savants over there. Piotr and I have already had some." She leans in for a whisper: "It's *good*."

Ted reaches into his pocket and feels a sense of dread. It's one of the bracelets. He missed it when he threw the others away. It's warm, like it's stolen the heat from his body.

"The security situation," Ted says. "It's getting worse." He describes Prasant's situation at the Aina Mahal, what he saw in Soniwad.

Lorraine purses her lips.

"Is there any way we can get a security patrol there? Or at least post a guard? It's—" Ted imagines Prasant and Karsan dozing off in the middle of the night, as men with crowbars approach them from behind—

"Ted," she says. "Do you need me to explain why I'm going to say no?"

All he hears is *no*.

"You're right," she continues, "the situation is terrible. And I appreciate you bringing it to my attention. But we have to stabilize the population first. Once we've taken care of that, we can concentrate on other issues."

The bangle cuts a circle into his leg.

"We'll get to it," she says. "We *will*. But we have priorities."

Ted understands the words; he understands the concepts behind the words. But it doesn't make it easier.

"Your next priority," she says, "is to eat. It sounds like you've got a rabid wolverine in your stomach."

Ted hasn't thought about how hungry he is.

She stacks the Styrofoam box on top of his cardboard box. "That's dinner. It'll probably last us for days."

"Do you want to split a can of Swedish cuisine?"

"No, thanks," Lorraine replies. "I'm trying to cut down on my penguin intake."

Ted swings by Andy's tent and finds him suiting up. Dark marks under his eyes make him look like a linebacker. He moves as if mired in molasses. It takes him a moment to register Ted's presence.

"Fancy seeing you here," Andy says. The other firefighters sharing the tent regard Ted with a certain suspicion, as if he were a female reporter in a locker room. Ted wants to hug Andy, but not in front of mixed company.

"Winding down?" Ted asks.

"Exact opposite, actually."

"You're going out? After curfew?"

"We got our exploration and listening equipment in. Need peace and quiet for it to work." The tent is thick with body odor. Grunting. Metal buckles fastening and unfastening. "We got permission to work at night, so"—he pulls his suspenders over his shoulders—"off we go!"

Ted moves closer, lowers his voice. "When do you think you'll be done?"

"Hard to say. When we're done, I reckon."

One of Andy's friends interjects, "Don't wait up," and Andy says, "Shut the fuck up, Reg," and Reg holds up his hands, *Oooh, so scared.*

"I'll stop by the fire," Andy whispers. "If you're there, great. If not, we meet another time, right?"

"I brought something for you. For you and your friends." He puts the cardboard box on Andy's cot. "I wasn't sure what sort of provisions you've been getting, but I figured you could always use some meat."

"You did, did you?" Andy flashes a devilish smile—the kind that makes Ted feel both giddy and decrepit. Andy pries back the lid of a can and exclaims, "Oh, man!" like he's opening a birthday present in front of the giver.

"I haven't had this since I was a kid," Andy says. "My mum would cook this up Sunday mornings before church. Not this brand, though—Mum always got Wilson's."

"What is it?"

"Blood pudding. You fry up a slice with bacon and tomato—that's how my dad liked it, anyhow." He sniffs the can as if it contained concentrated childhood. "I ate mine on toast with strawberry jam."

"Glad you like it," Ted says. "I'll see you tonight? Hopefully."

As Ted leaves, Andy announces, "Look here, you twats, look at what my friend brought." They murmur in response.

"Share some already."

"Are you really going to eat that?"

Andy replies, "Back off, back off. There's enough for everyone."

All Ted hears is *my friend.*

Final stop of the day: the medical tents. Ted watches Dev for a moment, moving from one patient to another. From afar, his medical coat seems luminous and white, but as Ted approaches, the stains become apparent: dirt accumulating on its bottom hem, in the creases of the elbows.

"I come bearing dinner," Ted announces.

"I did not expect to see you back here," Dev says.

"Have you eaten?"

"Some, yes. Let me finish, and I can join you."

A few patients have fallen asleep, but most face the night with open eyes. Dev kneels by one man, his left arm amputated at the elbow. The missing arm melts into the darkness. In their short time together, he had never seen Dev doing doctor things: making rounds, circling the hospital floors. For a moment, Ted wants to be the sick one, the one Dev comforts. Dev's fingers stroking his forehead. Dev's hip and leg forming a cradle in which his head rests.

Dev steps out. "So, what do you have for me?"

Ted lifts the top of the tub: tomato stew, polka-dotted with chickpeas, errant bits of coagulated oil. Condensation glistens on the underside of the lid.

"A step up from our normal fare," Dev says.

"What have you been eating?"

"Biscuits, mostly. The other day, we received packets of bread. The type for sandwiches. *Polite* bread. I have never seen that particular brand in Delhi. It may be local."

Bread that thanks you as you eat it. *Wouldn't you prefer me toasted?*

They sit on plastic crates, and Dev sweeps the bottom of his jacket out from under him, like a duck flaring its plumage. Ted produces two plastic spoons. Dev looks as if he's contemplating lecturing Ted about waste, but he says nothing. Ted stirs the stew.

"Thank you for sharing your meal," Dev says. He takes a spoonful.

"My pleasure. It's good to see you again."

"Likewise." Dev presses the spoon against his bottom lip until it bends into a U. "The Prince Hotel has opened to medical personnel. There's no running water, but they leave a bucket of water and a sponge in the washroom for rinsing up." Dev stirs the stew again. "If you want, you—or any of your colleagues, for that matter—are welcome to stop by. There's soap. There's towels." Dev doesn't look at him as he speaks.

An invitation. Nothing more.

"Stop in anytime, even if I'm not present," says Dev.

Ted wants desperately to bathe, but using water to wash is an inexcusable luxury. There's hardly enough to go around. In the morning, military water tankers slosh into Bhuj completely full and, by midafternoon, drive back out cavernously empty. From one end of Hamirsar Tank, people skim off brown, opaque liquid and in the other end, shit and piss into the same waters.

But a bucket and sponge—that's not wasteful. Ted's lichenous toes scrunch against his socks.

"I mean what I say about the hotel room," Dev says. "You can take a nap, stretch out on a real bed."

A real bed. Would his body even remember comfort? Only when he stops moving does he feel achy. "I might," Ted says. "How's—your wife?"

"She's in good health. Good spirits. I have a daughter now too. Arusha. She grows like a vine. She is the stars and the sky to us."

"Congratulations," Ted says. "I remember—"

Ted stops. What *does* he remember? Why must reunions involve reminiscing? For a time, he dreamed of changing Dev's mind. He relived his errors and tried variations of what should have happened. He should have apologized, early and profusely, even before he had something to apologize for. He should have made certain that Dev had forgiven him. He should have fallen asleep with his arm encircling Dev so that no escape was possible. Each scenario played out with the same end: he and Dev, living together, happy in a way that seemed hazy, effortless happiness, everlasting happiness, happiness as seen from a distance. It was happiness only because it was illusory, and knowing this, Ted reached for it anyway, as if it might come true. But—like the body aches—the things that troubled him at night disappeared when the time to work came.

Maybe this is what Lorraine means by "running away." You don't have time to relive your failures when you're expected to feed the desperate, the destitute.

"What is it?" asks Dev. "What do you remember?"

"Honestly?" he says. "I've forgotten what I was trying to remember."

So—that's it, then. The end. He still wants Dev; he will always want Dev; and this want will fade—over days, over years—as long as it takes. Irina had asked him this morning if he'd ever gone hungry. Oh—he knows hunger like it's an internal organ. Sitting next to Dev now, the tub balanced across their knees, he hungers. He knows that Dev loves him, and that this brief contact—his thigh touching Dev's—will be the extent of their love.

Their spoons scrape against the Styrofoam.

They chew in silence. They don't make a dent in the contents of the tub. It is, after all, meant to feed a family. There's more food here than they could possibly eat at once.

SIGNS OF LIFE

Four full days of corpses. It's been six since the earthquake, and three since they pulled out a survivor. Andy's prepared for this. Each UKFSSART team member undergoes counseling and psychological evaluations before and after every mission. "You will see," Dr. Cameron says, "many more dead bodies than living ones. But you have to focus on the living."

Right, then. Miracles. The 1985 Mexico City earthquake. Two weeks after the initial tremor, one woman was found alive in her collapsed apartment building. She had been at her refrigerator, and the refrigerator and kitchen wall collapsed toward each other, forming an inverted V. With the refrigerator door open, she had food, and rain brought a slow trickle of water. She lay there, in darkness, for *two weeks*.

But this isn't Mexico, and this isn't 1985.

The sun lashes Andy's skin. At first, he was glad to have it after a night in an acrylic blanket no thicker than a flannel shirt. But by afternoon, the heat becomes ghastly, a tongue on his back. In his full kit, he's a sweat factory. It collects in his boots, mixes with the dust and debris. When he takes off his boots at night, he pours out sludge.

For the past two days, they've used video

probes to search buildings, snaking the camera as deep as the cable can reach. The team works silently, except when calling orders. They are hypersensitive to sound. A slight scratching or tapping could be a sign of life. On-screen, he sees the obvious dead, heads flattened, bodies pinioned and pulverized, and on physical probes, he shimmies by them, sometimes coming close enough to see a face—dry, cracked lips, a final, frozen word there. He keeps a smear of VapoRub on his upper lip to block the smell. It doesn't always work.

He fears being *too late*. Through the grace of God, maybe someone's trapped in a survivable void, someplace with an air passageway and a steady drop of water from a broken overhead pipe. The rescues from previous days melt underneath the overwhelming possibility of *what if?*

"Positive thoughts," Dr. Cameron tells him. "Push other thoughts away. It's natural for you to have doubts, but don't let them distract you from your duty."

"We're going back to the Ashpura apartments," says Mike. "With the heavy-lifting equipment, maybe we can find some voids deeper in. We've got search dogs too." His voice sounds thick with dust, the skin beneath his eyes sunken. Around them are the newer arriving teams: the Russians, the French.

The dog handler is a Japanese woman, Emiko. "This is Momo," she says, roughing the scruff of one of the golden retrievers, "and this is Kami." She scratches Kami's muzzle, and he lifts his head to say, *Yes, yes.*

"Can we pet them?" Les asks.

"Yes, quickly," she says. "Before they start work."

Les reaches out tentatively and murmurs, "Hey, girl. How are you, girl?" Others pet the dogs as well, except for Colin, who crosses his arms, face turned down in a grimace, six days of beard speckling his cheeks and chin.

The men barrage Emiko with questions, which she answers with the patience of a schoolteacher: *Yes. Four and six years old. In high-stress situations, humans emit a unique chemical odor. Five rescues total.* The day holds its promise, thin and transient as the tongue hanging out of Momo's mouth.

The Ashpura apartments haven't changed since five days earlier. But Andy can't tell the difference: all ruined architecture is the same. The building is a sloppy layer cake, the top sheets askew, the ground floor and first floor collapsed under the weight of the upper floors. Cranes peel back layers of concrete. Orange jumpsuits and blue jumpsuits pick through the bricks.

Les helps Emiko out of the truck, and Momo

and Kami bound after her. The lads are smitten: *Such a pretty lady. And she loves dogs!*

Andy prepares for his day with the living and the dead.

The cranes expose new spaces where people possibly could have survived, but the possible soon gives way to the real. Momo and Kami clamber over the debris, noses close to the ground. When they finish, Emiko pulls rawhides out of her pockets, and the dogs chew them desultorily, as if disappointed in themselves. The sun beats on their pelts, tarnishing their golden sheen. Emiko cleans Kami's nose with a cotton swab, holding his head as steady as possible. Kami twitches, but doesn't fight. Back on the truck, Les scratches Momo's ears. He massages her forehead, her jaws, her neck.

"You look like you're going to kidnap her," Reg says. "I reckon Emiko would beat you senseless if you tried."

"I haven't had a dog since I was fifteen," Les replies.

"Missus won't let you have one?" asks Stewart.

"Says they're bad for the house. But not a day goes by that I don't find one of her cats mangling the carpet. She's afraid that a dog would be too rough on Maggie."

"You could get a little dog," Stewart says.

"Might as well get another cat for all the good

302

those little shit dogs do. Maybe when Maggie's older."

Andy had always been jealous of his classmates with pets, how they distracted themselves attending to something small and endlessly joyful. But since he was fourteen, Andy had his father to take care of.

Emiko calls to Momo: one short word, and Momo nearly knocks Les down as she bounds to rejoin Kami.

The Indian Army has begun recovery operations. Bodies wrapped in white sheets pave the road. Andy wonders how many of these people had been just beyond his reach, unable to hear him call out, "Hello? Please respond if you can hear my voice," unconscious, waking long after he'd left, alone in the dark, fear hanging in the air like a noose.

Andy never mentions these thoughts to anyone, including Les, because he'd be told to talk to Colin, who would tell him to see the brigade medical officer, and so on, until he was back to Dr. Cameron writing notes that said *Not fit for duty* and *Mentally unable to cope with stress.*

"Do you want to talk about your father?" Dr. Cameron asks.

"No," replies Andy, "I do not."

Andy brings his fists to his temples. He squeezes his eyes tight, hears nothing but

303

the truck crushing rocks beneath its tires into powder.

"You OK?" asks Les.

"Headache," Andy says.

"I've got a paracetamol. I think it's still in one piece." Les reaches for a water bottle.

"No need," says Andy.

"You're going to swallow it dry?"

Andy nods.

"Your funeral," Les says. The pill dissolves on Andy's tongue before scraping its way down his throat. Andy swallows again and again. Les turns his attention back to Momo.

"Andy," Les says.

"Yeah."

"Andy."

"What."

"I want to tell you something," Les says. "Keep this under your cap for now."

If anyone can keep a secret, it's him.

"Janice is pregnant," Les says.

Andy thinks he should give his congratulations but hesitates.

"I haven't run this by her yet but—I'd like you to be the godfather."

Andy can't imagine that responsibility. He remembers practicing on the infant CPR manne- quin. He blew too hard into its mouth, and the diagnostic system trilled as if he'd exploded

304

the baby's lungs, and after thirty compressions, Colin, loud enough for everyone to hear, said, "McGreevey, leave the baby some intact ribs."

"Boy or girl?" he asks.

"Girl," Les says. "A sister for Maggie."

"Have you named her yet?"

"We're still debating," Les says. "Have any suggestions?"

Andy thinks for a moment. "Victoria."

"Victoria," Les says. "Victoria, Victoria." He says it like he's trying on a new pair of shoes. "Not half bad. How'd you come up with that?"

"She was my favorite Spice Girl."

"Victoria," Les says again. "Anything but Victoria, then."

The cranes and lifts seem so unwieldy. They have no finesse, all pulleys and claws, knobs and levers. The engines whir with the screech of poorly oiled metal. But as long as the machines do their business, Andy has nothing to do but wait. His fingernails dig into his palms. They're on the sixth-day cusp—when people start to die of starvation. It's one thing to be swallowed whole by the dark, but it's another to be nibbled away by it. He can't imagine not eating for six days in a row. The most he's ever gone is a day, during those trying times right before his mother's next paycheck or his father's next suckle off the dole. He remembers sitting at the table, eating cheese sandwiches, and his mother finishing less than half of hers and announcing, too emphatically to be true, that she couldn't eat another bite, and his father reaching for the uneaten portion. It made him sick, how his father got fatter even when there was no food in the house.

Andy pounds his temples with his fists. His father is stuck in his head like a spike.

Emiko approaches, leading Momo and Kami.

"Problem?" she asks.

"Preparing myself," he replies.

Emiko gestures toward the dogs. "They brought me here."

"For what?"

She shrugs. "You tell me."

"No fooling those noses, eh?" Kami threatens to lick his face. "Are they happy doing this? Getting shipped halfway around the world to sniff around?"

"It's no good," Emiko says, "to think of happy or not happy. What they really want to do is chase squirrels." She wraps the leads around her hand to rein them in, then loosens them. Freedom and restraint. "But they do what they do because it is important. They understand."

Andy cocks his head. "Do they? Understand, that is?"

She holds Momo's head in her hand. "What do

you think, Momo? Do you understand?" She lets go, and Momo jumps onto him, all tongue and slobber.

An hour later, the cranes stop their work. It's time to explore. The setting sun turns the ground to lava, a molten road. But inside the wreck, the darkness consumes everything. Andy's right hand curls into a half claw, sore from clutching his torch. He calls out, "Anyone there? Can you hear us?" with as much strength as his diaphragm can muster. Sometimes, he thinks he hears someone calling back, and his heart seizes for a second before he realizes it's his own echo. And in that instant between hope and realization, his insides churn. He expects too much. Maybe saving lives is a drug. Maybe he's experiencing withdrawal.

Mexico City, Andy reminds himself. A fluke. A bona fide miracle. Bhuj is a city of unlucky bastards.

Dr. Cameron tells Andy to concentrate on reaching survivors. Think about the living—*yes*—but what can he do for those who give up? His father on the A682, just past Barrowford, the one-lane road, the ice in February, the tight corners, a lorry pressing into his lane—the cause didn't matter, because the result was the same: his dad flipped the car, shattered his legs, and went from selling medical equipment to requiring it. After the accident, it hurt for him to stand for longer than ten minutes. And—his father—just *gave up*.

He feels like shit for hating his father for something that wasn't his fault, but he hated the ugly blue Tesco shirt his mum had to wear because she had to go back to work, he hated living at home while doing his recruit course because Mum needed the extra money more than he needed his own flat, and he hated seeing his father deflate on the couch, becoming more globulous each day. The first time Andy came home in his recruit togs, his dad said, "Looking good there," in the same voice he used to greet the postman. But even if his father was proud, Andy couldn't reciprocate, and if what Andy had said in return made his father cry, well, that was that.

Momo barks.

"Here," Emiko shouts. "Over here!"

She stands next to a broken stairwell. Momo scratches at a crack in the ground.

"Are you sure?" Colin asks.

"Very likely," Emiko says.

"Maybe someone was in the basement when the building collapsed?" Les offers.

"Can we get a probe over here?" Colin says. "Hustle. Move!"

Sam brings the audio monitoring equipment

and snakes the microphone, thin as a whip, into the rabbit hole. He unspools the cable and jostles it to see if it will go any farther.

Colin looks at the purpling sky. "We need more light. Flood this area." Within minutes, army men carry two long pole lights. Colin clears the ground, kicking away pebbles. "Here," he says, pointing. "And here."

Sam gives a thumbs-up.

"Les," Colin says, "the honors?"

"Let Andy do it," Les replies. "He's been loafing around all day."

"I don't loaf," Andy says. "I do things."

"Likely story," Les says.

"Big talk from someone who's been playing with dogs all day. I've—" Andy stops because he realizes that Les is joking. Les's smile slips into puzzlement. Sam hands Andy a pair of comically large headphones, which Andy slips over his ears, and the world goes mercifully silent.

Dr. Cameron keeps pushing. Enough already. *Fuck.* OK, Andy had been the one to discover his father. That day, he'd been doing equipment-carry training, a relay race with coiled hoses and mocked-up light portable pumps, and the assessor stood there with a stopwatch, looking disappointed in everyone. Andy, knackered, ignored him when he got home. His father had the telly to *Top of the Pops*. Just a week before, his father had asked how things were going, and Andy said, "Jesus, why do you care? You're a fucking waste," and his dad said, "Don't you talk to me that way," and Andy replied, "Tell me I'm wrong. Tell me." This conversation replayed itself every time Andy passed his father, and that day, he had no desire to relive it one more time.

And if Andy hadn't noticed his father's pallid complexion when he'd gotten home; and if Andy hadn't stayed in his room until he heard his mother come home and scream, "Andy, Andy, come quick!"; and if Andy had hesitated touching his father's flabby neck to check for a pulse; and if Andy had performed chest compressions so violently that his father's sternum cracked—if all these things had happened or hadn't happened, what difference did it make?

"My father is dead," Andy tells Dr. Cameron, and Dr. Cameron responds, "I know."

"I hear something," says Andy.

"What?" says Colin. "What is it?"

"Scratching."

"Are you sure it's not static?" Les asks. "Sometimes the wires get staticky. Shite Chinese equipment."

"Everyone shut the fuck up!" says Andy. The men look at him as if he's never said a harsh word in his life. "I can't hear a fucking thing with all this noise."

"You heard him," Colin says. "Settle down."

Andy presses the headphones tight. Anything. Anything at all. *Just a sign. One sign and we can get you out.*

The sound is so faint that it could be a sigh.

"Someone's down there!" Andy cries. "I'm sure of it."

"Well, let's *be* sure," Colin says. "Get the video probe. We can't do much more heavy digging, or this place will collapse on our heads."

"The void down there," Andy says. "It's big enough to sustain oxygen levels."

Colin waves Sam over. "I believe you, Andy," he says. "But we have to be completely sure."

Andy's legs feel jittery. Fuck the shrink and his stupid diagnoses. He *is* concentrating on the living. Someone is down there, and Andy will move this building, piece by goddamn piece. Andy will go down into the void and brave the nail points poking out of walls and razor-sharp shards of glass, and he will climb deeper into the earth than he has ever gone, and he will come face-to-face with this person, this lonely, trapped soul, and look him in the eye and nod, just once.

Sam sets up the video equipment, which consists of holding lead cords and finding sockets to put them in. He turns on the video monitor, but nothing shows.

"What are you waiting for?" asks Andy.

"We need to know what condition the victim's in before we start moving things around," Les says.

"I know, I know—" But Andy is tired of corpses. The piles of ash on the road, the char marks like an exploding star. Those used to be people. The bittersweet stench—he's smelled it on burn victims, on remnants of hair singed away in a flash, on blackened skin peeling off in gooey sheets.

"We're go," says Sam, giving a thumbs-up. Andy wants to snap that thumb right off. The screen is a field of white. The camera, the size of his pinkie finger, points at nothing, and the light attached to the camera radiates outward, a single white dot.

"Feed the line in," Mike says. Les has coils of fiber-optic cable looped over his shoulder, and he spools it into the hole. "Follow the microphone line." Andy puts the headphones back on. If only he could send a message—*We're coming; we're coming*—through the microphone. Les waggles the cable. The on-screen blur makes Andy's eyes hurt. He understands why epileptics have fits. Overwhelming flashes of light.

"Left, left," says Sam. "OK, got it."

Andy concentrates. Blood whooshes in his ears. He can't remember the last time he was so conscious of silence, its utter emptiness.

Andy fills his life with noise from all directions, because if he's doing *something,* then he never has to stop, and if he doesn't stop, then he doesn't have to listen to the dull throb in his temples.

The screen goes dark. They've reached the void.

Andy eases up on the headphones. He's been pressing them so hard his ears ache. Everyone's mouths move without sound.

"Nothing on the monitor, sir," says Sam.

The team gathers around the screen, hushed by empty space.

"Give it a moment," says Les.

I heard something. I know it.

Les guides the camera deeper, unwinding it at a steady pace. The void is no larger than a sleeping bag, but on-screen, it seems without limits. If you were to wake up in a black space, how would you know if you were alive or dead? Maybe people in voids are neither living nor dead. It's not until someone finds them—hours, days, *weeks* later— that they become one or the other. It's worse, in a way, than death: this suspended animation, this not knowing. All it takes for you to live or die is for someone to *see* you.

The men crowd around the screen. From Andy's angle, all he sees is a shimmer of white on the screen, like the outer edge of a dream. Les points; Reg has his hands on Colin's shoulders, leaning forward; Emiko stands on tiptoe. All of them squint.

And Andy hears it: breathing. Shallow, so quiet that it might not exist if someone weren't there to hear it.

"Aspiration!" Andy yells. "I hear someone aspirating!"

Such a beautiful sound! He could listen to it all night. Inhale. Exhale. Someone is alive; there's been a miracle here after all; God is not cruel and capricious. It means they'll work all night, and that they'll bring someone out alive.

Everyone stays transfixed to the screen.

"Did you hear me?" Andy says. He stands, but the headphones yank his head back.

He looks at the screen. He sees what they see. The light shines on a small figure crumpled on the ground: a dog, lying on its side, its flank moving so imperceptibly that it might be screen flicker. The dog has its eyes open, its mouth open, and it moves its head as if to acknowledge the presence of the light, before it resumes its previous position in the void between worlds.

Mike gathers everyone.

"I'm proud of all of you," he says. "Everyone put in one hundred and ten percent, working hard and nonstop. We've saved lives."

"Sir," says Andy.

"We've earned a rest. New teams are coming in who are fresh and ready to go."

"Sir," repeats Andy.

"So as of now"—Mike looks at his wristwatch, making this act official—"I'm ordering the team to stand down."

"Sir!" says Andy, loud enough to be heard.

"McGreevey?"

"Shouldn't we try to save her? She's still trapped. I'm not sure how much longer she can survive." Andy hears her scratching, paws scrabbling futilely, searching for the ephemeral light. "We all saw it. She's still alive. She's all alone." He feels like he's inhaled helium, light-headedness, lack of breath. The others have stowed their gear, brushed themselves off, heaved themselves back onto the truck. Even Emiko is aboard, Momo and Kami in tow.

"We can't leave her," Andy says. "We can't."

He can do it by himself. The dog is maybe ten or twenty feet underground. He can dig out a passage. The dog is dehydrated, starving, but can live another day or so. He can work all night, all day tomorrow. Maybe some of the replacement teams can lend a hand. It will be hard, but he can save her. She's as worthy as anything else of living, isn't she? And that's what they do, isn't it? Save lives?

The team turns away from him. If it were Momo and Kami trapped down there, they'd

315

break their fucking backs to get them out. He hates them. Cowards, one and all: Colin, and his shitty, screaming brood; Reg, who called him a *poofter* in the squad room; John, without a gram of brain for every kilogram of muscle; Sam, who claims to have a girlfriend but is too ugly to admit that it's a lie; and Mike—fucking Mike—

"Andy," Les says, gently. Andy has been squeezing his fists so tight that his knuckles bleed. Les puts a hand on Andy's shoulder. Anyone else, and Andy would have socked him. But not Les. Never Les. "You've done all you can," Les says. And right then, Andy knows what it must feel like for that dog: a flash of light, an instant of hope before plunging, irrevocably, back into darkness.

When Andy arrives back at the tents, Ted is waiting with another box. Last night, he could only finish half of the blood pudding. The tinned meat reminds him of a housewife he passed earlier, her body the color of Ribena, striated and bloated. Andy vomits into his mouth, and he can taste the blood pudding again: the salt, the sour of his stomach acid, the slickness of the fat. But instead of letting it spew onto his cheeks, down his chin, he forces it down. He'd never really fancied blood pudding. His father

316

did—Mum made it for Dad. Andy had to smother his in jam to stomach it.

Andy drops his equipment onto his cot. He's got to repack. The bus to Ahmedabad leaves tomorrow afternoon, and they're on it. These clothes he's worn for the last five days straight? Burn them, a big fucking bonfire. He's got a change of clothes in his sack, at the very bottom, wouldn't you know. He holds a T-shirt to his face and breathes deep. He still takes his laundry to Mum every other week, and she says, "So the hero still hasn't learned to wash his own clothes?" She smiles when she says it.

"I wouldn't stick you with more blood pudding than you could eat." Ted takes cans out of the box—corned beef, fruit cocktail—and sets the box down at the foot of the cot.

"No need," says Andy. "We're through." He has a pair of Skivvies somewhere—ah, here. "Our mission is over. We're leaving tomorrow."

Ted stares at the can tops, as if wondering what to do with them now.

Tomorrow, they'll stop in Frankfurt for a one-day layover for debriefing and relaxation, and they'll have a hotel. He wants nothing more than a proper shit, shower, and shave. He wants to be presentable so that when Dr. Cameron asks him, *How was it?* he can answer, *It was fine,* and if Dr. Cameron inquires about his outburst at Ashpura, he can say, *Momentary stress overload.* And if

317

Dr. Cameron persists, *What's causing this stress?* what will Andy say then?

Christ, what do people want from him?

Tomorrow in Frankfurt, there will be steak. Tomorrow, there will be lager.

Reg says, "Come on, Les. Let's give Andy some alone time with his *boyfriend.*"

Andy reaches for a can and, before he has time for regret, hurls it. Reg is too shocked to raise his arms in defense. There are so many ways this could go wrong: the hard metal lip hitting Reg's eye could blind him; the can striking him in the mouth could chip a tooth, leave him with a torn and bloody lip. But as it happens, the can hits him broadside on the forehead with a dull thunk. Reg staggers back, and Andy looks at Les, whose mouth is wide with disbelief.

"You little shit!" Reg roars. He rubs his head. He starts for Andy, but Les restrains him.

"Andy," Les says, "get out of here."

But he's ready for a fight. His hands—cracked and scraped as they are—are fists. *I'll show you.*

Ted tugs his elbow. "Let's go."

Les says, "Leave!"

Reg yells, "I'll report you!" He strains like a dog who's come to respect the leash.

"Come on," Ted says. Ted grabs Andy's bag and pulls him out.

"You'd *better* run," Reg says.

But there's nowhere to go. Everything is

waiting to swallow him up. The night is a void; the sky is a void. Ted is a void. They go past the fire, past Ted's tent. They shouldn't even be out walking; curfew is in effect. But the final destination doesn't matter. It's still nowhere.

When they stop, Ted asks, "Why'd you do that?"

Andy shakes him off. "That cunt's been on my back for months."

"But that's no reason to—"

"Yes," says Andy, "it is." Andy holds out his hand for his pack. "I need to go back."

"I think you should cool off first."

"I don't care what you think. Just give it here." Andy tries to grab his rucksack, and Ted swings it behind his back. "I'm not playing." He wants to be rid of Ted, like when he sneaks out of a stranger's flat or when he kicks a stranger out of his own flat: *No offense, but I have trouble sleeping with someone else in my bed.* But he and Ted haven't slept together; they've only danced around one another, circling, sniffing. It's much easier to be rid of someone when you know what they need, and you fulfill that need.

"Don't go just yet," Ted says. "Come with me."

Oh—what the hell. A condemned man's last wish.

Ted leads Andy to a dark hotel. Men have paid for hotels before; men have offered to pay his way through life: men of means, men who form words

319

as crisp as freshly pressed sheets. And Andy can't say that he hasn't been tempted. He could have been like one of those Marylebone lapdogs: too pampered to even walk on the ground. Too helpless to do anything for themselves. He was fifteen when he first had to bathe his father. His mum usually did it, but a year after his father's accident, paralysis set in, as if the daily handfuls of pills hadn't just numbed the pain but everything else as well. That evening, Mum had worked a double shift, and she called for Andy to help, a half scream that made him think that maybe his father had slipped, split his head on the bathtub. But no: his father simply couldn't hold up his own weight, and Mum was too tired to support him any longer. "Get his feet," she said. His father—half-submerged—was naked, and his pasty skin floated on the surface like foam. He didn't seem ashamed that his wife and, now, son had to see him like this. His limp penis bobbed in the water like a lamprey. "What are you looking at?" he asked, and Andy said, "Nothing." His mother dipped a washcloth into the water, and the ripples shifted islands of foam onto his penis, a dead thing. "Wash his feet," his mum said, handing Andy the cloth. His feet were swollen and bulbous, the veins blue beneath the skin. His toenails disappeared beneath encroaching flesh. It was all Andy could do to touch him. The air smelled of the same soap he used himself, but it had a sour undertone, a smell Andy would always associate with hopelessness, failure. As the tub drained, his mum said, "Thank you, Andy," but his father said nothing—not even a nod of acknowledgment, as if this were an everyday occurrence in Andy's duties as a son—which it did, in fact, become. He doesn't want to say he felt relieved when his father died, but he doesn't know how else to describe it.

Andy's surprised that the hotel is intact. Most multilevel structures have been decimated, and still-standing buildings are only distant spots on the horizon, mirages of how things should have been. Inside the lobby, Tilley lamps glow on their lowest setting. It's a fire hazard, using those indoors. An Indian man rises off the floor to greet them. He picks up a nearby lamp, which casts a brief light on his family in the corner. His wife, fully dressed, curls around a young child. They sleep on a thin sheet. Even through his boots, Andy feels the cold marble.

Other families are clustered across the floor. The room wheezes, moans. The man leads them through, Andy's boots making a terrible thump as he walks. He's disturbing the dead. The man goes into a dark stairwell, and Andy looks for cracks, structural deficiencies. There are so many ways to get trapped. He wonders if he's heading into one now.

All men want something. His body, his good

looks, his vitality—from the bottomlessness of youth, he can provide these things. They run their hands over his skin and say, *So hot. So fucking lovely.* For a few minutes, he is everything to them. They are a cup, and he is a well. They are hungry, and he is flesh.

The Indian man leads them to a room and places the lantern on the ground, where it casts a buttery circle of light.

"Must be nice," Andy says. "Scoring a hotel room."

"It's not mine," Ted replies. "It's a . . . friend's."

"A friend—" Andy says, sotto voce.

"Get undressed," Ted says.

This is a familiar ritual. Andy knows the fasteners of his turnout trousers like he knows his own skin: the metal clip at his hip, the interior and exterior sockets for suspenders. He leaves the trousers bunched around his boots like he does at the station, ready to be jumped in and pulled up. He's imagined having sex with Ted since they met, the way he imagines himself having sex with all the men he meets. He pulls off his shirt, steps out of his underwear. The easy part.

Ted takes the lantern to the bathroom and calls, "Come on in." His voice diffracts, beckoning the entire room. He sits in the shower stall on a child-size plastic stool. He's rolled up his shirtsleeves. He holds out a hand.

Andy steps onto the tiles. It's like stepping

onto an ice sheet. Ted dips a sponge into a bucket near the drain and squeezes it out. He brings it up to Andy's chest and hesitates, as if hitting an invisible barrier, before touching it to Andy's skin.

"That's cold," Andy says, flinching. Andy's nipples are so swollen they feel like they could burst, and Ted spins him around to scrub his back. Andy smells the layers of sweat dissolving, scales of dirt and grime falling away. Droplets lance down his body, and each hair pricks up in response. The sponge squishes like wet footsteps. The lamplight catches different pieces of Ted's face: the flat plain of his cheek, a glow at the tip of his nose, a shimmer of his eye. But Andy can't put them together.

Andy asks, "What do you want?"

Ted doesn't respond. He wipes Andy's face, runs his wet, withered fingers through Andy's hair. Andy knows that Ted wants him. The weight of that want suffocates the room. But Ted continues to bathe him. Andy can't stand the silence. He arches his feet against the pooling water. If Ted were to say something, Andy would have some confirmation of desire, confirmation that this bath isn't just a duty. Ted has to be the one to say it. That something lies beyond this moment that they can look forward to.

Ted wraps Andy in a towel. The towel doesn't have a smell—not the overpowering florals of his mum's detergent or the bleach and industrial chemicals of cheap hotels. It smells neutral, the smell that's the absence of smell, as if it's waiting to absorb his smell like so much water.

He should get dressed and leave, find his way back to camp. Reg will have reported him; Colin's probably writing up a penalization form. What a palaver. He should tell Ted thanks and push on. Andy's skin is damp, mottled with goose pimples. He pulls on the clean T-shirt, a fresh pair of boxers. It seems foolish, considering that in a moment he'll hop into his grotty turnout trousers. But right now—

Ted says, "Stay with me. Just for a little."

Ted leaves the lantern in the bathroom, where it glows like a lost ghost. Andy can't see Ted's face. The bed sighs as Ted lies on it. "I understand if you can't." And it's true; he can't. Roll call will come at six sharp. This room is a hole, so deep, so far down that they'll never be discovered, and Andy crawls onto the bed, where he lies, legs bent, back hunched. Ted sidles against him. They sink into each other. Ted's warmth is like a blanket, and Andy pulls Ted's arm across his body as if covering up. Ted's breath on his neck, their heartbeats, the friction on Andy's skin as they shift incrementally: Would anyone hear these tiny things? Does anyone know they're alive?

Andy doesn't remember falling asleep. Exhaustion overtakes him softly and violently, like a cannon filled with feathers. It's a shock when he opens his eyes to an Indian gentleman in a medical jacket, arms crossed, staring. Ted is still wrapped around him. It's still dark, but Andy knows he's in a shit-ton of trouble.

The Indian fellow leans down and whispers, "It's time for you to go."

Andy doesn't head back right away, though he should. He stays in the shadows, where he's less likely to get nabbed by a patrol. He looks behind at the medical camps, the only source of electric light in the city. A beacon, sort of. In the opposite direction, the sky seems indistinguishable from the ground, a single expanse, and the stars have come to earth in the form of fires.

He sits, knees drawn up to his chest. He's royally fucked things up. He squeezes his arms tight around his legs, making himself as small as possible. Maybe he can disappear into himself. It was nice to melt into Ted, to not worry for a while. But that probably made things worse. The pendulum at camp has probably swung from anger to worry and all the way back to anger. In his immediate future: reprimands, disciplinary actions, first for attacking Reg and second for going AWOL. There's a reckoning coming.

But he can put it off a little while longer. This is the last time he's going to be here. This place should mean something more than his fight with

Reg. More than the woman he saved. More than Ted, even.

But as he waits, he becomes aware of the silence once again, how it stretches so far that he can hear how everything is connected. For instance, when he shifts his weight from one foot to the other, the dirt grinds underneath his ass, his clothes rustle, and items in his pack shift and clang. And sounds from far away become acute: from a temple in the distance, lit with torches, people chant, a mysterious susurrus, punctuated with a sharp, tinny sound. A bell. Someone's ringing a bell in the middle of the night. A prayer to silence. The temple sends forth such a tiny light, such a tiny sound, that it may as well be a firefly cupped in a divine hand.

Yeah, I hear you.

He dusts himself off. There are people in real pain, and here he is, acting mopey dopey. He's been gone for too long, and he's got to collect his equipment, prepare his reports, take his lumps. No more wasting time. His father used to say *daylight's burning* at night, trying to be funny, but he tried being a lot of things. Now the phrase is stuck in Andy's head. It's nearing daybreak: the sky has taken on a blue tinge, a blue that's almost black. Near the horizon, stars extinguish themselves. If daylight burns, then the fuse is blue. The sky waits to catch fire.

He hears voices behind him—whispery,

indistinct—and pays them no mind. Then he hears two loud cracks in the air. Gunshots. And before he can react, he feels an overwhelming force, a heat that knocks him forward onto his knees. And then, sounds stop altogether: all he hears now is a high pitch deep within his ear, a cochlear emergency tone. A warmth spreads over him, like he's being doused in Mentholatum. Brightness creeps into his peripheral vision. *Daylight's burning,* his father says. So soon? Look: past the boots surrounding him, the sky is still obviously dark. Any fool can see. He keeps his eyes fixed on the horizon, too numb to react. The warmth enveloping him is too much to bear. Hands pull the sack off his shoulder and pat down his pockets. It can't be dawn yet, but there's the sun, blinding. Daylight's burning. Come on. Let's go.

PRIORITY PATIENTS

—Priority patient, the nurse announces. —Priority patient coming in!

What the term really means is that a white person has hurt himself.

Médecins Sans Frontières has set up modular field hospitals, six surgical tents, side by side. The initial four Trigano tents used for surgery are still operational, but patients want to be treated in the newer tents.

MSF has also doubled the number of patient tents, all of which have filled to capacity. Sunlight illuminates the tents during the day, the translucent plastic glowing like an incandescent bulb. All injuries are visible. But at night, the soldiers dim the overhead lights so that the tents are trapped in eternal twilight. Electrical power, though restored, is intermittent. The temperature reaches a few degrees above zero Celsius, and the injuries become shadows, darkened murmurs that occasionally break through the painkillers.

Two paths lead from the surgical tents, both well trod, the ground sunken and compacted. The first leads to the patient tents. The other leads to where bodies are stacked to be buried or incinerated.

· · ·

Dev has seen two priority patients so far. The first was a Frenchman, who twisted his ankle constructing temporary housing. By the time he reached Dev, his ankle was black, and his foot had swollen to the size of a melon. Dev cut his boot off with surgical shears. The man was medevaced out, a waste of resources.

The second was a young American woman, a college student. She was having a panic attack, inconsolable, alternating between screaming and sobbing. She could not describe what had prompted the attack; she hugged herself while crying and pulled her hair while screaming. This continued for hours. None of the other patients, the "nonpriority" ones, could sleep. Eventually, Dr. Ferrell, the other doctor in the tent, also American, held her down, and Dev gave her an injection of phenobarbital sodium. She, too, was evacuated.

The only painkillers available are aspirin and morphine. No middle ground: no tramadol, no meperidine. Dev distributes aspirin like a garnish. A single soldier guards the morphine in an air-conditioned trailer. Only medical personnel know which tarp hides it. When Dev opens a box, the cardboard is so cold that his hands shake as he tears through the plastic wrap. The vials shake and tinkle like chimes.

If it weren't for morphine, no one would get any sleep at all.

A nurse parts the flap of Dev's tent. —Priority patient, she says. —An emergency.
—I heard. Bring him in.
The nurse ties back the tent flaps.
—Some action at last, says Dr. Ferrell.
Dev shrugs. Dev heard about, but didn't see, the priority patient who was slashed in the face with a machete.

The need for surgeons has shifted from emergency to orthopedic. Even in the best of conditions, medicine is not an exact science. Limbs set in haste are now as lumpy as poorly mixed dough. Many makeshift splints—wooden planks, bamboo poles, metal tubes—have not been replaced. Dev sees them and thinks, *That was mine; that was mine.* What he had done now needs correction.

Last night, an elderly woman with two skull fractures tried to rip the bandage off her head. After the first few layers, the gauze adhered to the dried blood and lymph, but before she caused herself serious damage, a nurse restrained her. Dev has heard the woman's story: during the earthquake, she had rushed inside the house for her grandchildren, but—all gone, all gone. Why is she alive? she demands. For hours, she fingers the edge of the bandage, like she wants to rip open her own head.

Dev, on arrival, worked over sixty hours continuously before resting. Then, a flood of foreign doctors, coming to take pity. One mistook Dev for a translator. *What is that man saying?* he asked. *Can you tell him that I'm here to help?*

Tell him yourself, Dev said.

People always take advantage of one's generosity.

With this surfeit of doctors, mobile medical teams rove the outlying villages. Things seem well taken care of. In a day or so, Dev will leave. He is finished here.

Dev washes his hands with water from a collapsible water jug and dons gloves with a snap. The latex pulls at hairs on his hands and wrists.

At New Delhi General, a *priority patient* means an ill dignitary or a Bollywood star having a "procedure," but here, in Bhuj, it suggests a hierarchy. Dev challenges any doctor to look a patient in the eye and tell her that she is not a priority.

They play a dangerous game, coming to "save" India.

—This way, this way, the nurse calls. Both Dev and Dr. Ferrell are prepped, though neither has been apprised of the incoming injuries. Another waste of resources: these gloves, this face mask, their time. MSF took control of the medical cluster to avoid duplicating efforts, but no one seems concerned about waste. Dev can think of ten efficiency measures off the top of his head. But he's only here to help.

Two soldiers appear, carrying an improvised stretcher, a blanket secured over two wooden planks. The priority patient has arrived.

Unknown subject, Caucasian male, approximately twenty-five years of age. Brought to field hospital at 9:11 a.m. Attending physicians, Drs. Khanna and Ferrell; assisting, nurses Sharma and Zinta. UnSub pale from blood loss, barely detectable pulse. Unconscious from shock, unresponsive to verbal commands. Intravenous morphine. Two gunshot wounds (caliber unknown) to lower and midabdomen, most likely 9 mm small arm. N. Sharma shears clothing, and N. Zinta inserts tube for stomach decompression. Exit wounds suggest left kidney and liver in danger. First unit of blood administered. N. Sharma sterilizes area with iodine. D. Khanna incises from bottom of sternum to navel. N. Sharma prepares portable battery-operated suction. After six-centimeter incision in peritoneum, N. Sharma inserts suction line. Tube occludes with blood clots but clears. Peritoneum set back and secured with plastic microvascular clips. Blood flooding cavity, more than mechanical unit can handle. Second unit of blood. D. Khanna requests N. Zinta to apply additional hand suctioning with Jackson-Pratt drain. Damaged liver apparent. Bile in cavity. Bowel also perforated, leaking contents. D. Khanna to concentrate on wound to upper and midtranspyloric plane; D. Ferrell to concentrate on lower. Third unit of blood. D. Khanna places swab beneath liver. D. Ferrell wraps gauze compress around bowel. Cavity rinsed with saline to improve visibility. Urine in catheter bag shows blood, suggests damage to left kidney. D. Ferrell repairs bowel while D. Khanna examines second bullet track. Fourth unit of blood. Pulse extremely weak. Damage to liver extensive. Momentary displacement of liver shows gallbladder also perforated. Forceps used to clamp hole in gallbladder. N. Zinta's bulb full; replaced to resume suction. Gauze beneath liver saturated, replaced. Fifth unit. Undersurface of liver has large, bleeding laceration. Attempt to close fissure with metal clamp results in crushing. Wide stitching used instead. Surface begins to clot. Lack of bile in cavity suggests biliary ducts intact, bile leakage from gallbladder alone. D. Ferrell examines intestines for additional holes, sutures as necessary. Heavily damaged sections (bruised, torn) will require bypass. Interior bleeding continues unabated;

blood pressure near undetectable. Sixth unit. Further examination shows second bullet track continuing past liver and into biliary system, possibly breaching inferior vena cava or portal/hepatic veins. Amount of blood lost greater than amount intravenously introduced. N. Sharma indicates UnSub declining precipitously. D. Ferrell pronounces left kidney unsalvageable, must be excised. Second gauze compress beneath liver removed, replaced. D. Khanna conducts examination of veins from lower transpyloric plane upward. Seventh unit. Inferior vena cava from renal vein onward appears intact. Possibility of bullet ricocheting off a rib and traveling transverse. Blood escaping at constant drip. D. Ferrell momentarily assumes J-P drain; N. Zinta to retrieve additional units of blood. Portal vein appears intact from superior mesenteric onward. N. Sharma announces UnSub crashing. Examination of hepatic veins shows that two have been completely severed by bullet; third under significant, possibly unsustainable strain. Blood pressure drops to zero. UnSub enters cardiac arrest. D. Ferrell suggests manual coronary palpitation. D. Khanna declines. Given current operating conditions, performing bypass procedure impossible. D. Khanna declares patient dead. 9:48 a.m., February 2, 2001. N. Zinta instructed to return eighth unit of blood to storage.

• • •

Death is not a switch. One is not *alive* one moment and *dead* the next. It is a biological process. His father taught him the four-point 1968 Harvard Committee definition: total unresponsitivity, no movement or breathing over a period of at least an hour, no reflexes, and, in the absence of severe hypothermia or central nervous system depressants, a flat encephalogram for twenty-four hours with no measurable change. These are standard evaluations for death.

To say, then, that this young man is *dead* is a lie. He has suffered a *clinical death*. His heart has stopped, and his respiration is nil. If they were in Delhi, Dev could put him on an artificial respirator to compensate for his collapsed lung. He could compress the boy's heart and keep the blood circulating. He could continue transfusions, more blood, more oxygen. It is possible to come back from clinical death. He has seen it. He has done it.

But Dev also knows he should have checked for the vein rupture before repairing the gallbladder and liver. No one would blame him, though, not in the heat of emergency. Not when *two* people were required for suction. Perhaps if his and Dr. Ferrell's positions had been reversed, Dr. Ferrell would have done the same. Who can say for sure?

After the point after which no revival is possible comes *biological death,* usually about four minutes after the clinical death. Brain activity ceases completely. Electrocerebral silence.

The nurse gathers the operating equipment—the scalpels, the hemostats, the clamps, twinkling stainless steel objects—to be boiled. Dr. Ferrell removes his face mask. His breath is audible, a low, stuttering grunt. Dev stares at the patient's face. At any moment, he will witness his biological death, irrevocable proof of failure.

Yet even after biological death, *cellular death* has not ensued. This is the basis of organ transplantation: not everything dies all at once. An excised kidney, for instance, continues to produce urine with a perfusion. It becomes a matter of keeping the tissue from necrotizing before it has been transplanted. This young man could have been a wellspring: corneas, pancreas, blood. Too many here have died of acute renal failure, after their crushed muscles flooded their kidneys with myoglobin. The dialysis unit of the Renal Disaster Relief Task Force has been delayed. In the meantime, medical workers have sent out the word: if your urine turns dark, seek help immediately. But the afflicted stay silent, as if accepting suffering were the same as minimizing it.

The nurse asks, —Can I aid you?

Dev shakes his head no. He yanks off the gloves with a single motion, before the blood can stiffen. The nurse holds a garbage bag for him. His fingers are damp, slightly slick. The boy's skin is still warm to the touch. His core temperature won't drop noticeably for at least an hour.

A waste, a terrible waste.

An act of nature he can understand: the unknown forces of the universe are blameless. But this—this was intentional. A conscious act of evil. He should have suspected the trajectory of the bullet. Maybe given another unit of blood. The nurse had it in her hands. Perhaps Ferrell had other ideas for resuscitation; something he'd learned at a conference while Dev ossified in clinical practice. But he had stopped, and now the boy continues to die multiple deaths.

The boy's comrades wait outside the tent for word about his condition. The sun casts their silhouettes against the thick canvas. This death, unlike the others, cannot go unremarked upon. This is grounds for an international incident, and Dev will be caught in its midst.

A grim duty, this knowledge.

But he has delivered unhappy information many, many times before. One grows accustomed to it. Back in Delhi, he once treated a *kabari* who had contracted HIV. His wife had sought help for him; she hadn't even known of HIV until one of the other ragpickers told her. She reeked of filth, and the admittance staff refused to let her enter the clinic. She was barefoot. It had taken her most of the day to walk there. Dev wondered if the man had contracted HIV from a prostitute, but in his line of work, scavenging through people's refuse, he may have been pricked by a syringe.

The next day, Dev and Preeta, the prevention-outreach worker, traveled to the Ghazipur landfill where the man worked. All eighty acres of it rose from the ground like a cliff face. The people here were ants, picking through the wreckage for whatever could be collected and sold. When people threw something *away,* this was *away.* The stench made Preeta gag.

Slum camps ringed the area, each specializing in a product: tangles of wire, bales of clothing, dizzying arrays of nuts and bolts and small shards of metal. But all Dev could see were iterations of death. Families leaving cooking fires burning, allowing the carbon monoxide to suffocate them in their sleep. Split-off timbers waiting to impale; crushing hulks of concrete balancing precariously overhead; rust-flecked metal cables promising tetanus.

The wife brought Dev and Preeta to a hovel, a latticework of bamboo poles and a roof of rewoven basket thatch, patched with plastic bags. The man was covered by a thin blanket with a Jet Airways insignia stitched in its corner.

He's wasting away, the wife said.

The man had Kaposi sarcomas on his arms

338

and shoulders, cancerous craters. His wife, too, was most likely infected. Her son, sporting a dirt mustache, ran up to Preeta and offered her a bent earring. He was no older than six. The woman instructed her son to settle down, and he went back to shredding plastic bags and stuffing the scraps into a larger bag. (Five rupees a kilogram, Preeta later told him.) The boy, too, might have been infected. He was severely anemic, malnourished.

Can you give my husband medicine? the wife asked. She clinked coins in her hand, surely no more than a few rupees. *Please,* she said. She held up her savings. Her hand was nicked and cut, the thin scabs crosshatching her skin. All she had were a few paise. Not enough, even, to buy the dust at the bottom of a pill bottle.

We will do what we can, Preeta said. She covered her mouth and nose with her hand, like she was trying to catch her own words.

As they exited, Preeta said, *Did you notice? Most of the trash pickers are women.* A refuse truck rumbled in. It dumped its contents with a pneumatic push, and in its wake, silence. But then, the cry of egrets circling ceaselessly overhead, and the steady crunch, crunch as people walked over the new offerings: half a toilet seat, discarded diapers, empty bags of chips. Cattle roamed the area. One boy found a carton of something and ate from it.

Over the next six months, Preeta returned to Ghazipur three more times for awareness sessions, emphasizing syringe safety. She told them to avoid medical waste. She taught them the biohazard symbol. She handed out pamphlets.

I'm sure those went directly into the recycling piles as soon as I left, she said. *But I had to try.*

On her final trip, before she left to take a job in New York, Preeta informed Dev that the man had died. His widow and son had disappeared.

Dev's gown is smeared with the boy's blood. He has no time to change into something more presentable, so he removes it, balls it up, throws it in the corner. They will preserve the boy's body for the inevitable inquiry. The blood bank will serve as a makeshift morgue. One nurse closes the incisions with hasty and uneven stitches, while the other wipes the body clean of blood. There's too much of it. Color has begun to drain from the boy's face. He is handsome, this boy, and immediately Dev feels shame heat his cheeks. Desire always comes unbidden, quick and vicious, like a mosquito.

—Are you well? a nurse asks. The question sounds odd coming from another person's mouth.

Dev nods. —I need to catch my breath, he says.

He sits on a child-size plastic stool, something Arusha would use. Decals are stuck to its surface, butterflies and bunches of flowers that have begun to peel away from the surface. The legs bow beneath his weight. He can't recall the last time he laid with Padma. Not since Arusha's birth. They sleep beside one another in their nightclothes. She makes no moves toward him, and they both breathe quietly, as if waiting for Arusha to make a sound. As a courtesy, he relieves himself outside of her presence, and never with another person. Not since Ted. Dev tries not to think of Ted at all. Ted is so distant that he comes from another era, when people like Dev were expected to kowtow to him. The world is no longer this way, and the sooner both he and Ted realize it, the better off they'll be.

Years from now, Dev will encounter Preeta at a conference in Washington, DC; Padma and the children will have come along. Arusha will be fourteen and defiant; sensitive, quiet Amrita will be a gangly ten; Arjun will be five. For them, it will be a vacation.

Preeta and Dev will greet each other with hugs—*Look at you! You haven't aged a bit! Liar!* She will live in New York City, still working in prevention and outreach. She will tell him, *You went to school with Mark Rifkin, didn't you? You know what happened to him?*

She will whisper, *He lost his license.* But not only that: he will have been arrested at the airport with illegal methamphetamines and have had criminal charges filed against him for treating patients while intoxicated.

Dev will know that Rifkin is not alone. Other doctors specializing in HIV have also fallen into addiction, depression, suicide. The tide they tried desperately to hold back swept them out to sea.

Back in the hotel, his family will prepare for dinner. Padma will have Arusha in the bathroom, teaching her how to apply eyeliner. Amrita will have given up trying to join them. Arjun will sprawl on the bed, watching cartoons. Dev has made the right decision. His family is a beautiful, precious thing. This is all a man can ask.

But even so, he will feel a violent clamor inside him, like a falling bell.

Amrita will approach and ask, *Are you well?* She will wipe a tear off his cheek with her palm.

Yes, darling, he will say. He will pick her up, put her in his lap. *Just remembering a dream.*

Was it a bad dream?

No, he will say. *It wasn't a bad dream. But it wasn't a happy one, either.*

—Shall we? Dr. Ferrell asks.

Outside the tent, the men are a puddle of uniforms, the same uniform he and Dr. Farrell cut the boy from. The uniforms disturb Dev, the color of jaundice, hepatitis, cirrhosis. The color

342

of excess bilirubin in the blood. Even before Dev fully emerges, they barrage him with questions: —How he is? Will he make it?

The tallest among them raises his arm to staunch the babbling, and they hold their breath.

—Your friend has suffered serious injuries, Dev says, and the rest of the sentence should come easily, but it does not. Dev is blinded by the reflective stripes on their uniforms, by their expectant faces, and as he moves his hand to shield his eyes, he realizes where he has seen these uniforms before: the boy wore one, of course. But Dev remembers the uniform from long before the boy was brought into the tent. He remembers it from when he came into his hotel room and saw Ted sleeping there with the boy, pressed against each other like clasped hands; he interrupted them, too exhausted to be angry, and as Ted sputtered apologies, the boy pulled up his uniform, the stripes on his shoulders catching the light from the lantern, shining fluorescent for one brief flash, an unmistakable brightness, and sneaked off. That boy now lies beneath a sheet, and the explanation dries in Dev's throat. The words choke away. He tries to keep his face neutral, but surely the men can read the failure on his face. They study him for answers, and the answers do not come. The boy's death should be no different from the hundreds and thousands that have come before; these men will grieve no

343

differently than the residents of Bhuj, survivors one and all, bereaved one and all. Dev himself should treat this death no differently, but he circles back to seeing this boy, asleep, in Ted's arms, and sadness overwhelms him, not because the boy is dead, but because he could have been in the boy's place had his life gone another way, but that life is dead, and the boy is dead, and, for once, he cannot find the words to explain this.

—His wounds were too severe, Dr. Ferrell says. —He died during surgery. You have my deepest condolences.

And now comes the mourning. Dev braces himself.

Ted needs to know. Dev owes him that much. The more Dev prepares, the less likely he will be caught off guard and stumble over his words. The easier it will be to look Ted in the eye and tell him that his lover is dead.

Maybe not *lover*. Maybe *friend*. It is impossible to say with certainty how one relates to another. He and Ted, for instance. Ex-lovers, friends, earthquake acquaintances—all these and more. There is something pitiable about Ted, a kicked man who begs forgiveness for getting in the way of the foot. He tries to make things better by making things worse. Ted reminds him a bit of Padma. There's an unwhetted softness to both, as if the world's cruelty were constantly surprising. He's been careless with them, and he will always regret that.

The boy's pockets were empty when he was brought in. Death in the commission of a robbery. So much suffering, and for so little. There is no way to describe how someone has died in vain. Dev is unsure why he feels compelled to tell Ted. Why this duty falls upon him, he cannot say.

Up ahead, two men repair their house. One stirs a bucket of plaster, and the other, standing on a chair and using a length of plywood as a palette, slathers it into the cracks with his hands. They make no attempt to smooth their work. The house grows bulbous gray keloids. They are resourceful, these two, to have secured building materials. But the handkerchiefs around their mouths are insufficient to keep from inhaling airborne particulates. Their alveoli will clog, and their lungs will harden. In years to come, they will develop respiratory problems, a cough that rakes the inside of their chests like a trapped rodent.

—Is it true, one man asks the other, —that the jail has been destroyed? I heard that the Pakistani terrorists escaped.

—Pakistanis, his coworker mutters. He clears his throat, lifts the corner of the kerchief, and spits. —Hey, he calls to Dev. —What are you looking at?

—You are fortunate, Dev says, —to still have your house.

The man with the bucket shakes his head, and the one on the chair laughs. —This is not our house, the lower one says.

The world has returned to its mercenary ways, so soon. The looters, these workers, the *kabari*—the feeling of camaraderie from two days ago has dissipated. It seems as though while the dust was still in the air, individual desires were veiled off from the heart, but now that people can see what they had and what they did not, the desires have returned, stronger than ever—stronger, now, with survivor's purpose.

Dev sees Ted first, but Ted speaks first.

—What I did last night was completely inappropriate and inexcusable.

Dev waves his hand, as if fanning away smoke. —It's not important anymore, he says.

—I took advantage of your hospitality.

—Please, Dev says. —I have pressing matters I need to discuss with you.

—Go on, Ted says. —I'm listening.

But what is within Dev will not emerge. Sadness has no destination, only a sheer drop.

—I—, he says. Dev's hands tremble, a quiver that runs throughout his body. —I—

—Take your time.

I am sorry for your loss. I offer my condolences.

Ted is wrong; there is no time, and they sit next to each other, silent, for what seems like hours. Ted looks prepared to say something, and Dev prays that he doesn't, because it's too late, Dev thinks. Too late. If he was ever angry at Ted, it was not because of what Ted was or because of what Ted did; it was because of what Ted represents. Ted is a path Dev could never have chosen, a life he could never have led.

So be it.

Dev takes Ted by the hand and leads him away.

They walk to the cold storage unit. As Dev grasps the door handle, Ted holds his breath. Dev does the same.

The inside of the unit looks as though it's draped with a red curtain. The blood is organized by type, from A+ on the far left to O− on the right. In the center of the floor is the unknown subject. The floor here is the same as the other field hospitals, black-and-white parquet over plywood. Near the walls, the parquet curls into a wave. A thin sheet of plastic keeps him from sticking. Someone must have replaced the sheet covering him. The one in which he had been brought was bloodied. This one is stark white, dusted with frost. The last evaporations from his body.

Dev can't remember the boy's face. When he tries to picture it, he only sees Ted. And then, unbidden, he sees Padma, then a gross aggregate of the two. It's as if he wished them both dead. Ted's breath coalesces in midair and dissipates, like his soul made visible.

Dev pulls back the sheet, like he's preparing Arusha for bed. The boy's hair has become hoary with ice crystals, and he is suddenly inexplicably older. Dev hears people say all the time, *He's lived a good, long life.* No, Dev will *not* say that this boy lived a "good, long life," or that anyone has lived a "good, long life." He will not see death as something other than it is: a waste.

Without a word, Ted leaves.

Dev finds him outside, standing near the abutting generator. The generators stay on as a contingency. The low thrum prevents Dev from hearing Ted cry.

—Ted? Dev doesn't dare touch him. The ground beneath Ted grows moist.

—Andy, Ted says.

Ted punches the wall of the trailer. Dev hears his hand crack.

Another priority patient.

Dev binds Ted's hand in gauze. Ted sits impassively, but the tears don't stop. He gives Ted an aspirin because morphine is no good for this type of pain. Dev knows only one cure for grief.

The cure for sadness is not happiness. No.

Happiness, to Dev, is a balloon tied to the wrist of a child missing both her hands. Nor is the cure for sadness less sadness: after all, Dev feels less sad when Arusha sits in his lap and burbles sounds that might one day be words. He feels less sad when Padma presents him a meal after an excruciating day at the hospital. His sadness lessens, but remains.

No—the cure for sadness is the elimination of desire. This is the Buddhist ideal, a patient once told him. K____ had traveled to Delhi from Arunachal Pradesh for treatment. He was a scholar of the region's endangered languages, and when he died, his knowledge of those languages—Digaru, Sherdukpen, Hruso, Puriok—died with him. Shortly before his death, he stayed awake twenty hours a day, feverish, writing in a notebook. He had told his colleagues at Rajiv Gandhi University that he was ill but not from what.

CMV retinitis had already taken his right eye, so Dev sat on his left side.

The antiretrovirals are no longer having an effect, Dev said.

K____ continued writing.

We have a few options—, but K____ shook his head.

No more, K____ said.

But your work, Dev said. His handwriting was steady, crisp, but the ink blurred.

It is here, he said.

Don't you want to complete it?

K____ shook his head, no more than a shiver.

I cannot desire more than what I already have, K____ said, *because the more I desire, the more I suffer.*

Dev desires so much. He desires a life that had taken a different path. He desires the impossible, the unattainable, and these desires cause sadness. But, most of all, he desires to hold this crying man, whose hand is white with bandages. He desires to embrace him, comfort him. Right now, he desires nothing more than to avert someone else's sadness, to limit it, reduce it. But that he cannot—this, too, is sadness.

NORMALCY BIAS

Normalcy Bias, Defined

A fact: most people underestimate the extent of disaster. Piotr is never surprised to hear victims delude themselves. They interpret ambiguities as optimistic signs. The Indian government, for example, promised to restore power eight days ago, and each flickering lightbulb seems proof of their success. But these brief illuminations are merely tests, random surges. The Central Electricity Authority is at least three days away from bringing the grid back on line.

But he understands the impulse to hope for the best. People make plans for when things get "back to normal." They think their lives will be unchanged. *Things will get better, won't they?* they ask, and they answer themselves, *Things will be fine.*

This is normalcy bias at work.

The Cold Room

Ted's Indian doctor friend leads Lorraine and Piotr to where they store bags of blood. The body is a bag of blood. He and Ted are bags of blood.

A bullet would drain them as surely as it would drain any other of these bags.

Ted stares at the body in the center of the room. The white sheet erases the body's features. A blank spot. "I made a mistake," Ted says. The world is full of errors: filing errors, rounding errors, estimation errors. This is a simple identification error. The nurses have gotten accustomed to Ted standing there. They carve footpaths in the frost around him.

The cold sinks into Piotr's joints. His cartilage refuses to yield. But Piotr shudders, as if he's breaking out of ice, and this movement starts a chain: Ted sobs, then crumples.

Piotr watches the door.

Correct and Incorrect Prayers

Ted is on his knees, like his skin has frozen to the floor. "Let's pray," Lorraine says.

Piotr hasn't prayed in years. He doesn't keep kosher, hasn't been to synagogue, and works religiously on the Sabbath. When he and Rana are invited to a seder, he keeps his head bowed and mumbles the blessings. Rana thinks him ridiculous. "Better you say nothing at all," she says.

The last time he remembers praying was during Mikhail's birth, a long, difficult labor, and though he never truly feared, he entertained for one horrible moment the possibility that he might lose one or the other. But he could not imagine raising a child without Rana. And equally, he could not imagine life with Rana, who had already lost so much, losing a child as well.

He prayed: *Please, God, if you must take one, then take them both.*

But as soon as he thought it, he wanted to renounce it, the way others renounced their own counterrevolutionary activities: *I was wrong, and I regret my statements.*

"Dear Lord . . . ," Lorraine recites, and Piotr mumbles something that sounds vaguely holy.

Protocol in the Event of Serious Injury or Death

The protocol begins with information: who needs to know, in the order they need to know it. The consulate in New Delhi, USAID, etc. The protocol also addresses issues of whether or not to perform an autopsy, and how to institute inquiry proceedings. Piotr calls Carter Lansdale, the DART liaison for USAID, the first person in the protocol. The satellite phone presses against his face like an iron.

"There's been a death," Piotr says.

Silence. Words take time to traverse the globe, despite the illusion of instantaneousness. This is not a conversation, but a simulacrum of conversation. "A death?" Carter asks, as if he misheard the word. Piotr imagines Carter wiping his brow with his hand.

"Yes," Piotr says. "A death."

"Don't tell me it's one of the midwestern missionaries."

"No," Piotr says, shaking his head. "A British rescue worker."

Static crackles, fire on the line. The world awaits instructions.

"Oh," says Carter. "So it's not our problem. The Brits are going to be in a world of shit."

Piotr has never liked the word "shit." Too simplistic. No resonance, no power.

Contrast that to Rana's command of insults. Once, at an Astoria supermarket, a man with a cart loaded with groceries darted in front of her at a lane clearly designated "Ten Items or Fewer." He laughed, as if thwarting Rana had been his intent all along. He said something in Croatian to his companion, and Rana shouted, *Da Bog da ti žena rodila stonogu pa ceo život radio za cipele!*" Piotr knew better than to ask what it meant at that moment, but later, on the subway, he nudged her with his elbow, again and again, until she smiled. This was how it was: her fury needed time to burn itself through, and once it had concluded, she returned to him.

"It means," she said, "may your wife give birth to a centipede so that you will have to work for shoes all your life."

Now that was a curse!

He asked her to teach him an insult in Bosnian. Nothing profane, nothing graphic, nothing that would get him into a fight. Just a phrase that he could deploy like an inflatable life jacket. She had him practice, *Sanjam da prdnem na tebe*, syllable by syllable, until he had committed it to memory. She showed him how to curl his tongue on the *nj*, how to stress *prd* so that it had the force of a fist waved in the air.

He uses the phrase in situations that warrant it—in line to renew his international driver's license, for example. While standing next to a young woman on the subway. While typing a report at work. He has absorbed the words into his being such that when he first held Katia, he wondered if, in her burbling, she was trying to shape the sentence: *Sanjam da prdnem na tebe*.

After his pronunciation lesson, Piotr asked, "What does it mean?"

Rana covered her mouth. "I dream of farting on you."

They laughed, long and hard, like teenagers.

Awake

Carter has been speaking, but Piotr hasn't heard any of it. Carter's voice, a pleasant hum, circles in on itself until Piotr understands what he's saying.

"Did you get all that?" Carter asks.

"Yes," he replies.

"I know you can handle it."

True—but Piotr's hands shake nonetheless. He has been daydreaming. He *never* daydreams. He isn't entirely sure that he even dreams while sleeping, though, surely he must. More precisely, he doesn't *remember* his dreams, because his mornings have a definite shape. He snaps into being at five and slips out of bed without disturbing Rana, without rustling the sheets or making the mattress squeak. In the dark, he dons his bathrobe and checks on Katia, who sometimes snorts in her sleep. Not a delicate baby snort, but a rasp, a snarl. He rubs the soft bulge of her cheek. She is his responsibility in these hours before work, and she wakes, hungry and fussy, as the sun breaks over the buildings of Manhattan. He looks up from the duties imported from the office to attend to her. By the time Rana shuffles out to greet him, her hair an intractable mass of spun sugar, he has prepared breakfast.

He wonders what shape the day takes when he's overseas—if Rana gets any rest, if Katia howls incessantly, furious at her father's absence.

Not Intended as a Diagnostic Tool

Michelle is the vanguard of MSF mental health counselors, here to identify local nurses, teachers, and social workers for outreach. She trains them to listen, to talk people through their problems. "I hope the others get here soon," she says. "This place could *explode* from all the traumatic energy." Piotr appreciates the necessity of counseling, but his focus is on the bottom rung of Maslow's hierarchy: the needs that sustain life.

Lorraine speaks about therapy as if she were getting her nails done. She tried to rope Ted into therapy as soon as he joined. But not with Piotr. Not in all the years they worked together. Why, he doesn't know. He supposes it no longer matters.

"Michelle," he says, "would you speak with my colleague Ted? I think he may have—injured himself."

"Of course." She looks at him as though he's had an amputation. "Piotr—are *you* feeling OK?"

Piotr wipes his face. The condensation from the cold room has collected in his hair, on the stubble on his chin, in his eyebrows, on his eyelashes. He probably looks as though he's been crying.

"I am," he replies. And after a pause, "Thank you for asking."

She reaches in her bag and produces a sheet of paper. "I'd like you to fill one of these out."

The Impact of Event Scale. On a scale of zero to four, with zero representing "not distressing at all" and four representing "extremely distressing," he rates how bothered he has been by certain . . . difficulties. *I am jumpy and easily startled. I think about it when I don't mean to.* Piotr and the IES are like old friends, old friends who forgive little lies.

Normalcy Bias, in Writing

"At the moment of disaster, people suffer cognitive dissonance, which they resolve by disbelieving external stimuli. Research has shown that, under ideal situations, the brain can take eight to ten seconds to process new data. Stress situations slow that further. Thus, the brain may fixate on a solution, which may not necessarily be the life-preserving option. Alternately, people may also refrain from taking direct action while awaiting additional information or external validation of the situation—resulting in what is known as 'analysis paralysis.' This reaction may have its roots in evolutionary biology, as predators are less likely to consume prey who are not struggling . . ."

Piotr will wonder whether or not to put this into his report. He will run it by Ted later. Out in the living room, Katia will play with her pet rabbit, which means keeping it from chewing through electrical wires. Mikhail will finish his homework. Rana will prepare dinner. They will know his work can be dangerous. He imagines them, frozen in place, having received news of his death. The world would not hesitate to swallow them whole.

IES Subscale: Avoidance

How are you feeling? People continually ask him, as if feelings were an adequate measure of health. Health-wise, he is fine. Feeling-wise, he is fine. Currently, there are four DARTs deployed around the world, including Lorraine's. There's another earthquake team in El Salvador. One in posthurricane Belize. Yet another in Java for the landslides. Maybe something else has happened that he does not yet know about. He wonders if they also get pestered about their feelings.

If he were really to answer how he feels, he'd say, angry. He's angry because Ted has hung out the laundry on a rainy day, and now he has that much more work to do. He needs to revise distribution maps. Tomorrow, he's supposed to test the city's water supply. And he must have *another* meeting with the military heads about security. His feels his right hand ball into a fist, and the hard plastic body of his mechanical pencil shatters. It sounds like a bone snapping.

"Piotr," says Lorraine. "Take it easy."

She pats his hands until they flatten. Hands upon hands: this is a language Piotr cannot decipher, and the more it speaks, the more it is gibberish.

IES Subscale: Intrusion

Rana has nightmares, terrible ones. She thrashes as if trying to gain a foothold in reality. Sometimes Piotr wakes to find her sitting up, staring at the space before her eyes. Or nothing. Or both. She disappears into the dark body of the apartment. When she returns, slipping into bed like a card folded into a deck, Piotr wonders if the time spent away indicates a particular state of mind. If he were to chart the ratio of the violence of her movements to the length of wakefulness, he might find a correlation. It would make more sense to administer an IES. Even so, there's a difference between knowledge and useful knowledge. He doesn't need empiric confirmation to know that she uses the time to walk off the violence in her heart.

One day, he fears the walk will not be enough, and she will return to bed, blinded, confused, unable to distinguish him from the faces tormenting her. He fears she will take a pillow and press it onto his face. Or take a knife and plunge it into his body, again and again, until she feels his warmth splashing her arms. And if this happens, he will not restrain her or move to stop her, either in word or action. First, he knows that if this happens, no words could break through her madness. There is no language that can speak to her demons. Second, and more importantly, he knows that he would rather surrender his life than bring harm to her.

Abnormalcy Bias, Defined

The flip side of normalcy bias is abnormalcy bias, wherein people expect only the worst. After disasters, people think only panic, shock, and looting can result. Piotr has seen all three. But the years of chasing bad news have made him blind to anything except bad news. Unlike Lorraine or Ted, he has little interaction with the populace. He joined Lorraine's team because she had a reputation for caution, because it would put him out of harm's way.

There are DARTs that are even less strenuous: ones dealing primarily with food aid, for example, or ones responding to health crises. Rana has never asked him to request a reassignment, but it's there, in the back of her mind. It must be. When it comes time for the winter holiday celebration, Carter will tap a plastic champagne flute with a knife. "Ting, ting, ting!" he'll say.

The room will quiet. "I'd like to take a moment to remember those who lost their lives in the line of duty." Everyone will bow their heads. Carter will read the list alphabetically. Rana will take Piotr's hand and squeeze it. The list will continue, and Piotr will never be surprised to learn how many people he knows who are now dead.

Recovery

For Piotr, *recovery* means the retrieval of dead bodies. One *recovers* one's dead. When he hears others speaking about recovery, it takes him a moment to understand that they mean the type of recovery that does not involve face masks, plastic gloves, or grave sites. It must be a relief to engage in recovery that involves talking rather than digging.

Therefore, he is confident that Ted will recover. Ted is very much like Lorraine: always talking. The two of them natter on incessantly, and now that Piotr's Walkman is broken, he doesn't know how he'll drown them out. Sometimes, when he was trying to ignore them, he'd hear a burst of laughter, a raucous joy, and he'd take off his headphones to see if he could glean what was so funny. But of course he was too late, and the moment had passed. It'd be superfluous to exhume the joke for his sake alone. Besides, he has plenty of things that make him laugh: Katia's increasingly desperate pleas for a pet, Rana's scolding when he only has one serving of dinner, or anything Mikhail does. He can think of any of those, and he laughs. Sometimes, it helps.

IES Subscale: Hyperarousal

This happened only once: an ordinary day. Months ago, it seems. Maybe almost a year. February. Yes, that was it, Chinese New Year. Funny to think back on it now. The sound of firecrackers, rapid-fire, startling. He had been caught off guard. But for a moment, he honestly thought he was hearing semiautomatic machine gun fire, and he's almost embarrassed to admit it now, again, only for a second, not even a second, a fleeting thought, a grim fantasia, but he was filled with a terrible dread, an unshakable certainty. His reason failed him, and he simply knew that, at that moment, armed men were storming his apartment, sending a fusillade of bullets into the air, into the walls, into his family, and he was too late to save them, and when he returned home, there wouldn't be enough for even dogs to find, and with that realization, he jumped up, startled, filled with so much rage and fear that his head felt molten, his body aflame at the incomprehensibility of it: Who would want to hurt his wife, his children? Though he already knew: it didn't matter. Chinese New Year. They were already dead.

And then Lorraine, she was clutching him in a bear hug, her tiny body belying a surprising tensile strength, yelling at him again, "Piotr, where are you? Where are you?" until the moment had passed, and the world came back into focus: the office, New York, reality. His clothes were soaked with sweat, and even though the moment had passed, the dread remained. Not because he feared his family's death, no, that was clearly a momentary hallucination, but because he knew that what he'd been teaching his children—how fears become smaller and smaller as they grow older—was a lie. Fears remained the same size, and it was only the love holding them at bay that shriveled, day by day, until it had become nothing more than a period at the end of a life.

Debriefings

"I'm sending Ted back," Lorraine says.

"Good," Piotr responds. "He's not cut out for this line of work."

Lorraine pauses. "That," she says, "is something for him to decide. At the very least, he's not much help right now with his busted hand."

Piotr returns to his work.

"I'm worried about you," Lorraine says. "You seem . . . distracted."

He waves his hand in the air, the way Rana does when she says he's being too smothering.

"Irina said that you sent her these distribution maps." Lorraine hands them back to him. He looks them over, but his eyes have difficulty focusing. He pinches the bridge of his nose.

These maps aren't even of Bhuj. They're of Orissa, after the cyclone he and Lorraine had worked two years ago. He isn't even sure why he has the maps. Perhaps he brought them to look at comparable village sizes or—

"A silly error," he says.

She takes his hands again. He hadn't realized they'd been shaking. "A lot has happened."

A lot. Such a vague notion, like saying *That's a lot of rice* or *That vehicle's had a lot of damage.* She makes it sound as though the past intruding on the present can be quantified. The past and present are an inseparable whole, a river, and memories are large rocks that occasionally break the surface when the water strikes them just so. They bare sharp edges; they break limbs; they capsize boats.

"You can't see all this stuff and not have it affect you," she says.

Stuff. He wants to laugh. If Rana were here, she'd have a few choice words! Piotr whispers under his breath, *"Sanjam da prdnem na tebe."*

The Right of Return

Piotr sees Ted off to the airfield, where he will fly to Delhi on a cargo plane. For a brief second, he has a feeling: *This is the last time I will ever see Ted.* But he shakes the idea from his head. Ted will come back; they will have another assignment; the world will continue to crumble and be rebuilt.

Ted asks, "Are you all right?"

Again, this question. He doesn't mind it per se, but its binarism suggests that one is either all right or not all right. The working assumption of the asker is that he, at this moment, is not all right.

"Yes," Piotr replies. "Of course."

Ted holds up his bandaged hand. "One day," he says, "I'll be made of iron like you."

Piotr shakes his head. "I doubt it."

Ted's face contorts, as if he's been insulted. Piotr hadn't meant it that way, but Ted says, "Yeah, you're right," and boards the plane.

Piotr should apologize. But he doesn't. He watches the plane take off and continues to stand there as other planes come and go, roar and screech. Live bodies arrive; dead bodies depart. The sun sets, and the after-dark curfew descends over the city. The moon makes its slow arc in the sky, nearly full. He needs to address the matter of the water supply. The government waste-removal services have dumped rubble into Pragsar Lake, which feeds the city's wells. A 450-year-old source—ruined. The waterway schematics have curled. It is the nature of paper to bend, to be malleable. He is not paper. He is the information. He is words, numbers, explanations. He is the shortest distance between Desalsar Lake and here. He needs to be *all right* for this.

But Piotr can do nothing; he's frozen in place. He can't move, can't think. Possibilities loom before him; the endlessness of them terrifies him. He wishes Rana were there to tell him what to do. He wishes Rana could tap his shoulder, lay his pencil down, and stop his information gathering, the ceaseless, distracting numeracy. He wishes she were there to tell him, once and for all, *Things will be fine.*

Normalcy Bias, as Defined by Rabbits

Piotr will read *Watership Down* to Katia. She chooses it because she loves rabbits, and she thinks single-minded determination will convince him to buy one.

He pauses when he reaches the word "tharn"—a made-up word from the made-up language of rabbits. He licks his finger and flips to the glossary. Tharn: *Stupefied, distraught, hypnotized with fear. But can also, in certain contexts, mean "looking foolish" or again "heartbroken" or "forlorn."*

He holds the book open in his lap.

Katia, in a tiny voice, says "Daddy?" She stares at him, at this creature that is not her father, because her father does not cry. He looks at her, sheets pulled up to her waist. Her eyes are wide as flashlights. She is transfixed, and he cannot move, not to hold her, not to comfort her.

Tharn. Yes, he thinks, *that is exactly what it is like.*

EPILOGUE

Sweet Unknown

I.

What time is it in the air? What time is it on the ground? How does time move forward when, every thousand miles, Ted loses an hour? Could the plane fly fast enough for time to run in reverse? Will they reach the moment before Andy dies? When would be the best time for Ted to warn himself, *This is where things go wrong?* Do he and Andy travel the same westward path, the slow arc over Asia and into Europe? When do they part ways, as Ted continues across the vast, black ocean? Is Andy cold there, in the belly of the plane? Does he have his own compartment, or is he braced against people's luggage, cargo, souvenirs? Who picks up his body in London? His mother? Does she even know what happened? Are two firefighters, in black double-breasted dress coats, knocking on her door now? Will they call him a hero? Will they tell her that he died valiantly? Will they comfort her? Will they give her a number to call? Do forms need to be filled out? Once they leave, what's left except the waiting? Why do the minutes stretch on and on, in the unending elasticity of grief? How does one survive the long hours until someone tells you what to do next? Will she sit in his old room, surrounded by his old things? Are magazine pictures of soccer players hidden and folded between the pages of a book somewhere? Are they stuck to his wall with tape, the adhesive yellowed and brittle? When she opens the door, do they fall to the ground and scrimmage in the breeze? Did Andy even like soccer? Why is it that the more he tries to remember Andy, the more Andy fades? Does forgetting happen that quickly? How long until Andy is a glimpse, a hazy memory? Occasionally, when the plane passes above a break in the clouds, lights flicker far below on the surface of the water—What are they? Ships? The moon reflecting off a cresting wave? How far away is Andy now? What unit of measurement marks that distance? Miles? Hours? Lifetimes? Did he say good-bye to Andy? Will he be invited to the funeral? Would Andy's colleagues want him there? How would they get in touch with him? Would he recognize Andy's mother? How would he introduce himself? And what does it matter anyway? Why imagine a life that never could have been? How would he and Andy have handled the distance? The age difference? What was he thinking when, on their second night together, his hand crept over Ted's? Why did he keep it there, the warm weight, his rough, stubby fingers? Why does it feel like cold has seeped into Ted's fracture, his joints, his marrow? Have the bones been set correctly? Will they heal crooked? Or at all? When can he return to work? Should he continue with Lorraine's DART? With USAID? What good could come of it? How long can he put off this decision? What will he do in the meantime? People continue like normal after their worlds have changed irrevocably, but is that any way to live? How long will he stay up above the weather, shuttling between one time and the next? Has it snowed in New York? Did the flakes fall from the sky, steady as an IV drip? Are the electrical lines covered so that the city looks like it's crisscrossed by conduits of bone? When the white and silence blanket the city, does everything beneath freeze in place? Is it like a scab? Does the city heal underneath the snow? Will it leave a scar? If Ted dies, who will inform his parents? How does one speak the language of grief? If he doesn't hear bad news, has it not happened? Would he rather be lonely than have someone mourn him? Why does he feel that, at any moment, he could burst into tears? And why can't he? What inside him feels like concrete? Why do his hands and feet feel leaden? Will he ever fall sleep? What demons await him when he closes his eyes? Should he take a sleeping pill? Two? A handful? Is it worse to sleep and run the risk of dreaming or to stay awake with endless questions?

Has it been another thousand miles? Have they lost another hour?

Will he recognize morning when it comes?

Why does it feel like Andy is still holding his hand? Will he ever let go?

How does the heart keep from breaking every second of every day?

II.

Today is the last day of the Mies van der Rohe exhibit at MoMA, and Ted decides to go see it and go into work late, because lately, the world has been blessedly free of calamity and catastrophe, and even though he and Lorraine and Piotr fill their days filing reports, great sheaves of papers to document who, where, when, and how much, an accounting that never concludes or balances, in these brief periods after disasters, they catch up and catch their breath, and on some days, the good ones, Ted doesn't think as much about Andy, or John, or Gujarat, or Arequipa, and the times when they do pull at him—a momentary shudder, a sudden vertigo, a burst of tears—Ted waits until this old friend has concluded his business and decides to move on, so today, Ted takes the L into town, but at Union

Square, the conductor comes on and says that, due to a shutdown, everyone needs to get off, and Ted doesn't mind, because this late summer morning is warm and dry, perfect for walking, and as he exits the station and walks up the stairs, he closes his eyes to the sunlight and emerges into the day, but as he walks up Fifth, he notices that everyone is looking south, and he's the only person facing north, and it's discomfiting, like he's being willfully obstinate in his refusal to turn around, like there's something wrong with him and not everyone else, and he's only passed four blocks when the noise comes, not a single noise, but an aggregate noise, as if the entire city were concentrated in this one sound, and when he turns to look, black smoke rises into the sky and—he can hardly believe it—the first tower sinks into the ground, as if deflating: the concrete collapses, the glass collapses, people collapse: this is the source of the sound, and it happens so suddenly that Ted almost doesn't believe it's real; no, it can't be real; Ted's throat is very dry, and he feels it crack like a brittle bone, and he wonders, *What can I do?* but he's too numb to move, and he stares at the space where *something* should have been, but there's nothing, just a trail of smoke that should have been attached to *something;* on the other tower, the second plume of smoke hangs there, as if waiting for a signal, and Ted, like the others around him, stands and watches as if there's nothing to do but watch: disasters cannot be prevented; they can only be witnessed; and so he witnesses the second tower's fall with another monstrous noise that makes him want to cover his ears and turn away, but he witnesses this too, and a numbness settles into him, into his chest, a cessation of thought, his mind stops its chatter, and in its place, an eerie stillness takes over, a stillness that feels as unreal as anything else today, and Ted sits on some nearby steps; in the distance, in the air, things flutter down, irretrievable things, motes of dust and ash, whispering sheets of paper, things that did not escape the destruction but just take longer to fall; Ted watches their final descent and loses sight of them in the cloud billowing on the ground, but even as he realizes that the cloud won't reach him this far uptown, he wonders, *What can I do?*—but there's nothing to be done; in the days and weeks to come, maybe, there will be things to be done, but right now, nothing, and as Ted sits and traces the path of objects in the air, a woman kneels in front of him, and she clasps his hand, sandwiches it tight between hers, and Ted has never seen her before in his life, this old woman, and she tells him, "It'll be all right," and Ted wants to ask, *Will it?* but he's too numb to speak; he'd almost say it's shock, but he sees too clearly for that: morning still overhead, the unblinking sun, traffic lights going through their cycles of stop and go, and everyone around him, themselves stunned, dazed by what they've seen, trapped in the same dream as Ted, a willful suspension of reality, and the old woman presses his hand tight, gives it a little shake, and lets go; *Why is she comforting me?* he wonders, and he decides that he should do something, though he's unsure what, so he keeps walking north, away from the unreal part of the city, the shrouded city, and reaches, at last, the Museum of Modern Art, but the revolving door won't revolve, and the entrance door won't open: they're closed; they might never have opened, and the workers inside huddle together, glowing by the light of a television, and Ted wants to knock on the glass, to catch their attention, but they don't see him, and he feels upset, not that he's missed the exhibit, but because life has somehow changed in ways he can't begin to foresee: here is the precipice of the unknown, and here he is, on its edge; here is the water, and here he is, walking; he fears this unknowability, and it rains down upon him like sunlight, like ash, and he continues farther north, into Central Park, where each tree seems unfamiliar and the smell of cut grass doesn't comfort him; it's late summer, and this will be the last mow of the season, and some of the leaves are dying on the trees, edges crisp and brown; the rest of the world has accepted this new order of things, and Ted—well, Ted continues toward Belvedere Castle, along the paths, and once again, he's the only one not facing south, but he blunders forth anyway, because what else can he do?—he feels like he too could collapse at any moment, disappear in a puff of dust and smoke, and as he approaches the sturdy brown stones of Belvedere Castle, looming in front of him, a park ranger waves his hands: "Go back, go back," the ranger says. "You can't come up here," as if the castle were also in danger of collapse, as if nowhere were safe, and Ted can do nothing but turn around and make his way south, though by now, the afternoon has passed him by, and the sunlight makes where the towers should have been a golden haze, and some people are crying, some people are discussing what has happened and what they should do now, and Ted walks through conversations, the detritus of words left in the air, and he hears speculations, fears, and angers—no different, really, from any other disaster, except that this one has happened to *us,* and *we* don't know what to do, and there, in Gramercy Park, he comes across movers who have stopped their work to stare, and they lean, wordlessly, on a heavy chest of drawers, as if it alone keeps them upright, and the dresser's owner pleads with them, "I'll give you extra to keep working," and Ted doesn't understand why they don't jump at the chance to do something that will, if only momentarily, give them purpose, and Ted, still purposeless, returns to Union Square to find the *L* back in service, and as the subway cars trundle underground, the passengers sit quietly, consumed by their own thoughts; couples comfort each other, and tears fill their eyes and spill out, and Ted thinks of what's above him, the feet, the tires, the flow; he thinks about people in other places of the world, how they've resumed their lives; maybe the missing buildings to the south are too far away from them to be real, and it seems, to them, like a mass hallucination because, for them, it's as if nothing has changed; and Ted wishes it were true, because if nothing has changed, then his course of action should be clear—but it's not; his path is occluded, like he hasn't fully woken yet; he's a sleepwalker in the city, and this dream has pressed down upon him all day and refuses to let up, and when he gets home, maybe he can get some sleep and the dream will finally release its grip on him, but when he reaches his apartment, he has six voice mail messages waiting; the first is from his parents: did he see what happened, and isn't it terrible?; the second doesn't leave a message, but dangles for five seconds before hanging up; the third is Lorraine, telling him that they're having an emergency meeting, she'll tell him all about it tomorrow, and be ready for—something, she isn't sure what yet; the fourth is another hang-up, a longer interval this time before clicking off; the fifth is obviously a wrong number, because a woman chatters in Spanish, breathless and excited, and Ted hears, in her voice, confusion, excitement, fear; and the sixth waits for what seems like a minute before speaking: "I'm just calling to make sure"—and Ted catches his breath, it's Dev, and Dev lapses into silence, as if all language were a failure, and in the background, Ted hears a child yelling and a baby crying—"to make sure you're all right," Dev concludes before pausing again, maybe suspecting Ted was screening the calls, and he lets loose an exhalation of breath that's almost a sigh, which cuts off as he hangs up, and Ted picks up the phone to hear a tone totally unfamiliar to him, a sharp, piercing sound that tells him that all the lines are busy, but he dials anyhow and doesn't get through: everyone in New York is calling out, and everyone in the world is calling in; the air is clogged with failed communication; cell phone towers melt under the strain, satellites overhead explode, unable to keep up with the demand, but he tries again, with still no luck; the news shows the planes flying into the towers repeatedly, as if repetition were a method of confirmation, and from where Ted sits, he sees the southern tip of Manhattan, an unreal city on a cloud, something out of a fairy tale, but Ted can't look anymore; he can't take it, he can't take the collapse, the damage, the dust; he wants to know that the world hasn't forgotten him; that, in this moment, someone will make sure the fracture isn't a break; that, in these moments after disasters, people are reaching out, so even though all the lines are still busy, all the lines are occupied, he tries, again and again and again, until—finally—he connects—

ACKNOWLEDGMENTS

For help with this book, I offer my thanks first and foremost to the members of USAID's Disaster Assistance Response Teams, whose spirits serve as my inspiration, as well as to the international aid organizations worldwide that do such important work, including the Abhiyan Foundation, the World Food Programme, and Oxfam International; to Abhijeet Bhattacharjee, Pramodkumar Jethi, and Kimbro Frutiger for sharing their stories; to the following books for research assistance, *The Disaster Gypsies* by John Norris, *Love in a Different Climate* by Jeremy Seabrook, and *Bhuj: Art, Architecture, History* by Azhar Tyabji; to Michelle Brower and Vivian Lee for being tireless champions of this book; to my alpha readers, Jennifer Sears, Mickey Hawley, Sam Miller, and Suzan Sherman; to my beta reader, Cruce Stark; to my omega reader, Wah-Ming Chang; to the residencies where portions of this work were written, the Jentel Artist Residency, the Hawthornden Castle International Retreat for Writers, and the Brush Creek Arts Residency; to my family for their generous support in the early stages of my life; to the National Endowment for the Arts and the Delaware

Division of the Arts for generous support in the later stages in my life; to my professors and friends from Johns Hopkins University and the University of Houston; to my colleagues at the University of Delaware; to Gramsci, Simone, Cixous, and the memory of Gwinny, who bring joy to my life; and, finally, and most importantly, to Matthew, whose love, patience, and understanding save me, every day, from disaster.

ABOUT THE AUTHOR

Viet Dinh was born in Vietnam and grew up in Colorado. He attended Johns Hopkins University and the University of Houston and currently teaches at the University of Delaware. He has received fellowships from the National Endowment for the Arts and the Delaware Division of the Arts, as well as an O. Henry Prize. His stories have appeared in *Zoetrope: All-Story*, *Witness*, *Fence*, *Five Points*, *Chicago Review*, the *Threepenny Review*, and the *Greensboro Review*.

| Books are produced in the United States using U.S.-based materials | Books are printed using a revolutionary new process called THINKtech™ that lowers energy usage by 70% and increases overall quality | Books are durable and flexible because of smythe-sewing | Paper is sourced using environmentally responsible foresting methods and the paper is acid-free |

Center Point Large Print
600 Brooks Road / PO Box 1
Thorndike, ME 04986-0001 USA

(207) 568-3717

US & Canada:
1 800 929-9108
www.centerpointlargeprint.com